THE VANISHING

Violinist

Also by Sara Hoskinson Frommer

Murder & Sullivan
Buried in Quilts
Murder in C Major

THE VANISHING

Violinist

A Joan Spencer Mystery

Sara Hoskinson Frommer

St. Martin's Minotaur
New York

Library of Congress Cataloging-in-Publication Data

Frommer, Sara Hoskinson.
    The vanishing violinist : a Joan Spencer mystery / Sara Hoskinson Frommer. — 1st St. Martin's Minotaur ed.
        p.   cm.
    ISBN 0-312-24104-6
    I. Title.
PS3556.R5944V36   1999
813'.54—dc21   99-27228
                                                             CIP

First St. Martin's Minotaur Edition: September 1999

10   9   8   7   6   5   4   3   2   1

For Charles and Joe

Acknowledgments

Special thanks to:

Peggy T. Alper; Charles Brown; Ann and Richard Burke; David Canfield; Rose and Marcos Cavalcante; Flo Davis; Karen Foli; Gabriel Frommer; Janelle Johnson; Laura Kao; Susan Kroupa; Laura Lynn Leffers; David McIntosh; Joe Morales; Eileen Morey; Bill Pomidor; Rhonda Riesefeld; Anne Steigerwald; Swedish Club of Andover, Illinois; Luci Zahray; and to Stuart Krichevsky, my agent; and to Joshua Kendall, my editor.

Author's Note

The quadrennial International Violin Competition of Indianapolis is real and exciting, and the stakes are high, but this book is fiction from beginning to end. Although Josef Gingold's likeness is indeed on the gold medal of the real competition, all the characters named or referred to without a name are imaginary, as are all the events in the story.

All the music played in the book is real, except the compulsory solo. The real competition commissions a piece from a famous composer for each new group of competitors. So I "composed" one for this group.

I've scheduled concerts and rehearsals as needed for the story, and taken a few other liberties with the details of the competition.

Sara Hoskinson Frommer
sfrommer@juno.com

1

*W*aiting for Rebecca seemed like such a simple thing to agree to at the time.

Joan Spencer hadn't expected to marry again after Ken died. During the rough years when she was bringing up two children alone, she had occasionally let herself fantasize about a stranger with their father's slender build, dark curls, and pixie grin. Nothing could have been further from the man of her dreams than the one on her sofa, nibbling her ear after she'd fed him lunch. Yet she felt absolutely right about planning to share the rest of her life with the bulky blond policeman with crinkly eyes.

"Only don't rush me, Fred," she said.

"Rush you!" Detective Lieutenant Fred Lundquist pulled away and patted her hand the way she occasionally patted the hands of the old ladies at the Oliver Senior Citizens' Center she directed. "I wouldn't dream of it. Now that you mention it, we'd probably better wait a few more years. You'll need grandchildren first, to throw rose petals."

"You!" She punched him lightly on the shoulder. At the moment, she was feeling anything but grandmotherly. Besides, she devoutly hoped grandchildren were a long way off, what with Andrew in his sophomore year at Oliver College and Rebecca still trying her wings in New York City. "But, Fred,

I'm serious. We haven't even talked about the practical things."

"Like what?" He moved back to her ear, sending shivers down the back of her neck. She tried to concentrate.

"Like—like where we'll live."

Fred looked around the living room of the modest house Joan had inherited from her parents, who had once planned to retire to this little southern Indiana college town. Her eyes followed his. Nothing was new, but her books and old furniture welcomed her every time she came home, and the built-in cherry bookshelves glowed.

"This looks fine to me," he said.

"You wouldn't mind?" Many a second marriage had foundered on disagreements about territory, she knew. Add those to the problems that happen when two people with long-established domestic habits try to make a go of it, and it's no wonder, she thought.

"Why should I mind? You never lived here with Ken. And I'm certainly not attached to my place."

That was true, Joan thought. Since his divorce, as long as she had known him, Fred had been more or less camping out in the smallest of apartments, in an area inhabited mainly by Oliver undergraduates who rejected the college dorms.

"We'll need a bigger bed." Ken had been several inches shorter than Fred.

"Sure!" He nuzzled a spot that made her tremble. "Come on. What else is so important?"

She knew there had to be lots of things to consider, but she couldn't think of a single one. Not with him making his way along her body like that.

"I don't know," she said finally. "Just give me time to plan a little. I wouldn't want an elaborate wedding, but I want to know we're married."

"Trust me, you'll know." He sat back, and his eyes crinkled at her. Of all the ways he knew to turn her on, those blue eyes got her every time.

"Fred, I do love you."

"And I love you," he said, running his fingers through her thick brown hair, long since released from its clasp to fall around her shoulders. "What do you think your kids will say?" he asked. For the first time he sounded hesitant.

"You think they don't know already?"

"Well . . ."

Now it was her turn to reassure him. She stroked his high forehead and the beginnings of gray over his temples. "They'll be all right. You won Rebecca over when she was here, and Andrew always did like you. They've probably been making book on how long we'd take to get around to it."

"So? How long will we?"

"I was thinking maybe the end of December. That's more than enough time to plan a wedding, and Andrew will be on Christmas break. I don't know about Rebecca . . . but then, I never know about her. What about your family?" Fred hardly ever talked about them. She knew that he was from a Swedish community even smaller than Oliver, up in northern Illinois, where both his parents still lived.

"They're going to love you. My folks are pretty creaky these days, though. Maybe my brother could bring them. Or we could go visit them. It'll be quiet here, with the college between semesters. I ought to be able to get away then."

"I'd like that."

"You know what you're getting into, Joan." For the first time he sounded serious. "My life isn't my own, and that's going to interfere with yours."

"I know." How different could it be, she'd asked herself, from her previous life as a minister's wife, with unexpected emergencies that had always come during dinner, late at night, or when the children were sick? Plenty, she realized. No one ever shot at the minister. I don't want to think about that. I know how he felt when I walked into danger last summer. At least I don't do it for a living.

"Are you all right?" he asked, as if he could read her mind.

"Fred, don't get hurt."

"I can't promise that." He hugged her gently. "I wish I could."

"I know. Be careful, though, okay?"

"Okay."

They sat in silence while it ate at her. Where is my head? she thought suddenly.

"Fred, I don't think I could bear it if you got yourself killed while I was waiting for the perfect time. Let's not wait."

"You want to run off this weekend?" he asked. There went the eyes again.

Did he mean it? "Can we do it that fast?"

"Today's Monday. Sure."

"Yes. Yes, I do. We can celebrate later. And who knows, maybe Rebecca could come anyway."

"Go ahead—call her and find out."

"At twelve-thirty?" The frugality that had seen her through the rough years was so ingrained in Joan that calling long distance before five in the evening seemed wildly extravagant.

"I'll treat. Tell her I'll even buy her plane ticket." Now Fred was laughing at her. We haven't talked about money, either, she thought, but she no longer cared.

She was reaching for the phone when it startled her by ringing. Probably someone who wouldn't be able to make Wednesday's orchestra rehearsal, although they didn't usually call two whole days in advance and give her a chance to find someone else to cover the key parts. Her second, part-time job, managing the Oliver Civic Symphony, involved reacting to everyone else's emergencies with a calm she often didn't feel. She shrugged and picked up the receiver.

"Hi, Mom."

"Rebecca! I was just about to call you." She smiled at Fred and took his hand.

"Are you sitting down?"

"Yes." Joan leaned back against Fred's warm body and wondered what her daughter would say if she could see them. "What's up?"

"Mom, I have wonderful news." Me, too, Joan thought,

4

but Rebecca didn't pause. "I've been seeing a special guy, and well, Mom, we're getting married!"

"Married! Oh, my." You're right, she thought. It's a good thing I'm sitting down.

"Mom, you're going to love him, I just know you are."

I'm not ready for this. But would I ever be? She's older than I was when I met her father. "Tell me about him."

"Well, his name is Bruce. Bruce Graham. He's a violinist studying at Juilliard. But he went to Oberlin, first, Mom, just like you."

"The college or the con?"

"The what?"

"The conservatory of music." Joan's own music making was strictly amateur. She had attended the college.

"The conservatory, of course. He's a wonderful violinist. You should hear him play, Mom. In fact, you can. He's about to go to Indiana."

"University?" IU had a huge music school in nearby Bloomington, Joan knew, with plenty of graduate students.

"No, he was accepted into the International Violin Competition of Indianapolis. He'll be competing against the best in the world. It's the perfect chance for you to get to know him."

"Sounds as if he'll be pretty busy." And a little tense? she wondered. Hardly the time to meet your prospective mother-in-law.

"Well, sure, but they place all the competitors with host families. I figure now that he's about to become part of our family, you'll want to host him. I know you'll just love him. And he won't be any trouble. He's great around the house." Was that the old insecure child Joan was hearing in Rebecca's adult voice? And did that "great around the house" mean they were already living together? Joan and Fred weren't. Would Rebecca say she was prudish? Maybe, she thought. Tough. Besides, we're having enough trouble sorting out our life together without complicating it ahead of time.

"Sure, we could give Bruce a place to stay," she told her daughter now. "I'd love to meet him."

"It's more than that, Mom. The host families take them everywhere they have to go. You wouldn't mind, would you?"

Joan's hand tightened around the phone. Oh, Lord, let me do this right.

"I'll be happy to do anything I can, Bec. Is the competition over a weekend?"

"Oh no, it lasts a couple of weeks. They start out with lots of competitors and narrow the field in stages, until they get to the finals. It takes a long time to go through that much music."

"Yes, it would. Rebecca, I wish I could have him here, but I have to work during the week at the senior center and with the orchestra on Wednesday nights. I can't take off to Indianapolis nearly as often as I suspect he'll need to be there." Joan held her breath, but to her surprise, Rebecca reacted cheerfully.

"That's what Bruce said."

"He what?"

"He said no one with a job could do what they ask host families to do. He was amazed anyone was willing to do all that stuff."

"I like him already." Joan grinned into the phone. "Look, Bec, even if I can't host him, I ought to be able to go up and hear him play. And if he can spare the time, maybe we could get together for a meal or something while he's out here. Andrew will want to meet him, too, you know."

"Oh, Mom, isn't it absolutely wonderful?" Rebecca's joy flowed through the wires.

"Yes, dear, it is. I'm so happy for you. When is all this happening?" And do you plan to include your family? she didn't ask. After a couple of years of keeping them at more than arm's length after she took off to be on her own, Rebecca had thawed when she'd brought her risqué sleeping bag to enter in Oliver's big quilt show. Since then Joan had had her daughter's phone number. Still, she didn't take anything about Rebecca for granted.

"The wedding? I don't know. He leaves here Friday, and the competition starts next week. After that's over, we can

6

think about wedding plans. We don't want to wait, that's for sure. Bruce doesn't believe in long engagements. I just wish I had someone to give me away. Andrew's younger than I am, and Grandpa Spencer's much too old. I suppose I could ask Uncle Dave." She sounded dubious, as well she might. Joan hadn't seen her brother for years. Childless himself, Dave had never showed any interest in his only niece and nephew, much less affection. She doubted that he would even accept an invitation to see her marry Fred.

"How would you feel about asking Fred?" Joan took his hand and smiled up at him.

"Fred?" Rebecca sounded puzzled. "I like him. But he's not in the family. If it can't be Dad, it should at least be someone in the family."

Here we go, Joan thought. She smiled at Fred and plunged in.

"That's what I was about to call you about—I have some news of my own. Fred and I are planning to be married this coming weekend. I was hoping you might be able to be with us." She held her breath again. Prickly Rebecca—so much her father's daughter—could she possibly accept Fred?

"Mom, that's great!"

Whew.

"What does Andrew say about it?"

"He's in class. We'll tell him when he comes home."

"You mean you told me first? Gosh, Mom." Rebecca sounded genuinely touched.

"Do you think you can come?"

"I don't know how. I've been trading hours with one of the girls at the bank for things not half so important. I'm so far in the hole now that the dragon who schedules us told me I'd lose my job if I did it again in the next month. I can't even come out to hear Bruce play. I'm sorry, Mom. Couldn't you wait until I can be there?"

"We were going to, but then we just couldn't."

"You're not . . ." Rebecca's voice trailed off.

"Not what?"

7

"You know."

Rebecca, shy? Joan laughed out loud.

"Oh, for heaven's sake, Rebecca, I'm not 'you know.' "
Fred was grinning broadly. Another thing they hadn't gotten
around to discussing—what if he wanted a family of his own?
Could she face starting over again? "We're just ready."

"I wish I could come. Couldn't you wait just a little while,
till I can?" It wasn't a whine; more a plea.

Joan didn't want to start justifying herself to her daughter.
Hadn't they gone past that stage on Rebecca's last visit? She
didn't want to make her anxious about Fred, either. Bad
enough that I am, she thought.

"Don't worry about it, Rebecca. Fred's family probably
won't be there either."

"I didn't know Fred had kids."

"He doesn't, just a brother, a sister, and his parents. Andrew will have to represent you all. We'll celebrate with you
whenever you get here. At least you *know* Fred—I haven't even
met his folks yet. We may go up to see them at Christmas."

"Well, you'll meet Bruce long before that. And, Mom, tell
Fred I'd be honored to have him give me away when the time
comes. Wait till I tell Bruce he's going to have a cop for a
father-in-law." Rebecca's laugh burbled forth.

This from the girl who for years had looked daggers at
any man who paid attention to her mother. Again, Joan let
out breath she hadn't known she was holding. When she hung
up, she filled Fred in on the parts he'd missed.

"Fred, she sounds so genuinely happy that it's spilling over
onto us. I think this young man may be good for her."

"Sounds like it. Bend a little, Joan. We don't have to rush.
I'll be careful around the bad guys, and you're not 'you
know.' " He grinned.

She smiled. "No."

"Go ahead," he urged. "Call her back and say we'll wait."

2

The call the next Saturday wasn't from Rebecca, but from a woman whose voice Joan didn't recognize.

"Mrs. Spencer?"

"Yes," she said into the telephone. For a while yet, anyhow. That's another thing we haven't discussed—names. She looked over at Fred, standing in the sunny front bedroom she had chosen as her own because she loved it, even if she did have to go upstairs to shower. At the moment he was hanging up his winter clothes in what soon would be his closet. Thank goodness they weren't going to have to share one. Her little house was short on some kinds of space, but rich in closets.

"This is Polly Osborne. You won't know me, but my husband and I are hosting one of the violinists at the Indianapolis violin competition, and he's asked us to invite you to the picnic we're giving this evening with a couple of the other host families." Polly talked fast, but her voice was warm enough.

"You mean Bruce?" What was Bruce's last name? Would it be Rebecca's?

"Bruce Graham, yes. I understand he's engaged to your daughter?" A half-question.

"That's what she tells me. This is all a little sudden."

"I would have asked you sooner, but I didn't know until he mentioned it today."

That's not what I meant, Joan thought, but she didn't quite know how to say so. Polly Osborne didn't pause.

"I hope you can join us anyway. It will be very informal. Just a little get-together before the competition actually begins. The violinists are all so tense, but they have to eat, don't they? And of course your son and Mr. Spencer are invited too."

"Thank you. I'm sure my son will want to meet Bruce. But his father died some years ago. I could bring my fiancé, Fred Lundquist." It felt strange, but good, to say it out loud.

"Of course. We'll be glad to have him."

"Just let me ask him. Picnic up in Indy tonight, to meet Rebecca's Bruce?"

Fred nodded, pointed to his watch, and raised his eyebrows.

"We'd love to come," Joan said. "It's past noon now. What time did you have in mind?"

"We'll be gathering between four and five. But it's very informal—you come whenever you can make it. Our next-door neighbors, Harry and Violet Schmalz, are hosting another violinist, so we're getting together at their house." She gave Joan an address in Indianapolis, and directions.

"It's good of you to include us. What can I bring?" In Oliver, such a picnic was sure to be a "pitch-in."

"Not a thing. We'll see you there!" And Polly was gone.

They took her at her word and set out about half past three with nothing but the casual clothes on their backs and an old photo album that Joan tucked into the car at the last minute, in case Bruce turned out to be interested in seeing Rebecca as a small child.

"Mom, she'll kill you for that," said Andrew, who had showed up in time to go along.

"She won't know unless Bruce tells her. And if he tells her, it'll be because he wanted to see them. She'll like that." Seeing a glance that seemed to say *women* pass from Andrew to Fred, Joan smiled to herself. Fred hadn't needed to worry about Andrew.

Indianapolis welcomed them on a large sign planted between fields of soybeans and dried cornstalks—Marion County's Unigov system produced strange contrasts between the official city limits and the beginnings of anything even remotely suggesting a city. Soon, though, the tallest downtown buildings came into view, and then they were following the directions Joan had jotted down, through a section of rundown older houses, some of which were boarded up, to a near-northside neighborhood of restored Victorian elegance.

Multicolored balloons floating over the wrought-iron railing marked the house they wanted, a two-story brick building with curved stone porches and tall windows. Fred parked his Chevy on the street a short way down the block. This little get-together was turning out to be considerably larger than Polly Osborne had made it sound. Joan checked the back of her hair for stragglers. Fred patted her knee and kissed her.

"You look lovely," he said. "Sexiest mother-in-law for miles around. Come on, let's go meet the man."

Andrew hopped out of the back and held Joan's door for her. They followed another family up the driveway and around the house toward the people in animated conversation in the backyard.

Why didn't I ask Rebecca what he looked like? Joan worried silently. She suddenly felt shy.

A young man broke away from the crowd and came toward them. Taller and thinner than Fred, he sprouted a shock of hair as straight and red as Rebecca's was dark and curly, and his eyes were the same startling blue as Fred's. A few freckles dusted his fair skin, and a rough red mark below his left jaw labeled him a violinist. He wore jeans, an Oberlin T-shirt, and a wide smile.

"You must be Andrew," he said. "And you're Rebecca's mother."

"Bruce?" Joan said, and held out her hand. "I'm so happy

to meet you." Rebecca must have shown him our pictures, she thought. She introduced him to Fred and they shook hands all around.

"How did you know us?" Andrew asked.

"Easy." Bruce grinned. "Rebecca told me to look for her face on a guy."

It's true, Joan thought. Both Rebecca and Andrew are cut from the same pattern as their father. Bruce will certainly widen the gene pool. As would Fred, if I could face going back to night feedings and colic. If *he* could. Except that for him it wouldn't be going back. Will mine be enough for him? Could I live through it all over again? Women past forty do have babies. But I'd be over sixty by the time that child was Andrew's age. And Fred would be past retirement.

She jerked her attention back to the moment.

"I've been living that down for years," Andrew was saying. "Everyone expected me to be just like my dad and sister."

"But you're not?" Bruce's eyebrows tilted upward.

"Nope. It's better now, though. Nobody in Oliver does that to me."

"Don't worry, I won't, either. One Rebecca is enough!" The warmth of his laugh reassured Joan, who wanted this young man to be good to her daughter.

They had stopped a little distance from the rest of the picnic crowd, but now a petite blonde in a denim skirt had left the others and was bearing down on them. Up close, her skin betrayed her as considerably older than Joan.

"I'm Polly—are you Joan?"

Bruce stepped forward to do the honors. "Polly Osborne, Joan and Andrew Spencer and Fred Lundquist."

"Thank you so much for having us," Joan said.

Polly's handshake was quick and firm. Her eyes sparkled, and her face and bearing conveyed a boundless energy.

"It's our pleasure. Bruce is a fine young man. I know you're just getting acquainted, but do come join the others. The steaks are on the grill."

"Steaks!" Andrew said. "Sounds great!"

Joan beamed thought waves at him. *Andrew, if you say we never eat like that at home, I'll throttle you.*

"I like a man with a healthy appetite," Polly said. "Come on, Andrew." Putting her arm through his, she led him toward the crowd. Bruce crooked his elbow for Joan, and Fred followed in their wake.

Introductions to the other competitors followed thick and fast and left no question about the international nature of the competition. After exchanging greeting with violinists from Montreal, Budapest, and Osaka, Joan risked a few words of German with Uwe Frech, a cheerful, tall, blond violinist from Stuttgart, and was gratified when he praised her accent. His own soft consonants sounded like her Grandpa Zimmerman, who had brought his bride from the Black Forest to southern Indiana.

"Do I say *Hals- und Beinbruch* to a violinist?" she asked.

"No." He grinned. "I think only actors worry about breaking their necks and legs. Violinists worry that we will break something more important, like a finger."

Bruce introduced them to Violet Schmalz, a neatly dressed woman on the dumpy side who was carrying a tray of cantaloupe and watermelon slices from her house out to the table, and to Dr. Bob Osborne, Polly's husband, a handsome, graying man in a denim apron who waved a friendly fork in lieu of shaking hands. After accepting thick steaks from Bob and filling their plates from the ample buffet table, they sat together at one of half a dozen large redwood tables scattered on the lawn.

"Dr. Osborne's in family practice," Bruce said, "like my dad. At first I thought that was a coincidence, but they put Nate Lloyd and his mom with the Inmans, the third family that's hosting this picnic. They live a couple of houses down that way." He pointed across the street. "Nate says Mrs. Lloyd's a Realtor, like Gail Inman, so maybe they do it on purpose."

"Lloyds of London?" Andrew asked with a grin, and picked up a forkful of food.

"No, Louisville." Bruce grinned back. "Nate and I may be the only Midwesterners, but there are quite a few other Americans in the competition, and more than a few of the international competitors are already studying or working in the U.S."

"Did many of the violinists bring their folks along?" Joan asked. She wondered whether Bruce's parents would come, but she didn't want to pry.

"Some did. There's a Korean family, I know, and I think Hannah Weiss's dad will be here—she's from Israel."

"Will they stay with the host families?" Joan said, and took a bite of Bob Osborne's perfect steak.

"If they want to. Vivienne Rambeau says her parents will come down from Montreal if she survives to the semifinals, so they gave her a family that speaks French and had room for her parents, too."

"Sounds as if they'd done everything they could to make you all feel at home."

"They really have. It's not like the Tchaikovsky in Moscow. We didn't have families there, or much of any help in finding our way around. It's plenty stressful in your own country, and even worse if you have a language barrier to boot, as most of us did there. It was especially bad in Moscow because they kept changing things suddenly. There's enough tension without that kind of worry."

"How did you do there?"

"I came in fifth. An also-ran."

Rebecca had said he was good, but it hadn't sunk in that he might be that good. The Tchaikovsky was a world-class competition. "You're too modest."

He shrugged. "First or even second will help your career, but nobody cares or even knows who's that far down the list."

"I'm impressed," Fred said. "Why would you come to this one after that?"

"Are you kidding? The prizes are great, and the competition is at least as stiff. We have medalists here from several of the big competitions." He pointed to the Hungarian they'd met earlier. "Arpad over there was third at the Queen Elisabeth of Belgium, and he thinks competing here is worth the risk of not winning this time."

"What happened, Bruce? You were going to save a seat for me."

Joan looked up and saw a tall, golden-skinned young woman with a perfect figure and warm brown hair waving down her back to just above her skimpy shorts. Only the violinist's callus beneath her jaw marred her beauty. She played the fingers of one hand along the back of Bruce's neck while balancing her plate and drink dangerously close to Joan's left shoulder. Her voice had sounded wounded, but the smile on her lips and in her huge brown eyes suggested an altogether different emotion.

"Camila!" Bruce scrambled to his feet. Fred and Andrew followed suit. "Please, join us. I want you to meet some special guests. Joan and Andrew Spencer, Fred Lundquist, meet Camila Pereira. Camila's from Brazil."

At Bruce's right, Joan thought for a moment that Camila expected her to move over and make room beside him. But Camila nodded pleasantly enough and took the empty seat beyond Andrew, who was on Bruce's left.

"I didn't see *you* at the governor's reception," she said, turning those liquid eyes on Andrew.

"Where?" he asked, tearing his gaze from her formfitting top.

"Andrew's not in the competition," Bruce told her.

"No wonder," she said to Andrew. "I didn't see how I could have failed to notice you." She laid her hand on his, and Andrew blushed through the remains of his summer tan.

"The governor had a reception for all the violinists this morning," Bruce explained. "They make a big fuss about us here."

"It's a good thing I didn't try to put you up," Joan said, looking around. "It wouldn't have compared to this." The lawn, the food, the matched lawn tables and chairs, and the real china and silver for a crowd this size overwhelmed her.

"Come to Heeoh, and we will take you to the beach." Camila's smile was aimed at the men.

"Where?" Andrew said again. It was only a short step up from "uh."

"Rio de Janeiro. A very beautiful city."

"Heeoh," he imitated. "I love the way you say it."

He's a gone gosling, Joan thought, but she was more concerned about Bruce, who still hadn't really told this fascinating creature who they were.

"Tell me, Bruce," she said. "How did you two meet?"

"At the reception, I guess," he said. "And Camila's staying here, with the Schmalzes. The Osbornes live next door there." He indicated a tree-shaded yard. "So that makes us neighbors." He smiled at Camila, and got a flash of white teeth in return.

"That must be convenient," Joan said. She didn't want to grill him, but she felt obliged to stake her daughter's claim in the face of this marauder. "But I meant how did you meet Rebecca?"

Fred smiled, but didn't say anything.

He knows exactly what I'm doing, she thought, but she didn't care.

"I went into the bank a time or two to cash a check, and there she was," Bruce said. "I quit using the bank machine after that."

"Who is this Rebecca?" Camila asked him.

"My girl in New York. She's not here this week, but these folks are her family."

"Is she very beautiful? Do you have a picture of her?"

"I wish I did. She looks a lot like Andrew."

"There's your cue, Mom," Andrew said. "Mom brought along a whole photo album, Bruce. Baby pictures and all. You want me to go get them?"

"Do I!" The spark in Bruce's eyes left little doubt about his affection for Rebecca, even if he hadn't mentioned marriage in Camila's presence.

Fred tossed Andrew the car keys.

"I'll come with you, Andrew," Camila said. "I want to see this girl who looks like you." She clung to his arm as they threaded their way between the tables.

Joan rolled her eyes at Fred, but she couldn't tell Bruce what she was thinking. "This is quite a place, isn't it?" she said, instead. "Who did you say lived here?"

"The Schmalzes," Bruce said. "Camila's host family. I don't know much about them, but they've been good to her. And here come Gail Inman and Nate and Cynthia Lloyd. I think I told you—the Inmans are hosting this picnic with the Schmalzes and the Osbornes." He waved to a young man accompanied by two women old enough to be his mother. "Nate! Over here! We have room!"

They brought their food over. Joan's head was swimming with names by now, but she trusted there wouldn't be a quiz. Still, she practiced them. Nate Lloyd was the violinist from Louisville. Gail Inman and Cynthia Lloyd had to be the two Realtors Bruce had mentioned earlier. Both were attractive middle-aged women who obviously spent more time on makeup than Joan did. Gail had salt-and-pepper hair, dimples, and a certain softness around the middle. Cynthia resembled her son; slender, dark, and gangly, Nate looked more than a little like the drawings Joan had seen of Paganini. He tossed his black hair as Paganini might have done, often enough to suggest a nervous mannerism. Hardly surprising, with the competition so close. The real wonder was that the other violinists they'd met so far seemed relatively relaxed.

"This is Joan Spencer, who came up from Oliver," Bruce told them.

"Just call me Cindy," Cynthia Lloyd told her.

"Oliver's a lovely little college town," Gail Inman said. "I have a new listing down there. Do you know the old Dayhuff house? It's on Prospect, near the park."

Joan had noticed a real estate sign on Prospect, on her walk to work. "Is that a brick house, a lot like this one, only smaller?"

"Yes. The old folks died, and the children live up here."

"That's right. Some of my people at the Oliver Senior Citizens' Center were speaking of them only the other day." Actually, the old people had been complaining at how seldom the Dayhuff children had visited their elderly parents, especially considering how close Oliver was to Indianapolis, and how often the senior Dayhuffs had baby-sat their grandchildren while they were still able.

"I'm about to marry Joan's daughter, Rebecca," Bruce said. "And this is Fred Lundquist, who's about to marry Joan."

Joan had wondered whether they'd pussyfoot about what Bruce should call her before settling on some awkward name, but maybe world-class violinists were comfortable first-naming everyone. At least he didn't pussyfoot about Rebecca this time.

"Congratulations," Gail said.

"Thank you," Fred said. "I'm a lucky fellow." He reached over and gave Joan a sideways hug.

"So am I," Bruce said warmly. "Now if my luck can just hold for a week or two, I'll clobber all these other fiddlers first." He grinned at Nate. "I'd like to say present company excepted, but I can't very well, can I?"

"Don't expect me to lie down and play dead for you," Nate said with the beginnings of a twinkle.

"Nathan's an exceptional violinist," Cindy Lloyd told them all as if he weren't there.

"Don't jinx me, Mom," he said. He was smiling, but the twinkle was gone, and he tossed his head again.

"Don't be silly, Nathan. I knew it when you first picked up that little violin." She turned to Joan. "When Nathan was born I took one look at those long fingers, and I knew he'd either be a surgeon or play the violin. Can you believe it, he was only three when we got him a darling little sixteenth-size instrument."

Nate rolled his eyes and mimed playing a miniature violin with his thumbs and forefingers. The muscles at the corners of his jaws tensed.

"You mean they wouldn't trust you with a scalpel?" Fred said, and Nate laughed.

"He never looked back, did you, son?" his mother said. "He made his debut with the Louisville Orchestra when he was only thirteen, and he's gone on to bigger and better things every year since. He'll win here, too."

"Mother!"

Joan thought Nate Lloyd's face would have stopped the average mother in her tracks, but it didn't faze Cindy, if she even saw it.

"When they hear you play, they'll know I'm not exaggerating."

Andrew had returned to the table with the photo album. He was alone; Camila must have found someone else.

They excused themselves, and thanked Gail Inman for the picnic.

"It's our pleasure," Gail said, but her dimples were gone. Following her gaze, Joan saw Camila near the driveway with her arm around a middle-aged man, who was lifting tendrils of hair from her face. Gail strode off toward the driveway.

Watch it, girl, Joan thought. This lady's not going to give up her man without a fight.

With Andrew still carrying the photo album, they circled around the other families.

"Where's a good place to look at this thing?" Joan asked Bruce. "I'd feel awkward about going into the house."

"I'm sure it's okay," he said. "The Schmalzes wouldn't mind. I don't see them right now, but they want us to make ourselves at home."

"You think they mean indoors?"

"I'm sure they do. These three families are really close. They share house keys and run in and out of each other's houses all the time. I've been doing it, too."

"I'll take your word for it," Joan said.

They were approaching the stone porch that curved around the back of the house when a Frisbee sailed out the back door and narrowly missed Joan's left ear. Andrew dropped the album on the ground and lunged for it.

"Got it!" He flipped it back toward what looked like leaded glass windows.

Joan cringed, but instead of the breaking glass she was dreading, she heard laughter. She looked up in time to see Uwe Frech, the German violinist she'd met earlier, run out the door and dive for the red disk. He held it up, even while his body continued to slide toward a stone planter at the top of the porch steps.

"Good catch!" Andrew said.

But the Frisbee rolled down the steps and Uwe lay still. Then he began to scream.

3

 red reached him first. This is the violinist Joan spoke
German with, he thought, but he couldn't remember the
name of the stocky young man who lay curled into a ball,
hugging his body with both arms.

"Don't try to get up, son," Fred said. "Where are you hurt?"

Already blond and fair-skinned and with no summer tan,
the German was even paler now. He had stopped screaming,
but his breath came in gasps.

"My hand!" he choked out. "I think I broke my hand!"

"Arms and legs okay?" As far as Fred could see, nothing
was displaced.

"I don't know—it doesn't matter. I tell you, it's my
hand!" Cradling his left hand in his right, he began a rhythmic
rocking and keening. Fred looked closely at his left hand. The
fingers were already beginning to swell.

"I'm going after Dr. Osborne," Bruce said. "And some
ice." He loped off toward the grill. Andrew ran after him.

"Oh, Oo-veh, I'm so sorry," Joan said. Her hand reached
toward his shoulder, but she didn't touch him.

Oo-veh? Fred thought. Oh, Uwe. If you're right about that
hand, Uwe, my boy, you've just missed this year's competition.

"I'm too old," Uwe mourned.

Too old? "You're not too old to heal," Fred said. "You'll be back for the next competition."

"I can't! Four years from now I'll be thirty-one." Uwe's careful "th" degenerated into an "s."

Fred raised an eyebrow at Joan.

She nodded. "He's right, Fred. There's an age limit. He won't be eligible again."

"This was my last chance! And now, nothing. I can't even earn my ticket home doing program in the schools!" Uwe began rocking again. "God, it hurts!" Tears streamed down the white face, whether from the pain or the lost opportunity, Fred couldn't tell.

While they waited for the doctor to reach him, Uwe worked himself into a state, trembling, weeping, and generally carrying on, as Fred's mother used to say. Fred couldn't blame him. These kids—they were scarcely more than kids—had worked intensely for this opportunity. For Uwe to have it snatched away before he could even begin to compete had to be a severe blow.

The rest of the competitors and their host families crowded around when Andrew brought Dr. Osborne, still wearing his denim apron. Fred automatically shooed them away.

"Come on, folks, stand back. Give the doctor room to work." The people yielded to his natural authority, although many of them stayed to watch and listen from a few feet away.

Bob Osborne knelt beside Uwe, checked him over quickly, and helped him sit up, with his feet resting on the first step below the patio and his arms resting on his knees.

"I'm pretty sure only your hand is injured," he said.

"*Only* my hand!" Uwe's voice was shrill. "My hands are my life!"

"We have excellent hand specialists right here in Indianapolis. But first"—he forestalled another outbreak from Uwe—"first I want to get some ice on it."

"Here you go." Bruce was at his elbow with a plastic bag filled with ice cubes and closed with a twist tie.

Bob looked up, nodded, and placed it on Uwe's hand. He

smiled at Bruce. "I don't suppose you brought splints."

"A couple of magazines? Best I could find." Bruce held them out, and the doctor nodded.

"Good enough." With the adhesive tape the resourceful Bruce pulled from a back pocket, Bob Osborne wrapped the injured hand, ice bag and all, in a firm cylinder of slick pictures. "That ought to help," he told Uwe. "I've sent my wife next door for my bag. Soon as it comes, I can give you something for the pain."

"You can't give me my hand. You can't give me my life!" Uwe flailed out with the magazine-wrapped hand as if oblivious to the physical pain.

"Calm down, son. You don't want to make it worse."

"How can it be worse? Don't you understand anything?" And he flailed again.

He's falling apart, Fred thought. The gathered crowd, which had been relatively quiet, had begun to murmur. He saw Cindy Lloyd approaching. Not now, he thought. He glanced down at Joan. She shook her head and Andrew rolled his eyes.

But Cindy was nothing like the stage mother they'd met earlier. "Bob, would this help?" she said quietly. She climbed the steps and held out a prescription bottle. He took it and read the label.

"Lorazepam? It probably would calm him down, but it might get him in trouble with any other sedation." He returned the bottle.

Cindy nodded her understanding. "I'd be happy to drive him. My car's just across the street." She gestured to a white wagon with the logo of her firm on the front door.

"Thanks, but Polly's already bringing ours. You stay here with him," the doctor told Bruce. "Send someone after me if there's any problem. I'm going to call one of those hand specialists." He disappeared into the next yard.

Bruce sat down beside Uwe, who had buried his head in his good hand. He was speaking to him, too softly for Fred to hear. Uwe nodded a couple of times, but didn't raise his head. With nothing more than eye contact and a shake of the head, Fred restrained a couple of young people who looked as if they were planning to run over. Uwe was too unstrung for visiting, he thought. Bruce was doing fine all by himself.

Bob Osborne was back in only a few minutes, this time with his medical bag. After he gave Uwe an injection, he and Bruce helped him into a dark blue Volvo wagon that had pulled into the driveway beside the house. Fred saw Polly Osborne at the wheel. This host family got more than they bargained for, he thought. Then he remembered that Bruce, not Uwe, was their violinist. Bob climbed into the car beside Uwe, and Bruce closed the door behind them.

"That's some fella Rebecca found herself," Fred said to Joan.

"He is, isn't he? I won't worry who will take care of her."

Bruce came over to them. "Sorry I had to ignore you."

"Heavens, Bruce, don't worry about us," Joan said. "We were just talking about what a good job you did with Uwe."

"Where'd you learn all that?" Andrew waved at the steps, as if Uwe and his makeshift splint were still there.

Under his freckles, Bruce's fair skin reddened. "Dad says anyone can do first aid in an emergency room, but that's not where people get hurt. He taught us to improvise."

"I guess he did," Joan said. "How'd you improvise that tape?"

"That was the one thing I got out of their medicine cabinet." Bruce smiled. "Any strong tape would have worked, but the bathroom was right there. I didn't have to poke around much. I know the Schmalzes said to make ourselves at home, but they probably didn't want someone going through their desk drawers."

"But you would have?" Fred said.

"I'm glad I didn't have to." He would have, that was plain.

With the need to protect Uwe now past, Fred stood back out of the crowd while the other violinists surrounded Bruce. They were subdued, even as they pumped him for more than he could know. If their worst nightmare had happened to one of their number, it could happen to them.

Joan picked up the photo album and shook her head. Fred could read her mind. Their chance to meet Rebecca's intended had gone sour. Or had it? he thought. The young man had showed himself to be compassionate, calm, and resourceful in an emergency. An evening's chitchat would hardly have drawn that kind of information out of him.

"It's too bad," Joan said.

Fred nodded. "Poor kid."

"Oh, Fred, I'd already blocked Uwe out of my mind—isn't that awful? I was just thinking how sorry I am we didn't have a better visit with Bruce. I'll come up to hear him play, but it won't be the same."

"Did you like him?"

"How can you help it? And to see him helping one of his rivals like that says good things about his character."

"Not anymore," Andrew said.

"What do you mean?" Joan asked.

"Uwe stopped being a rival the minute his hand hit that planter. Bruce could afford to be nice to him."

"Andrew!"

"Don't get me wrong. I like him, too."

Joan's eyes were begging Fred to take her side.

"He seems like a fine young man," he said, and wondered whether he should tell her he was planning to run a check on him Monday.

Eventually they visited a little more with Bruce, who even remembered to take a quick look at Rebecca's baby pictures. But darkness was falling, and the party had broken up. In the end, they settled for promising to come back to hear him play as often as they could manage.

I'm acting like a father already, Fred thought on the drive home to Oliver. But why not? Joan's kids are all the family I ever expect to have. We could do lots worse. She's never mentioned wanting more, but her biological clock doesn't have a lot of years left. Is she waiting for me to bring it up, or would she be upset if I did?

4

*J*oan had to miss hearing Bruce play his first round of competition. When the violinists had drawn numbers for the order in which they would appear throughout the competition, Bruce's high number had put his first round on Wednesday, the last night of the preliminary phase. But Wednesday was orchestra rehearsal night in Oliver, when Joan not only played in the viola section but had duties as the paid manager and librarian of the Oliver Civic Symphony.

Occasionally, she could arrange for someone to take her place, but not for this first rehearsal of the season. She wanted the first rehearsal to run as smoothly as possible, and she especially wanted people to sign out their rehearsal folders. If they didn't, she'd have a hard time tracking down the music that didn't make it back after the concert. At best, that would mean extra work for her. At worst, the orchestra would pay substantial fines for lost or late rental music.

She would call Bruce afterward, she told Nancy Van Allen during the break on the stage of the Alcorn County Consolidated School. Nancy, who played trombone, was the only sixth-grade classmate Joan had remembered from the long-ago sabbatical year when her professor father had taken his family to Oliver.

"You really think your daughter's going to marry this violinist?" Nancy asked. "Just like that? How long has she known him?"

"Not long. Rebecca doesn't say much, except how wonderful he is."

"What did you think, when you met him?"

"He seemed like a very nice young man."

Nancy laughed. "You sound a million years old!"

"That's how I feel sometimes." And then there are the times with Fred, Joan thought. Why don't I tell Nancy about us?

But she knew why: Telling Nancy anything was tantamount to telling everyone in Oliver. Even though Bruce had announced their plans freely up in Indianapolis, where they were strangers, she and Fred hadn't made a general announcement at home yet. Nancy could wait.

Snacking on the cookies and punch served by the orchestra board during the break, most of the players were exchanging news and greetings after a summer apart. For Joan and the others who had played in the pit orchestra for Gilbert and Sullivan's *Ruddigore* during the summer, September had come all too soon. Joan hoped that meant she wouldn't be as tired at the end of this rehearsal as she often was after too long a period of little practice and even less extended playing. What must it feel like, she thought, to be in the shape Bruce and the other violinists at the competition had to be in? Not only would the music flow more easily out of your fingers, even if you weren't a virtuoso, but your back and shoulders wouldn't ache after an ordinary rehearsal.

At the end of the break, Joan introduced and welcomed the new players, some of them Oliver College students who might or might not stick with the orchestra when they began feeling pressured by papers and exams. A few always did, though, and there was no way to predict who they would be. She made her plea about signing out the music. Then she turned the rehearsal back to the conductor. Alex Campbell, a pudgy woman with a fuse as short as she was, hadn't blown up at anyone yet tonight. A good beginning, Joan thought.

A couple of the pieces they'd be playing in this concert were real warhorses: Nicolai's Overture to the *Merry Wives of Windsor* and one of Joan's all-time favorites, Schubert's Unfinished Symphony. Alex was actually smiling when she invited them to take out the Schubert. Maybe it was her choice.

But Alex's benevolent mood didn't survive the Unfinished. The cello section sounded ragged in that most familiar of lush cello passages. She gave them a second crack at it, but when they failed again to achieve the lyrical lines she wanted, she lit into them.

"How can you call yourselves cellists if you don't already have this in your fingertips?" she railed. They don't call themselves cellists, Joan wanted to say. They're amateurs, and they know it. But she knew better than to interrupt the tirade. Alex finally wound down and ordered them to "practice as you've never practiced in your lives between now and when you come back next week."

I hope they even bother to come back next week, Joan thought. We're already short in some sections for this concert, and maybe for the whole season. If the cellos start giving up, we'll be in real trouble. But Alex thinks that's the manager's problem. Mine. She looked at her partner on the second stand of violas. Bald, middle-aged, and feisty, John Hocking was far more likely than she to fight back, but he was hunched over his viola, half dozing. Tired? or just tired of this nonsense? she wondered.

By the time Alex finally released them, the orchestra's mood had darkened. Joan's mind was already wandering to Bruce, who should have finished his first session by now. Would he have gone back to the Osbornes' right away, or would he stay to hear the others? She hoped he wouldn't stay so late that he'd hesitate to call her.

Did she care for Bruce, or for Rebecca's future husband? Both, she thought. Of course she wanted only good for the man Rebecca loved, especially if he was going to be part of her family. But after watching him cope with Uwe's injury and soothe his outbursts, she was sold on this redheaded fiddler for his own sake.

She carried her viola into the house about ten o'clock and returned to the car for the awkward boxes of folders, now considerably lighter without the ones people had taken home to practice. Rebecca called almost immediately.

"Mom, did you hear from Bruce?"

"I just got home. Has he called you?"

"Yes. He said it went well. He won't know till tomorrow morning, but he thinks he made the first cut. Well, not really. They made the *first* cut from a couple of hundred audition tapes. But this will be the first cut of the fifty or so who are competing live. He's feeling pretty sure he'll be in the semifinals."

"Oh, Rebecca, I hope so."

"So, can you hear him then?"

"Any night but Wednesday."

"Then you can! The semis are from Friday to Monday. Bruce will probably play Sunday or Monday. I'll ask him to get you tickets. Should he get three? Do you think Andrew and Fred would go hear him?"

"If they can. We all like him."

"And he likes you."

5

*B*ruce did make the semifinals and, to Joan's relief, was scheduled to play on Sunday afternoon. Nice, she thought, not to have to rush up to Indianapolis after work. When Fred and Andrew both turned out to have conflicts, she decided to attend the evening session as well. This time she drove directly downtown, left her old Honda in a parking garage, and walked to the Indiana Repertory Theatre, on Washington Street near Monument Circle.

On this bright blue day, jet trails were diffusing slowly overhead. Top-hatted drivers from several different companies offered carriage rides behind matched white teams outfitted with manure catchers.

Joan went in to pick up her ticket. Opposite the ticket windows of the restored movie palace, posters and cast photos announced upcoming plays. Then she saw one of the International Violin Competition of Indianapolis, with photos of the famous violinists who would judge it and a painting of the gold medal.

A matronly African-American woman in a black skirt and white blouse, wearing a diagonal sash with the violin scroll and name of the competition in gold, told her she could sit wherever she liked.

"Aren't some of the seats reserved for the judges?"

30

"Don't you worry about the judges. They're up in the balcony, where the rest rooms are. Nobody else sits up there but the big donors."

"You'd think the judges would be right down front."

"I guess they are, some places. Here's your program." The usher handed her a glossy book of at least a hundred pages. "It's for the whole competition."

"I don't know whether I'll get to come back after today," Joan said, wondering whether Bruce would survive this round.

"I'm usually at home with the kids, but I wouldn't miss any of this!" The woman's dark face shone. "That's why I usher!"

After paying a quick visit to the elegant ladies' room on the balcony level, where a sash-draped dragon guarded the door to the reserved balcony seats, Joan walked back down the long staircase and picked a spot in the center of the small theater, about a third of the way down.

The seats were beginning to fill up. In front of her, a visibly pregnant woman was speaking French, slowly, with a couple who rattled it back like native speakers. Joan wondered whether they were related to a competitor. Hadn't Bruce said the family of a violinist from Montreal would come? But these people could be from Paris; she knew she wouldn't be able to hear the difference. For this afternoon's concert, at least, most people were casually dressed. Many were middle-aged or older, but there were a few children. Joan hoped they wouldn't disturb her, or the violinists.

They must be videotaping the concert. A crew member in jeans and a T-shirt was taping wires down onto the stage. A tripod leg stuck out from behind the curtain over on the side, and another camera stood in a side aisle. Over the center of the house, about six or eight rows back, a microphone hung suspended. The curtains were open, and the stage itself was edged with ferns and white chrysanthemums. Nothing fancy, Joan thought, but festive. It was empty except for a grand piano and padded piano bench, and a page turner's chair behind the stool. The piano lid was propped half open.

She looked at the program booklet, but saw no programs—only photographs and information about the competitors, who had a page apiece in alphabetical order with their ages, addresses, a history of the awards they had won in other competitions, their professional training, and their teachers. Also on the page was a list of pieces the competitor had chosen for each phase of this competition. Of course, Joan realized. They couldn't print programs for each concert ahead of time because they didn't know who'd be eliminated and who would be left to play at any particular stage of the competition. She flipped through the alphabet to Bruce's page, and there he was, smiling widely, with only the scroll of his violin showing, rather than playing with soulfully downcast eyes, as were many of the others.

"Joan?"

She looked up, startled. The tall, blond young man with his left arm in a cast and sling who was standing over her was also staring up at her from the program on her lap. Uwe Frech's picture was on the left-hand page, opposite Bruce Graham's on the right.

"Uwe! How are you?" She patted the empty seat beside her, and he took it.

"Much better, thank you. They operated on my hand, and I have almost no pain."

She was afraid to ask the question that mattered most, but he answered it without prompting.

"The surgeon says I will play again."

"Oh, Uwe, that's wonderful! I'm so glad to hear it! I couldn't help worrying that you wouldn't." And that the whole thing had happened because Andrew threw that Frisbee at him. She hoped Andrew didn't feel responsible for what was, after all, an accident, but she hadn't been able to block the idea from her thoughts. This was really good news. "It's bad enough that you had to miss this competition. I'm a little surprised you stayed on."

"They said I could speak to the schools, after all. Some

violinists don't like to talk to children, but I'm happy to do it. And I need the money."

"You don't have to play?"

"No. It is always optional, they say. So I show the kids my violin and tell them about it, or maybe a little about Germany. At the school where I went on Friday, they all asked about my hand. One boy asked, did I insure my hands for a million dollars?"

She grinned. "They watch a lot of television. What did you tell him?"

"I said I wish I had."

At the last minute, the Osbornes arrived and sat in front of them, next to the pregnant woman and the French couple.

Uwe leaned forward. "How is Bruce?"

Polly Osborne swiveled around. "Hi, Uwe. Hello, Joan. I don't think he's quite as nervous as the first time. He only threw up once today."

Bruce throws up before a competition? Joan thought. She wondered whether he felt that bad every time he performed, or only under this kind of pressure, but the lights dimmed before she could ask. Polly turned to face the stage, and a disembodied woman's voice announced, "Good afternoon, ladies and gentlemen. The next performer is Bruce Graham. He has chosen the Beethoven Sonata Number 6 in A major and the Ysaÿe Sonata Number 6, Opus 27. He will begin with the commissioned work by Gerald Quigley. Thank you."

Dressed in dark trousers and a white shirt open at the throat, Bruce walked onstage alone; apparently the commissioned piece was for unaccompanied violin. Joan clapped with the rest of the audience, except for Uwe, who slapped the armrest of his seat with his good hand. After a quick nod to the audience, Bruce stood quietly for a moment before putting his instrument under his jaw and raising his bow.

The first notes he drew from the violin were low and sure, with a warm vibrato, and Joan leaned back in her seat. Of course he could play; she'd known that all along, but hearing was believing. Pizzicato accents broke into the long lines. Then came arco runs, spiccato arpeggios, and left-handed finger pizzes. The original theme recurred, sometimes a single line, sometimes double stops, always different, but always musical, carrying her through changing harmonies, complex rhythms, and grace notes with ponticello, tremolo, and a virtuoso passage of down-bow staccato. As if that weren't enough, the theme continued in a passage of double-stopped harmonics, which to her ears, at least, sounded precisely in tune. Bruce ended on a whisper.

He shut his eyes and took a deep breath. The audience paid him the compliment of silence before breaking into prolonged applause.

"It's wonderful," Joan said to Uwe while she clapped and watched her almost-son-in-law bow. "I didn't expect to like it, but it's wonderful."

"Bruce makes it sound like music," he said. "Not everyone can. I had a hard time with it. Especially the down-bow staccato and those killer harmonics."

"I can see why." There was no way she was going to tell him that she even attempted to play an instrument. If ever there was a time for humility, this was it.

Bruce had left the stage. Joan watched a stagehand move the music stand from behind the piano to center stage, and so she was not surprised when Bruce returned carrying music. A young Asian man followed him and sat down at the piano after they both acknowledged the applause of the audience. Calmly, or so it seemed, Bruce set his music on the stand. The pianist sounded the A, and Bruce tuned lightly. Then he raised his bow, nodded, and they began together.

After the effort of listening to the commissioned work, Joan let the familiar, lyrical Beethoven flow over her. The pianist was no slouch, she thought, nor did he overwhelm the violin. They played together as if they'd known each other for years, even though they could have had at most a couple of rehearsals. She knew from the program that the competition provided the pianists.

In the first movement, they echoed each other's rippling notes. In the second, the piano's simple chords and arpeggios supported Bruce's long, sweet lines with sensitivity. Here was no show-off stuff, but music that stood on its own. Bruce's bow danced over the string crossings in the third movement and attacked the down-bow chords with authority, not harshness. By the end, the pregnant woman in front of Joan was nodding her head with the rhythm, and a child across the aisle was conducting in the air.

"Lovely," Joan said to Uwe when the applause let up. "But then, I always did love Beethoven. What do you know about the Ysaÿe?"

"It's beautiful," Uwe said. "Violinistic and demanding. Ysaÿe was a Belgian violinist."

"So it's appropriate to play his music here," Joan said.

"Yes. But many of us choose Ysaÿe because of Mr. Gingold."

"Who?"

"Josef Gingold, the father of this competition. The gold medal shows him playing the violin. He studied with Ysaÿe and loved his music. Mr. Gingold was one of the most famous and best-loved violin teachers in the world. He taught for many years at Indiana University. I wanted to study with him."

"Why didn't you?"

"He died before I could afford to come." He looked wistfully at his broken hand. "I missed that chance, too."

Bruce walked back onstage alone and without music. He bowed to the audience, launched strongly into a trill, and scarcely paused until the end of the piece. Fiendishly difficult, the Ysaÿe was full of Gypsy fire and fast double stops. Joan thought one or two double stops might be off by a hair, but they didn't throw Bruce. This was high-risk playing, and he didn't hesitate. He gave it his all, and ended with a flourish.

The audience loved it, and he bowed low. Polly Osborne turned around and winked at Joan, whose hands were sore from clapping. Bob, looking dignified in coat and tie today, kept yelling "Bravo!" Even Uwe had a silly grin on his face.

"Where will he be now?" Joan asked during the break. "Can we go backstage to congratulate him?"

"No," Uwe said. "I could go back, with my ID, but not you. They worry about protecting our violins. Some of the competitors play wonderful old instruments, much better than mine. But he will come to the lobby to sign autographs."

"Autographs?" Like a movie star? she thought. Amazing. "Who wants them?"

"Lots of people," Polly said. "Especially the children. It's wonderful, seeing them get turned on by music like that. Some of them even bring their little fiddles with them, like kids who wear their gloves to the ball game."

Joan considered going to the lobby to watch, but stayed put and chatted with the Osbornes and Uwe. After the intermission, they sat through another violinist. All the semifinalists had to play Quigley's commissioned piece, and Joan soon realized what Uwe had meant about making it music. Arpad Nagy played with flamboyant gestures and Hungarian fire, tossing his hair on the loud notes and closing his eyes on the long ones, but she thought he missed his aim a few times too many to be in the same league as Bruce. While Arpad was scrambling for the notes, the music fell by the wayside. And he lacked the expression Bruce had brought to the piece. By using his powerful vibrato on all the sustained notes, rather than letting some of them float into the air, as Bruce had done, he produced a sameness instead of the intensity he was surely aiming for.

When, in spite of even more noticeable intonation problems, Arpad brought much of the crowd to its feet with Sarasate's Concert Fantasy on *Carmen*, the Osbornes kept their seats and Polly muttered to her husband, "Most of them have never heard it before."

"Flash gets them every time," he said.

"Never mind," Polly said. "It won't fool the judges. Let's take Bruce home to supper. Can you come with us?" she asked Joan. "Or did you have plans? We have plenty of food."

Joan didn't hesitate. "I'd love to. I was planning to come back tonight, though. Maybe I should take my own car."

"Oh, we'll bring you back," Polly offered quickly. "We don't want to miss tonight. Do you have a way home, Uwe?"

"Thank you. My host family is picking me up."

"That's all right, then," Bob said, and stood up. "We'd better go find the man of the hour."

Bruce was already making his way down the aisle toward them. He paused on the way to sign the program of the little boy Joan had seen conducting. She was pleased to see that he listened to what the child told him and did more than scribble in his program. Uwe reached him before she did.

"Good job," he said quietly, and went out.

"Bruce, you were wonderful!" Joan said.

As often as he must have heard it, he blushed. "Thank you. It's a relief."

"Only the finals to go," Bob said.

"That's up to the judges." Bruce sighed. "At least this part's over. I'll eat supper and then come back to hear Camila and Nate."

"Is that who's playing tonight?" Joan asked. "They're the last two?"

"They are now," he said. "The ones who drew the numbers after theirs didn't make it this far."

6

As soon as they reached the Osbornes' house, Bruce excused himself to make some phone calls.

"He'll call his folks and your daughter," Polly told Joan. Bob chuckled. "Probably not in that order."

Sunshine still streamed through the kitchen windows while Bob whisked covered dishes from an enormous side-by-side refrigerator to the built-in microwave. Polly put on the coffee and set out what looked like homemade dressing and a big green salad in an oiled teak bowl.

"Can I help?" Joan asked, impressed by their efficiency. With the next concert coming so soon, they needed it.

"Sure," Polly said. "How about tossing this?"

Joan added the dressing and tossed the salad while Polly set another place at the table and Bob stirred sour cream into hot beef. By the time Bruce returned, supper was ready. He dug into the tangy beef Stroganoff as if he hadn't eaten all day.

He hasn't, really, Joan thought, if he lost his lunch. To see him cracking jokes with Bob now, it's hard to imagine that he was ever in such a state.

After helping clear the supper dishes, Bruce said, "I think I'll go next door and wish Camila well."

"Are you sure?" Polly said. "You wouldn't have wanted visitors at this point."

"True," Bruce said. "But Camila's a different animal. I think she'll be glad to see me. I'll be right back." And he went out the kitchen door.

"He's such a friendly young man," Polly said. "The violinists we've had in other years have been more single-mindedly devoted to their own careers."

"You think he isn't serious about his?" Joan asked. Looking out the window, she saw Bruce lope across the lawn to the Schmalzes' back door as if he'd dropped in on Camila more than once. Rebecca doesn't have a thing to worry about, she told herself sternly.

"Oh no," Polly said. "He's by far the best musician we've hosted. He just . . ." She turned to her husband, who was rinsing plates.

"He's serious, all right," Bob said. "Even intense. But he doesn't take himself too seriously."

They carried their coffee to the living room and settled down in comfort to wait for Bruce. Like the rest of their house, the Osbornes' living room said "touch me." Without a qualm, Joan put her feet up on a leather ottoman that she suspected cost as much as all her own furniture put together.

"How does Bruce compare to the other competitors?" she asked. "I mean, there was no question this afternoon. He was far and away the better of the two."

The Osbornes looked at each other.

"That's true," Bob said. "But wait until you hear these two tonight."

"If Nate's half as good as his mother thinks he is, you're right," Joan said.

"Actually, he is," Polly said, and laughed. "And Camila's amazing."

"You know they call it the Olympics of the violin," Bob said. "I'm convinced that these three kids will medal."

"We've never hosted a medalist before," Polly said. "I'm really pulling for Bruce."

Joan learned that the Osbornes had been hosting violinists ever since the first competition, when they thought it would be a good experience for their children and a way to support young talent. Now their children were long gone, and they had grandchildren scattered all over the country. Joan admired a wall of photographs and tried to imagine herself as the grandmother of Bruce and Rebecca's children. Finally she looked at her watch.

"Are we going to be late? When does the concert start?" What is he doing over there so long? she wondered.

"Time to go!" Bruce breezed in through the kitchen. "Sorry I took so long. I had to wait down in the music room— Camila was upstairs dressing. She and Nate took a walk before supper to get rid of the jitters, she said. Sure never worked for me."

"How is she?" Joan asked.

"She seems okay. She's playing first tonight, so she and Harry Schmalz took off in a rush."

Bob hurried them out. They'd make it on time, Joan thought, but they might not be able to sit together.

"What about Violet Schmalz?" Polly asked from the front seat of the Volvo as they pulled out of the garage. "Didn't she go with Camila and Harry?"

"Camila said Violet apologized all over the place, but she had an old commitment she couldn't get out of."

"It happens," Bob said, and turned south into traffic. "I'm glad I haven't had any emergencies during your concerts so far. I'll bet Violet doesn't miss Camila's finals, though."

"Camila's sure to make the finals," Bruce said.

"So are you," Polly said warmly.

"I don't know about that." But he smiled at Joan as he said it.

He's feeling more confident now, she thought. I wonder whether Bob's right about those three.

When Bob dropped them off at the Indiana Repertory

Theatre, Bruce slipped out of the car. "Save me a seat," he said.

The house was almost full, but Polly and Joan found four seats together on the left aisle, near the back.

"There aren't any bad seats in this house," Polly said. "The acoustics are great."

Bob Osborne found them in only a few minutes, but the lights were already dimming when Bruce slid into his seat and whispered something Joan didn't catch. At the last possible minute, she recognized Cindy Lloyd as she scooted down the aisle to a seat halfway to the front. She slid in next to the man Gail Inman had taken off to rescue from Camila's charms at the picnic. That's right, Joan thought, the Inmans are Nate's host family.

"The next performer will be Nathan Lloyd," the loudspeaker announced.

"But I thought Camila—" Joan said to Bruce.

"There's a problem with her violin. Nate's playing first."

What could have gone wrong with Camila's violin? Any violinist could replace a broken string. The bridge, maybe? Or the tailgut, which anchored the tailpin with all the strings to the endpin? Once Joan had opened her case to find all her strings loose and the bridge lying flat on the viola. It hadn't taken Mr. Isaac, who ran the violin shop in Oliver, long to replace Joan's old gut anchor with a new one of some synthetic that would last for many years. But even a little job like that would have delayed Camila's performance, as late as she must have arrived at the theater. It made sense to switch the order, especially if Nate was ready. Nice to know the judges didn't disqualify a participant for a small disaster.

The voice didn't wait for the audience to stop buzzing before announcing that Mr. Lloyd had chosen the Brahms Sonata Number 3 in D minor, Opus 108, and the Ravel Sonata in G Minor.

Wearing a dark gray suit and a white silk turtleneck, Nate came onstage with the pianist who had played with Bruce. He planted his feet and played the Brahms from memory. The first high notes were sweet, and he quickly demonstrated solid control. Joan watched his bow circle as he wove back and forth between strings, made huge leaps, and landed precisely on pitch. She found herself pulling for him the way she pulled for ice-skaters jumping triple axels.

In the simple, lyrical second movement she thought, I could probably play most of these notes—until the double stops, anyway—but I could never make them sound like this! The violin began the third movement with afterbeats to the piano's dancing tune, but soon Nate was dancing in double stops. In the fourth movement his rapid, forceful chords, syncopation, and driving rhythm brought the sonata to a rousing ending.

"Wow," Joan said to Bruce. Her palms were sore. "He's up at your level."

"You better believe it." Bruce was clapping just as hard.

"Going on suddenly doesn't seem to have thrown him."

"He's a pro."

The pianist left, but Nate stayed onstage and raised his violin even before the applause stopped. The audience quickly hushed, and he began Quigley's commissioned piece. Like Bruce, he made it music, not a mere succession of unconnected technical feats. His tempo was generally more relaxed, if anything about that piece could be called relaxed, Joan thought. The effect was equally lovely.

"How can the judges possibly choose when you're all so good?" she asked when the applause died down.

Bruce smiled. "At this level, you don't know how they decide. Not everyone likes the same approach. You can't read the judges' minds."

"And would you, if you could?" she asked gently.

"I don't know. I hope I'd play it the way I think it should be played. Only sometimes I can think of more than one good way to approach a piece." He grinned. "I wouldn't mind a little nudge in the direction that would help me the most."

Only after Nate returned to the stage with the pianist, and

the audience hushed, did Joan realize that she'd forgotten to ask what was wrong with Camila's violin. Nate tuned to the piano again. In the first movement of the Ravel, the piano rippled while the violin played long, lyrical lines with a warm tone, and some unbelievable softs. Joan watched Nate's index finger bend into his bow to go from ultra-soft to a mere pianissimo. Like the end of the Quigley, the end of this movement was a long whisper. The second movement was a syncopated blues with driving rhythms, and Nate's body moved to them. In the last, his bow flashed in a perpetuum mobile with fire and wonderful dynamic contrasts. Before lowering the violin at last, he raised his chin and let out a great breath.

This time it was Bruce who said "Wow!" Cindy Lloyd jumped to her feet, as did much of the audience.

"*C'est incroyable!*" cried a woman behind them, and Bob Osborne was yelling "Bravo!" again.

"He's got to be a finalist," Joan said. "Maybe a medalist."

"You never know," Bruce said. "But if he isn't, there's something wrong."

When Nate left the stage, Joan chose again to avoid the crush of the lobby. She and Bruce stood to let the Osbornes pass them, and stayed upright to unkink their legs. Toward the back, she noticed the French-speaking couple from the afternoon. Their pregnant friend must have gone upstairs to stand in line for the ladies' room.

At last Joan remembered to ask Bruce about Camila's violin. He answered so softly that she had to strain to hear him over the general chatter, "It's missing."

"It's *what?*" Joan couldn't believe her ears.

"Missing," he said, still too softly for his voice to carry to the next row, not that anyone seemed to be paying attention. "There was no violin in her case. Her bows were there, but no violin."

"When?"

"When she arrived here and opened it. I went to wish her

luck one more time because she asked me to, back at the house, and she was just standing there, with tears running down her face."

"How did it happen?"

"I don't know," he said. "You'd think she would have noticed that the case was too light."

"If she even carried it. Maybe Harry Schmalz put it in the car for her."

"He did. Or maybe it happened after she got here. Someone who saw it in the first round might have made plans to steal it. I just don't know."

"How much is it worth?"

"Plenty. Camila plays a Stradivarius, from the Golden Period. It's probably worth a million. Maybe more."

"A million dollars?" No wonder they didn't let people go backstage.

"Yup. Her father is a wealthy banker in Brazil, and he bought it for her from a collector. Most of us have to mortgage our souls to buy our violins."

"She'll have insurance, won't she?"

"Oh, sure. But it's not as if she could run down to the corner violin store and plop down her insurance money for a new Strad. There *aren't* any new Strads." He shook his head mournfully.

The noise level in the theater rose steadily as people returned from the lobby. Joan saw Bob and Polly Osborne making their way unevenly back down the aisle. They kept stopping to talk along the way, and the noise kept increasing.

"Look at them," Bruce said. "They know."

"Everybody's going to know, Bruce. You can't keep a thing like that quiet." And why would you want to?

"Of course not. I was hoping that if there weren't too much hubbub tonight, she might be able to pull herself together enough not to get bumped out of the finals. She's a fabulous violinist, Joan. Much as I want it, I thought she'd probably win this thing. But now . . ."

She understood. "It's like Uwe's hand, isn't it?"

He nodded. "I want to beat them, but not like this."

"So what violin will she play tonight?"

"I don't know. One of the judges, I don't know who, is lending it. You know, like the concertmaster handing over his instrument when the soloist breaks a string in the middle of a concerto. All the judges have fine violins, but it's not the same as playing your own, especially hers."

Then Polly and Bob Osborne arrived at their row. "Did you hear about Camila's violin?" Polly said breathlessly, and when they nodded, she said, "The lobby's full of police. I don't know what they think they can do now. It's not as if anyone else had a violin back there to steal."

The Osbornes couldn't tell them anything new, and soon the lights dimmed and the voice announced that Camila Pereira had chosen Prokofiev's Sonata Number 2 in D major and Sarasate's *Zigeunerweisen*. Another flashy piece, Joan thought, but a wonderful one, if she can pull it off tonight.

The tall, golden-skinned beauty with the flowing hair strode onstage in a formfitting dress, followed by a man who was considerably shorter and rounder. They bowed to thunderous applause—at least partly sympathy, Joan suspected, although many of these people would have heard her in the first round and would be applauding her earlier performance. The pianist turned the little wheels on the sides of his padded bench to raise it and sounded the A for Camila to tune.

Camila began with the Prokofiev. Wisely, Joan thought when she recognized it by ear, though she hadn't by name. If the strange violin bothered Camila, Joan couldn't tell it by her playing. In the first movement, her tone was vibrant and the notes clean and sure. She had set the music on the stand, but turned the pages only between movements, when she also re-tuned. She took the rollicking second movement at a breakneck tempo. Some of the tension left her face, and when they finished the movement in unison, the pianist smiled at her. Like the man who had played with Bruce and Nate, he was far more a partner than an accompanist. Joan thought their communication was especially nice during the echoing in the third movement. Giving no quarter in the fourth, Camila flew above the piano's strong beats and ended powerfully.

The applause thundered again. She's all right, Joan thought. The little pianist smiled, bowed briefly, and left the stage. Camila set the music stand out of her way, tuned one more time, and began the Quigley piece almost before the applause had died down. She, too, made music of it. By now the notes were familiar enough that Joan knew when the hardest places were coming, but she didn't worry about triple axels with Camila. Only the harmonic double stops gave her pause, as if she were making very certain of their position on this unfamiliar instrument. Maybe she would have paused there anyway, Joan thought. It was not unmusical rubato.

Camila left the stage briefly before the Sarasate.

"She's doing it," Bruce said. "I don't know how, but she's doing it."

She returned with the pianist for the *Zigeunerweisen*. Sarasate's Gypsy airs were even flashier than his *Carmen* fantasy, but Joan thought there was no comparison between Arpad's and Camila's playing. When her bow finally raced to the finish, the audience stood, roared its approval, and generally made it plain that the judges might as well skip the rest of the competition and hand out the gold medal right then and there.

Whatever she's feeling about her missing violin, Joan thought, Camila has to be happy with her performance tonight and this response to it.

Smiling broadly now, the young woman tucked the violin under her arm and bowed again and again. They were still calling when she left the stage.

"Bruce, I don't know how you can fight that," Joan said when they stood to leave.

"It's all right," he said. "I'm not done yet. At least I won't feel I have to hold back."

"You'd do that?"

"Probably not." He grinned. "But I might feel I ought to. Now I'm free to lay into her and everyone else in the finals. If I even get to the finals."

No wonder Rebecca loves him, Joan thought.

Polly was right—the lobby was filled with police officers, who added to the heat and crush of the crowd. Bruce tried to go backstage to Camila, but not even his ID admitted him. Polly's wrong about one thing, Joan thought. There *is* at least one fine violin worth protecting back there tonight—the one Camila borrowed.

While they waited for Camila to appear, the Osbornes congratulated Harry Schmalz, who responded as warmly as if she were his daughter.

Joan congratulated a beaming Cindy Lloyd on her son's performance. "You must be so proud of him."

"Yes," Cindy said. "And relieved that I got to hear him. I was on such a tight schedule after showing a house in Louisville that I had to fly low on the drive back. It's a good thing I didn't know he was going to play first. I would have been a nervous wreck."

At last Camila emerged from the locked door, violin case in hand. The crowd surged toward her and followed her outside. Joan thought it was odd that the police made no attempt to hold them back. She waited near the front doors, welcoming the cool evening air whenever anyone left. Two young women who looked vaguely familiar—from the picnic?—pushed their way out, making catty remarks about Camila's dress and hair and even her playing, which they categorized as overdone. Her standing ovation, they said, was nothing but sympathy.

"I wonder who stole her violin," one said.

"I don't know, and I couldn't care less!" said the other.

"Did you see the way she was carrying on with my boyfriend at the picnic? She didn't even know him, but she knew he was mine, all right."

Bruce came, then, and walked Joan to the parking garage. He told her that the case Camila was carrying contained only her bows. No one would send her home right now with a precious instrument belonging to someone else.

"How will she practice for the finals?"

"I don't know. If it turns out that I don't have to practice for them myself, I could lend her mine."

Joan smiled. "That's sweet of you, Bruce, but I believe you're going to need it."

"I sure hope so."

7

The disappearance of Camila's violin made the national news. The live broadcasts of the finals would be carried on public radio stations, though only the awards ceremony and concert would be televised at all. But this kind of news brought out the networks and put the competition on the front page of the Oliver paper, which until now had run only one routine story listing the countries from which the competitors came and the awards for which they were vying.

Much was made of the value of the missing violin, variously estimated from five hundred thousand to five million dollars. Joan wondered whether the press and broadcasters made up their figures as they went along.

"Such an instrument can't be replaced by money," said an impassioned official of the competition in a plea for the return of the violin. "It's a priceless treasure that should be played by a master musician, in this case the fine young Brazilian violinist from whose hands it was torn."

"Is that the way it happened, Mom?" Andrew asked at breakfast. "Did they come right up to her and tear it out of her hands?" With expertise born of experience, he caught the toast that flew out of their old toaster and began slathering jam on it. No wonder he had good hands for a Frisbee.

"Not according to Bruce, and he talked with her. He said

she didn't even know it was missing until she opened the case to play it last night."

"Good." Andrew scribbled on a scrap of paper. "I needed an example of hyperbole for class."

Joan still had one ear on the radio, but in the excitement over the violin, the announcer hadn't mentioned the names of the finalists. No, this was only Monday. The judges' decision wouldn't be made public until Tuesday morning.

She was leaving for work when Rebecca called. "Mom, can you go up to Indianapolis?" she said. There was panic in her voice. "They're accusing Bruce of stealing that girl's violin!"

Bruce? "Who's accusing him?"

"How would I know! But he's so scared."

"Did they arrest him? Does he have a lawyer?"

"I don't know. I don't think so. Please go, Mom. I would if I could. You'd go if it were Andrew."

Below the belt, Rebecca. But I hear you. "I'll call work. If I can, I'll go up. But, honey, I don't know what good I can do him."

"Just *be* there, all right?"

Andrew had already left for class. Come on, Fred, Joan thought while she dialed his number on her mother's old, slow kitchen wall phone. At least she wouldn't have to fill him in. She had called him after making it home in one piece Sunday night. Fred, not generally overprotective, had seen too much carnage on the road to take any highway driving for granted, and so she'd promised. After the events of the evening, it had been good to know he was expecting her call, and to be able to unload the full story.

He picked up on the third ring.

"I was halfway out the door. What's up?"

Joan told him. "Can you help him?"

"I don't know anyone in the IPD. But we ought to try— the kid's squeaky clean."

"What are you talking about?"

"I wasn't going to say anything, but I ran a background

check on Bruce after we went up there, and I couldn't find so much as a parking ticket. Don't be mad."

"Mad!"

"I didn't want to interfere, but hell, Joan, it's Rebecca's whole life."

"Fred Lundquist, I think you're turning into a father." She smiled into the mouthpiece.

"That's the general idea."

She could imagine his eyes. But was she so possessive, to have made him worry like that about how she'd react to his concern? Never mind, she thought. "So you think I should go."

"Absolutely."

"Good. I'll call the center. And I'll see you when I see you."

She left a note for Andrew and told the Oliver Senior Citizens' Center she had to be gone for the day, knowing, but not caring, that some of the old women would confabulate romantic reasons. At the last minute, just in case, she threw an overnight bag into her Honda. She didn't have to tell anyone it was there, but having it gave her some feeling of control.

Having been a passenger instead of the driver until now, Joan wasn't sure she could find the house where Bruce was staying, but she had kept Polly Osborne's good directions and made it to the neighborhood without difficulty. Once she recognized the Schmalzes' curving limestone porch, which matched the porch out back on which Uwe Frech had broken his hand, it was easy to find the Osbornes' house next door.

Polly opened her front door only a crack at first, and then held it wide.

"Come in," she said. "I'm so glad it's you! I keep expecting to see a TV truck in the front yard, or the police with a search warrant, or worse."

Worse? Mobs, maybe? "I should have called," Joan said. "My daughter phoned this morning, and it sounded as if I'd need to bail him out of jail." She could hear a violin playing

Mozart somewhere in the house. At least Bruce was still a free man.

"No, no, he's here. Trying to keep his mind on his music and practice for the finals. I'll tell him you're here."

"Couldn't you fill me in first? I hate to break his concentration."

Polly took her into the comfortable living room, where Joan reclaimed the ottoman. She had to accept a cup of steaming coffee before Polly would sit down and talk. It smelled fancier than any coffee she ever bought, and tasted as good as it smelled.

"Well, you know almost all of it," Polly said. "After you left, there was lots of talk about Camila's violin. We were all too tired to hang around, so we went home. Before we went to bed, though, the police came to our door, asking for Bruce. They asked us all about his movements last night, and they read him his rights before they talked to him. They'll want to talk to you, too."

"I don't know anything about Camila's violin!"

Polly laughed. "No, of course not. But you were here. You know that Bruce went over to the Schmalzes' house before we left for the concert."

"I saw him go," Joan said carefully. "All I know about what he did there—all you know—is what Bruce told us. The police can ask him that for themselves." Why am I backing off? she thought. Am I afraid to talk to the police? But I can't testify to what I don't know for myself, can I? Is giving information to the police the same as testifying? Or am I fooling myself? Don't I trust Bruce? But he's such a sweetheart. Even Fred says he's squeaky clean.

"They already asked him," Polly was saying. "And they asked us separately. More than once. As if they were trying to catch someone in a lie."

"I suppose they are." Fred, where are you when I need you? "I'll do my best for him. There's nothing to lie about."

"No. We've already told them the truth, and that's why

they came back this morning and put us through it all over again."

"They what?" Joan set her cup down so hard that a few drops spilled onto Polly's oiled walnut coffee table. She swiped at them with her hand. Polly didn't seem to notice.

"Don't you see? Bruce was there by himself at the critical time. He could have taken Camila's violin when she was upstairs getting dressed."

"But he wouldn't!" Joan was surprised by the passion in her own voice, especially after her first wishy-washy response.

"I don't believe it, either," Polly said. "But of course, we don't really *know* Bruce, do we?"

Fred knows more than the rest of us, Joan thought. And if he could find it out that quickly, the Indianapolis cops can, too. The music had stopped, she realized suddenly, and so it didn't startle her to see Bruce standing in the doorway to the hall. His hair stood up in a red cowlick, and she thought he looked tired around the eyes. She wondered how much he had heard.

"Joan!" he said, and came over to her. "Rebecca said she'd call you, but I didn't expect to see you here on a workday."

She stood up and hugged him. "I almost didn't come. I didn't see what good it would do you to have me traipse up here, but Rebecca thought it would help. So here I am."

"Rebecca's right!" He hugged her back, and they all sat down, Bruce plopping onto the ottoman to face Joan and Polly on the sofa. "Not that Polly and Bob haven't been great, but they're kind of stuck with me." He shook his head. "I'm sorry to put you all through this."

"It's not your fault," Polly said quickly. Was she, too, hoping he hadn't heard her qualify her support?

"I didn't take the violin, if that's what you mean," he said. "But it was stupid of me to run over there and hold Camila's hand last night. She even talked me into going backstage right before the concert, when I can't imagine why she'd want anyone. I sure wouldn't."

She's a natural flirt, that's why, Joan thought, and she's making you feel important to her. Watch out, Rebecca. This guy's in over his head.

"Maybe Camila's got something up her sleeve," Polly said. "And she wanted you there to throw people off."

"You can't be suggesting that she stole her own violin," Joan said. "Why would she?"

"I don't know. Maybe someone offered her a price she couldn't resist, and she's greedy enough to want the insurance money, too."

"No," Bruce said flatly. "I saw her right after she opened that case. It wiped her out."

"Not for long," Joan said, remembering the radiant young woman who had wowed the audience. "A few minutes later, she was playing as if nothing had happened. She must have known someone would lend her an instrument."

"I don't think so," Polly said. "She'd have to be willing to risk not getting to play. But if she sold it and declared it stolen, she'd be getting twice the value of the violin. The thirty-thousand-dollar first prize is nothing compared to that."

"Camila's father is a wealthy banker," Bruce said. "How could she possibly need money so badly? You know her violin will increase in value every year. And what will she do for an instrument now? Even if she faked a theft for the insurance and kept the violin, she could never play it in public again."

"Neither could anyone else," Joan said. "So why would anyone buy it from her, once it's known to be stolen property? For that matter, why would any violinist steal it? Doesn't that rule you out?"

"Well, sure," Bruce said. "I mean, even if I would do such a thing. Who would want a violin he couldn't play?"

"Collectors," Polly said. "For some people, possession is enough."

Joan shivered. "Isn't it bad for a violin, not to play it?"

"That's the conventional wisdom," Bruce said. "But there's debate about it. Some people believe you can wear them out by playing them. And mine has a wonderful tone, even though it hadn't been played for years when I got it."

"How did you find it?"

"I didn't. It found me. The woman who owned it heard me play, and offered it to me."

"Just like that? Free?" Joan was dumbfounded.

He laughed. "Hardly free. I'll be paying on it for years and years, unless my career really takes off. She liked my playing, and she was willing to let me have it on a schedule I could afford." He shrugged. "I didn't argue."

Women fall all over themselves for this guy, Joan thought, suddenly doubting him again. But he *is* a superb violinist. "How did this woman happen to have it?" she asked.

"It was her father's. He played first violin in the New York Philharmonic and the Titan Quartet until he died, years ago. I guess she'd been waiting to find someone—well, worthy of it." Another shrug accompanied the red rising in his fair skin. He ran his hand over the cowlick, which popped back up.

Good as he is, he still feels awkward about praising himself, Joan thought, and her doubts receded again. She reached over and patted his hand.

"I can understand how someone might feel that way, Bruce, about a violin and about you. What I can't understand is how a person who plays as well as Camila would think of a Stradivarius as nothing more than a piece of property." A man, maybe, but not a Strad.

"I suppose not," Polly said. "It was probably a real thief. People do steal these violins, you know. I seem to remember that Erica Morini's violin was stolen when she was on her deathbed. And a few years back, someone stole a Strad and another valuable violin out of a Rolls-Royce in midtown Manhattan in broad daylight."

"For heaven's sake, how?" Joan said.

"I think the driver was using the car phone, and they distracted the passenger."

"But no one distracted Camila. And who would know

where to find her violin unguarded?" As soon as she'd said it, Joan wished she hadn't.

"No wonder they think I took it." Bruce seemed to shrivel, and his voice cracked as if he were on the verge of tears. "I don't know how I'll ever prove I didn't."

Joan wanted to argue him out of it, but the words wouldn't come. Let's face it, she thought, the odds are low that the police will come up with the violin or the thief, either one. And if they don't, Bruce is right. He'll never be able to clear his reputation, even if they can't prove he did it. A cloud will always hang over him—and over Rebecca, if she marries him.

The doorbell made her jump. Feeling foolish, she hoped nobody had noticed.

"I know," Polly said sympathetically. "I've been like that all morning." She went to the door.

8

$\mathcal{I}$t wasn't the police, but Uwe Frech, smiling broadly and carrying a violin case with his good hand. Setting it down, he greeted Joan with a handshake and a little nod that hinted at German formality of years past. "Are you ready?" he asked Bruce.

"Sorry, Uwe." Bruce wore his usual wide smile, but stayed put. "Maybe another time. I've got company." He gestured toward Joan.

She didn't see a shrug. Did she hear it in his voice, or was it only her overactive imagination? "What were you going to do?" she asked Bruce, and bit her tongue. I'm butting in. I knew it. Just like a mother-in-law.

"I was going to visit a school with him, but I didn't know you were coming. I probably ought to stay here anyway and try to get some practicing in."

"You could come with us," Uwe said to Joan. "The woman who is driving us has a big car. I'm sure she won't mind."

"Go on, Bruce," Polly said. "It will take your mind off this whole miserable business."

She didn't have to push hard.

Bruce shrugged. "I wasn't going to get any work done today. Come on, Joan."

Joan was soon confused by the diagonal streets the Indianapolis volunteer driver negotiated with ease. Arriving eventually at an inner-city elementary school, they were escorted to a large room in which posters from the competition and children's drawings of violins covered the walls. Almost a hundred children, who looked to be between eight and ten, were crowded into a semicircle on the floor, giggling, whispering, poking each other, and pointing at the new arrivals. Joan found a chair behind the children while one of their teachers introduced Uwe, who parked his violin case on a low table.

"You're probably wondering how I can play the violin with only one hand," he said, and drew both laughs and sympathetic noises. "The secret is, I brought my friend Bruce along. He's an excellent violinist, and if he doesn't try to catch a Frisbee and fall down, the way I did, he has a good chance of winning the big Indianapolis violin competition—the one they call the Olympics of the violin. In a few minutes, Bruce will play for you. But first, I need help to show you my violin." He had the children help him open his case. Then, holding the violin between his knees, he asked them to pluck the strings while he tuned them. He let them rub his cake of rosin along the bow hairs and even unscrew the bow, so that they could see the loose hairs looking like the tail of the horse from which they had come.

"You know what the rosin is good for?" he asked. Most of them shook their heads, but a tiny girl with her hair in cornrows waved her hand in the air.

"Ballerinas rub it on their toe shoes," she said.

Uwe nodded. "Why do they do that?"

"So they won't slip and fall."

"You are right!" he said, and she squirmed with self-importance. "So why do I rub it on my bow? Am I afraid the bow will slip and fall?" They laughed. "But what if I rub butter on my bow instead of rosin? What kind of sound will the violin make then?"

There was silence. No one raised a hand.

"That's absoultely right!" he said. "It wouldn't make any sound at all, because the bow would slip across the strings instead of rubbing them and making them vibrate. Remember how they vibrated when you plucked them?" Lots of nods and eager agreement. "A bow that's sticky with rosin can make them do that, too. The vibrations make the music."

Uwe's a natural, Joan thought. He continued to involve the children until he turned the violin over to Bruce, who unhesitatingly flew into a Paganini caprice as exciting as the Gypsy airs with which Camila had brought the competition's audience to its feet. Chills went down Joan's spine. Bruce, you're really good, she thought. Maybe you *can* beat her, after all.

"Now it's your turn to ask us questions," Uwe said, when the applause for Bruce died down. The dam broke.

"Is that violin worth a million dollars?" a boy with hair as red as Bruce's demanded.

"Yeah," said another boy, before Uwe could answer. "Like the one that got ripped off?"

"Naw," said a third. "That was *two* million!"

"Good violins are expensive," Uwe said, "but mine didn't cost that much."

"Is there gonna be a reward?"

"I wouldn't be surprised," Bruce said. "If my violin were stolen, you bet I'd find a way to offer a reward. Anyone who tells the police something that helps them find this one is going to be a big hero, that's for sure. Keep your eyes and ears open. Sometimes kids see and hear things that grown-ups miss."

They left the children abuzz. On the way back to the car. Joan said, "Put that part about helping find the violin in your act, Uwe, even if they don't ask about it. The kids loved it. Besides, who knows, maybe one of them really will notice something."

After stopping for a sandwich, they repeated the performance at another school in the afternoon. By the time the volunteer driver dropped Bruce and Joan at the Osbornes' house, Joan had persuaded Uwe to take his act to Oliver, if she could set something up in the school and the senior center, and if she could arrange it with the people running the competition. They agreed on Wednesday afternoon.

"I think they won't object," he said from the car. "They feel sorry for me. But Bruce needs to practice. I'm sure he will be a finalist."

"I couldn't practice this morning anyway," Bruce said after Uwe left. "Good thing I don't have to play for a couple of days, even if I make it." In a little while the melodies of the Brahms violin concerto were floating through the house, but only after Bruce had persuaded Joan to accept Polly Osborne's urging to stay for supper. She followed Polly into that shining kitchen to see whether there was anything she could do to help and was soon peeling carrots and potatoes.

"I didn't want to tell you while he was listening." Polly was snapping the ends off fresh green beans. "But the police do want to talk to you. They're coming back."

Joan felt oddly better about staying, as if talking to the police were a greater justification for taking a day off than being a comforting presence to Bruce. The more she thought about what she had to tell them, though, the deeper her peeler dug into the carrots.

When a single soft-spoken detective arrived to take her statement before supper was ready, she was glad to get it over with. Yes, Bruce had gone out before Camila's concert. He said he'd gone next door to wish her well. No, Joan didn't know whether he'd spent time alone with Camila's violin. No, he hadn't been carrying anything when he returned. No, she hadn't seen or heard any unusual activity over at the Schmalzes' house.

"I didn't see or hear anything over there at all," she said, but promised to report anything that occurred to her later. After the man left, she was sure that nothing she'd told him could have made a difference one way or the other. So why were her hands shaking?

It's not as if I were afraid of policemen, she thought. Maybe I do think of Bruce as family.

Right now there was nothing she could do for him. He was working on the cadenza from the first movement of the Brahms, one of her all-time favorites. With the table set and the stew on the stove, Polly had changed into running shoes.

"I'll be back," she said. "But you don't have to do a thing."

I ought to move my body, Joan thought. She'd never been a runner, but ordinarily at this hour she'd be walking the mile home from work. She wandered into the living room. I'm a little tired, she thought. Maybe I'll put my feet up for a minute first.

The cadenza sounded wrong. Technically wonderful, and beautiful, to be sure, but the familiar notes led into others that were not what she expected to hear. What was he doing?

And then Bruce was patting her shoulder. "Wake up, Joan," he said. "Supper's on the table. You've been sleeping for almost an hour."

Embarrassed at falling asleep in the living room of people she hardly knew, but feeling rested, she joined the Osbornes in the dining room, where they kept the conversation away from what was on all their minds. At last Joan heard more about Bruce's family. His father, she already knew, was a general practitioner in Canton, Ohio. His mother, she learned now, was a serious amateur violinist who played in the Canton orchestra.

"She loves it that I'm into music. Both Sally and Tom care more about science, like Dad. And they're both jocks. Sally's on the high school track team, and Tom plays football. But they all cheer for me."

"Sounds like a great family."

"I'm lucky," he said. "And so is Rebecca. She's really happy about you and Fred, you know."

After supper Nate stopped by and offered Bruce encouragement. "It'll all blow over," he said.

"I hope so." Bruce smiled. He sounded doubtful, but Joan thought he looked more cheerful than he had all day, except while he was helping Uwe with the schoolchildren. The afternoon had done him good, she was sure.

"Hello, Nate." Polly Osborne came into the living room drying her hands. She'd shooed Joan out of the kitchen once the dishwasher was loaded. "How's your mother?"

"She had to go home to work. She'll come back if I play in the finals."

"You will," Polly said. "You and Bruce and Camila. I'm sure of it."

Nate and Bruce looked at each other. Nate shrugged, but he didn't toss his hair.

"I wish *I* were sure," Bruce said.

"Well, I am," Joan said loyally, even though she hadn't heard many of the other semifinalists.

"If they don't arrest me first."

"Bruce, they can't arrest you on no evidence," Nate said.

"They can't have any evidence, because I didn't do it."

"So who do you think did?"

"I don't know. But you're safe, Nate. You and Camila were out together until right before you both had to change for the performance."

The two violinists began to speculate, but came up with no ideas Joan hadn't already heard. Catching herself yawning, she thought she'd better not wait much longer to drive home. It was past nine.

"Thanks so much for coming," Bruce said when she told him. "It meant a lot."

"Anytime. You take good care of yourself." It felt perfectly natural to reach up and hug him.

She was in the front hall saying good-bye to Polly Osborne when the doorbell rang a few inches from her ear.

"Another one?" Polly said. "All this visiting is unusual. Mostly they all shut themselves up to practice." She opened the door to Harry Schmalz, whose forehead was wrinkled up into what must once have been his hairline. "Hello, neighbor," she said.

"Is Camila here?" he barked instead of greeting her.

"No," Polly said. "Why?"

"She's disappeared."

"Disappeared!" Polly stepped back. "Come in, Harry, and tell us what happened."

Joan followed them back into the Osbornes' living room. Polly introduced them quickly. "Harry Schmalz, Joan Spencer. I think you met at the picnic."

Harry nodded to Joan, but he addressed his words to Polly and the two violinists. "She said she was going out shopping with one of the other girls this afternoon to try to take her mind off the violin, but she didn't come back. At first Violet waited supper for her, but finally we went ahead and ate. Violet was kind of teed off. Camila runs on Brazilian time, but she knows how we feel about mealtimes. We sure weren't going to give her any grief about it today, though." His face softened.

"And then you got worried?" Polly said.

Harry's wrinkles climbed back up. "She's just a kid, you know? And she's a long way from home. So Violet started calling around. Turns out Camila didn't go out with any of the other girls. A couple of them talked about it with her, but she never called them, and they haven't seen her all day. Violet's been on the phone trying all the fellows. No luck. Your phone was busy, so I came over."

"Bob had some calls to make," Polly said.

"I was out with Uwe this afternoon," Bruce said. "We sure didn't see her. Then I came home to practice."

"I was just talking about going over to your place," Nate said. "If there's anything I can do . . ."

"That's the hell of it," Harry said. "I feel so damn responsible, but I don't know what to do. It's only been a few hours, and she's over twenty-one. The police would laugh in our faces."

"Not after what happened last night," Joan said. "I'd call them."

9

*A*s Joan had predicted, the Indianapolis police responded quickly to the disappearance of the woman whose rare violin had been stolen only the day before. The quiet detective returned, this time with a partner, an older man with a louder voice and grim face.

"Detective Richardson," the quiet man introduced himself. Joan had missed his name before. "And this is Detective Richards."

Really? Joan thought, but she wasn't even tempted to smile.

Sitting in the Osbornes' living room again, they listened to the little that Harry Schmalz could tell them. Joan propped her feet up on the ottoman and leaned her head against the soft back of the sofa. It was turning into a long evening.

"You wouldn't have a photograph of her, would you?" Richards said after taking down Camila's general description.

"Are you kidding?" Harry smiled for the first time since appearing at the door. "She's got a press kit you wouldn't believe. Plenty of pictures over at my house."

"Here's one," Polly said. She reached into the drawer of an end table and handed them her program booklet for the competition, open to Camila Pereira's page. "It tells you a little about her. Mostly where she's studied and performed."

"Rio, huh?" Richards said, looking down at Camila, who flashed white teeth at them from the booklet. His grim face softened. "What do we know about her?" Richardson asked. "Besides the violin?"

"Her family's wealthy," Bruce said. "Her dad's a banker. We were talking about that last night."

"She called home every night," Harry said. "The connection was always terrible, and she kept us awake, shouting in Portuguese."

Joan noticed the past tense. As if Camila were dead.

"It was awful last night," he said. "I couldn't understand what she was shouting, of course, but I had the impression they were blaming her for losing the violin. I can't imagine what they'll do when they hear we've lost their daughter."

"Let's not jump to conclusions, sir," Richards said. "She may have gone off on her own."

"God, I hope so," Harry said, shaking his head.

"We'll do our best to locate her," Richardson said softly. "But we need to ask all of you if you have any idea who might want to harm her."

They fell silent. Joan thought of the jealous words she'd overheard in the lobby. What do I know? Nothing, really. That young woman didn't say anything about Camila I didn't think myself. She's a flirt, period.

Richardson's eyes seemed to bore a hole through her. "You think of something?"

Joan sat straighter for a moment, but left her feet up. "Only that I heard a couple of cracks from some girls who were clearly jealous of her. Camila flirted with their young men."

"She flirted with everybody," Bruce said.

"And that got to you, did it?" said Richards, turning on Bruce. "You still willing to talk without a lawyer?"

"I don't need a lawyer," Bruce said. "I didn't do anything."

"Where were you this afternoon?"

"Practicing something I take seriously." His eyes flashed.

"Don't get cute with me, son. You practice all afternoon?"

"No. First I was out with Mrs. Spencer here and Uwe Frech, another violinist. We went on a school visit—lots of witnesses. When we came back here, I started practicing. I kept at it until Mrs. Osborne called us to supper."

"I heard him," Joan said. "Brahms and Mozart." But I didn't hear all of it, she thought. I fell asleep. Do I have to tell them that? Surely Bruce didn't stop practicing, do something to Camila, and come back in to wake me up for supper.

Richards nodded and turned to Polly Osborne. Joan's eyelids drooped, and she was having trouble following his questions. The only policeman she wanted to spend time with right now was at home, in Oliver. She sat up again and chewed the inside of her lip to stay awake. Why was she so tired? Sure, it had been late before she got home last night, but she'd slept this afternoon. Stress, maybe? Then how must Bruce be feeling by now?

"If you were fixing dinner, you didn't see him play," Richards was saying to Polly. "You just heard him."

"What's that supposed to mean?" Bruce asked. "You think I put on one of my tapes and took off?"

"You have tapes?" Richardson asked.

"Sure," Bruce said. "Audition tapes, and tapes I make so I can hear how I sound. You can catch a lot of stuff that way."

Joan didn't doubt it. That's why she never intended to tape herself playing viola.

"One night during supper we played a trick on him," Polly said. "We put on a tape of one of the famous judges playing one of Bruce's pieces, and told him it was a tape we'd made of him practicing that piece. He was horrified—said, 'I sound like *that*?' But when I couldn't keep a straight face, he knew."

A smile flickered across Bruce's face but left him sober again.

"So it *could* have been the tape recorder," Richards said.

"It could have been, but it wasn't." Bruce's voice was steady, and he looked the man in the eye.

"Let's move on," said Richardson. "What can any of you tell us about Miss Pereira's personal life?"

"Not much," Harry Schmalz said. "She had a serious boyfriend back in Brazil. God, she called *him* every night, too. She'd keep us awake half the night and then sleep in, when we couldn't."

Hardly the ideal houseguest, Joan thought. Hard to imagine that young woman as the violinist I know she was—is. Now *I'm* doing it.

"You think she'd run home to her boyfriend?" Nate asked.

"Not after the way she played last night," Bruce said. "She wasn't about to give up."

"We'll check the airport," Richardson said.

"And the shopping centers?" Harry Schmalz put in. "She told us she was going shopping with another violinist, but we've talked to all of them, and she didn't. Maybe she went out alone, and someone recognized her from the TV last night and kidnapped her. By now everybody knows her family has money."

"Have you seen a ransom note?" Richards said. "Or had a phone call?"

"Hell, no," Harry said. "But that wouldn't do them any good. It's her father who's the banker, not me. Besides, Violet's been on the phone all evening. The kidnappers couldn't have gotten a word in edgewise."

"Maybe she's had an accident," Nate said.

"We checked the hospitals before we came here," Richardson said. "And we'll put out an alert, in case she's brought in as a Jane Doe. We'd better go see the rest of those pictures and take a look at where she was staying." The two detectives stood up.

"Sure," Harry said. But when Polly opened the door for them, Violet Schmalz was standing on the front porch. "Violet!" Harry said. "Did you find her?"

"No," Violet said, and came into the living room. "I

called everyone I could think of," she quavered. "The only people I didn't call were the ones who run the competition. Oh, Harry they're going to be furious at us."

"Not half as furious as her family," he said.

"I feel so guilty." Violet turned to Polly. "You remember how much I griped about the crazy hours she kept, and when she took over my kitchen to cook that mess of Brazilian stuff with the black beans and rice. I even told you I wished she'd hurry up and leave, but I didn't mean it, not really. I meant it right that minute, all right, but she was really a sweet girl, and I was rooting as hard as anybody for her to win."

"I know," Polly said. "You were both great hosts."

"I'll say," Bruce said.

"Camila said so herself," Nate chimed in.

Joan couldn't stand it any longer. "You're all talking as if she were dead!" she burst out. "And you—" She turned to the detectives. "You've been quizzing Bruce as if you thought he'd killed her. Why don't you start by looking for Camila, alive? She probably took a walk and got lost. I could get lost on these crazy streets!"

"Maybe she thought she spotted someone with her violin and took off after him," Nate put in. "She'd be lost in no time. But she might be in danger, too, you know," he said to Joan in a calm, reasonable voice, the kind she'd used many times to head off an explosion from her children. "They've got to consider that possibility."

"Ma'am, we consider this an urgent case," Richardson said in the same infuriatingly calm voice. "We have to look in all directions at once. It's just routine."

"I know. I'm sorry. I'm just tired. If you don't need me here anymore, I'd better go home." She hugged Bruce and Polly and escaped to her car with as much dignity as she could manage. On the way home, she wished she could talk with Fred.

She wondered about the Schmalzes. Camila must have driven Violet wild. Wild enough to drive Camila off, or worse? She'd surely flirted with Harry, too. Had Violet seen her as a threat to her marriage? Was Harry more concerned about Camila, or did he suspect his wife of doing something drastic? Did Violet have a short fuse, or a long, slow one with a big bang at the end? Or how about Harry himself? Did he have a history of doing inappropriate things to young women? How would he respond to this one in particular?

It would be a relief to talk it all over with Fred. But when she finally called him, only his machine answered. He must have had some late-night emergency.

Well, that's what I'm getting myself into, marrying a cop. "Hi, Fred," she told the machine. "I'm home safe and sound, and really tired. Talk to you tomorrow."

No sign of Andrew, either. She showered, brushed her teeth and hair, pulled on a clean nightgown, and crawled into bed, meaning to read herself to sleep. When she flicked the switch on the reading lamp, though, it refused to turn on, as it had for the last three or four nights. Rats. She kept meaning to change the bulb, but the extra bulbs were down in the furnace room, an inconvenient fact she never remembered until she was barefoot.

I'll remember to bring one up tomorrow. I hope I'm tired enough tonight to go to sleep without a book.

Yawning once, she curled up and knew nothing more.

10

The boys who called 911 on Monday had reported "a dead man curled up in the gutter." From the location, at the very end of a shady street that ran past the campus, Fred had expected to find a young faculty member at Oliver College, or maybe a student. The students called these the "tree streets," and the upperclassmen who moved out into older houses that had been divided into apartments paid a premium to live on them. Not the kind of neighborhood that ran to dead men in gutters.

With Officer Jill Root driving, Fred had wasted no time getting there, but the ambulance had arrived first, and the fire fighters who doubled as paramedics were performing the obligatory CPR. Fred sighed when he saw them laboring over the man spread-eagled several feet from the gutter. They'd already compromised the crime scene—if there had been a crime.

Showing his badge, but keeping out of the way just in case the paramedics were right this time, and there was life left in the too-still body, Fred circled around to get a look at the face.

Root, who beat him there by inches, cried out, "Kyle! My God, Lieutenant, it's Kyle Pruitt!" She was trembling, but didn't interfere.

When the fireman bending over the head paused between puffs, Fred glimpsed the sergeant's flaming hair and round, freckled face, often florid, but now abnormally pale. Fred had been putting some pressure on Pruitt to work off some of the extra pounds he'd carried around at least for the couple of years since Fred had arrived in Oliver. Never one to turn down food, Kyle had claimed in recent weeks to be jogging and biking five and ten miles a day, but Fred had seen little result.

Dammit, Kyle, he thought, you drove me crazy sometimes, and I still don't know how you made sergeant, but you didn't deserve to have your life cut short like this. Did you collapse of a heart attack because you pushed yourself too hard? Or worse, because I pushed you too hard? Shaking his head sadly, he watched the useless effort to revive a dead man. You couldn't dissuade these guys. He had seen paramedics attempt CPR on a man with his chest shot away.

The firemen finally stopped, as Fred had been sure they would. But then, checking Kyle's heart one more time, they put an oxygen mask over his face.

Fred was suddenly hopeful. "Detective Lieutenant Lundquist, Oliver Police. This is Sergeant Kyle Pruitt. He's alive?"

"Yeah, we've got a thready pulse," one man said. "I know Kyle—went to school with him. He's awful banged up."

"Banged up?" Not his heart, then?

"Someone plowed into him pretty damn hard," said the other man, now splinting Kyle's left leg. "This whole leg is a mess. And he must've hit his head when he hit the ground. Might be a skull fracture."

I didn't do it, Fred thought. Relief flooded over him, and with it, new guilt, for caring almost more about his own responsibility than Kyle Pruitt's life.

Root had pulled herself together and herded the little crowd of students gathering in the street back onto the sidewalk.

Fred radioed the dispatcher. "It's a hit-and-run," he told her. "I want Ketcham here. The victim's on the job." He omitted the name so that the Pruitts wouldn't get the news from some scanner-happy neighbor, but he knew the department would send everyone it could spare to investigate this particular hit-and-run. Steady, intelligent, middle-aged Sergeant Johnny Ketcham was Fred's first choice.

"Were the kids right?" the dispatcher asked. Fred translated: Is he dead?

"Not yet. He's not moving, but they're still working on him. And what happened to the kids who called it in, anyway? Did you get their names?"

"Negative—they were too scared. They sounded young—you could tell they were boys, but their voices hadn't changed. I told them to go back there and wait for you, Lieutenant."

Fred didn't see anyone younger than a college student.

"Anybody see what happened here?" he asked, but no one volunteered. "Anyone here before the ambulance arrived?" he tried.

"Only me," said a young man on rollerblades, wearing an Oliver College T-shirt. "The rest of them came later. But I didn't even notice the guy until the sirens stopped and the ambulance pulled up beside me."

"Did you see them move him?"

"Oh, sure. They pulled him out of the gutter and rolled him over to do CPR."

The gutter—so the kids were right about that, at least.

"Which way was he facing before they moved him?"

The young man frowned. "The curb, I guess. Or down, I don't know. I didn't notice him, you know?"

"No, I mean which direction was his body aimed? Against the traffic? Or with it, the way he is now?"

"Oh. Yeah. With it—he never saw what hit him. That's why I skate the other way."

Fred skipped the lecture about staying out of the street. "He never saw it—but did you?"

"I told you. All I saw was the ambulance."

"Did you notice any kids around?"

"A couple, but they didn't go near him. They came from

over there," and he pointed in the direction of the college library. "They took off when the guys got out of the ambulance."

"You see where they went?"

"Uh-uh." He shook his head. "I was watching the action here."

"What did they look like?"

"I don't know. Just kids, a boy of maybe ten or twelve and a bigger one about fourteen or fifteen. The big one stood yay high," and he held his arm about five feet from the ground. "Grubby jeans, Indiana T-shirts. Both real blond—towheads. The little one had an old beat-up bike with a banana seat. The bigger one had a ten-speed he had to stand up to ride."

Even with Fred's pumping, he came up with no more details. His attention had shifted quickly from the boys who had left to the drama happening in front of him. Fred took down his name, dorm address, and phone number, and handed him a card. "Let me know if anything else comes to you."

"Sure thing, Lieutenant." The student glided off down the street, facing the occasional cars that Oliver thought of as traffic. Even half an hour earlier there would have been more witnesses, but the college offices had emptied at five, and most folks were home eating supper. Just bad luck. Or maybe someone had seen it happen but didn't want to get involved?

The paramedics were loading Pruitt into the ambulance now, with a backboard under him, an oxygen mask over his face, a brace around his neck, and a blanket covering the rest of him.

"How's he doing?" Fred asked.

"He might make it to the hospital," the man who had gone to school with Pruitt said. He climbed into the back of the ambulance with the stretcher. When the other paramedic slammed the doors and climbed into the driver's seat, and the siren wailed, the students dispersed quickly and silently, leaving Root standing alone on the curb.

"I can't believe it," she said. "Kyle. He's so young." She

turned her face away for a moment, and then faced Fred, her eyes shining. "Sir, I'd like to go to the hospital."

"As soon as Ketcham arrives." Heading back to the unit she had driven, Fred quickly scanned the street for skid marks. Nothing. The driver hadn't even tried to stop. It wasn't dusk yet. No way the creep wouldn't have seen the heavy, red-headed Pruitt.

Three units pulled up. Fred quickly filled Johnny Ketcham in on the little they had. "Only witnesses might be those kids, but I'll give you odds they didn't see it happen." He left the investigation of the scene in Ketcham's competent hands. It didn't look as if he'd find much, but you never could tell.

"Okay, Root, let's move it," he told her, deliberately keeping it brisk. Was she emotionally involved with Kyle? He had no idea. "I'm afraid Pruitt's going to be the only one who can tell us who hit him." If he lives.

In the hospital's limited emergency room, it quickly became apparent that they weren't going to get anywhere near Kyle Pruitt for some time. A soft-spoken, middle-aged nurse, whose ankles bulged over the tops of her white oxfords, told them he was alive, but still unconscious. They were welcome to sit in the waiting room. Fred pulled rank on her.

"I want Officer Root closer than that, in case he regains consciousness," he told her. "She won't get in your way, but I want her to hear anything he says, even if it doesn't seem to make sense. It's important. Sergeant Pruitt is the victim of a hit-and-run driver."

The nurse sighed. "I don't think it's going to do any good," she said. "But you can stay if you want to, honey," she told Jill Root. "We'll give you a chair where you'll hear him if he makes any noise. You want some coffee?"

"Maybe later," Root said. "Thanks."

"You know his family?" the nurse asked her. "We're going to need someone to sign the forms."

"I'll tell them," Fred answered. "You let me know if anything happens, good or bad."

The nurse was opening her mouth to respond when Root said, "Yes, sir."

"And you take it easy," Fred told Root. "This could be a long night. I'll send another officer to let you go for some supper."

"I'll be all right."

"I know you will. But you won't do us any good if you fall asleep."

"Maybe I'd better have some of that coffee, after all." She looked uncertain.

Fred nodded, and left. He stopped in at the station to get the Pruitts' address and fill the others in, especially Captain Warren Altschuler, his chief of detectives. They'd already heard some of it from the dispatcher. With a wave of his hand, Altschuler okayed whatever overtime was needed.

"Keep me informed," he said.

"Okay if I go with you?" Detective Chuck Terry said, his brown face grim and his voice even huskier than usual. "Kyle's dad was my Scout leader."

"I'd appreciate it, and I'm sure they will." Times like these made Fred feel more than ever how much a stranger he still was in Oliver.

Kyle Pruitt, pushing forty, though he looked younger, still lived with his parents in the modest frame house in which he had grown up. The Hoosier bungalow was L-shaped, with a long porch inside the L and two doors from the porch, one into a room with a double bed visible through the window, the other into what looked like a living room. Terry knocked on the living room door.

It was opened by a short, round, graying woman whose smile showed teeth too perfect to be her own. She was wearing a full-length flowered apron not unlike the demin one Fred wore for serious baking. Wiping her fingers on it, she took Terry by the hand.

"Well, hello, Chuck," she said, apparently not at all alarmed to see two police officers standing together on her front porch. She stood back and held the door wide. "Come on in. Kyle's out, but I expect him back any minute. He's late for supper now, and he knew I was fixing fried chicken and biscuits. It's all ready. Can you stay?" Her warm smile included Fred. "You always loved my biscuits, Chuck."

"Yes, ma'am, I do," Terry said, and stepped inside, with Fred following. "Is Mr. Pruitt at home?"

"Well, sure. Sam, come see who's here!"

The man who came into the living room was Kyle, aged by twenty years or so. The red hair was faded with gray, and flab had turned to downright fat. But Fred would have recognized that wide grin even out of context. He hated what had to come next. At least they would hear it together.

"Mrs. Pruitt, Mr. Pruitt, I'm Detective Lieutenant Fred Lundquist," he said. And before they could glad-hand him, "We have some bad news." He paused, and saw the fear enter their eyes. They were as ready as they were going to be.

"About Kyle?" His father tightened his lips.

"Yes, sir. He was hit by a car this afternoon."

Mrs. Pruitt gasped. "Is he—"

"No, ma'am. He was still alive when I left the hospital, but it's very serious."

"We'll take you over there," Terry said. "Let's just turn off your stove." He ducked past them into the next room as if he were a member of the family, and Mrs. Pruitt hurried after him, untying her apron behind her back.

"What happened?" Sam Pruitt asked. "It was that bike, wasn't it? He did some damnfool stunt on that bike."

"No, sir," Fred said. "He wasn't on his bike."

"I ought to know if my son was riding a bike," Pruitt said, his tone increasingly angry.

"There wasn't any bike when I saw him," Fred said carefully, but he didn't doubt Mr. Pruitt. What had happened to Kyle's bicycle? It certainly explained a lot. Most of his injuries had been to his leg, low on his body. And the force of his fall made more sense if it had started from the seat of a bicycle.

"Whaddya mean, when you saw him? There sure as hell

was when he rode off on it. Did you ask the guy who hit him?"

"No, sir, we couldn't. The driver didn't stop."

"Didn't stop! Oh, my God." Pruitt's face crumpled. "Did you hear that, Barbara?" he asked Mrs. Pruitt as she came back into the room with Terry. "He didn't stop. Hit our boy and didn't even stop." He reached out to her blindly. Shorter by inches, she pulled his head down to her shoulder and held him while he wept.

11

At breakfast the next morning, Joan learned what Fred had been doing the night before. OLIVER POLICE OFFI-CER NEAR DEATH the local headline screamed, and beneath it, HIT & RUN DRIVER SOUGHT, with a fresh-faced, serious picture of Kyle Pruitt at the ceremony when he was promoted to sergeant and another of him looking even younger, as smiling Officer Friendly, surrounded by big-eyed children at the elementary school. In a third, Fred and Charles Terry, the tall black detective who had interviewed the Gilbert and Sullivan pit orchestra last summer, were escorting Sergeant Pruitt's parents into the hospital.

The accompanying story emphasized the gravity of his injuries. It quoted Fred as saying that the police were searching for clues to the driver, and asking anyone with any information about the accident to contact the Oliver Police Department immediately. They urgently needed to find the bicycle Sergeant Pruitt had been riding, for the evidence it might yield about the automobile whose driver had left the scene after hitting him. And especially, they hoped to talk to two boys who had called in the accident, but not left their names.

"Turn on the radio," Joan said to Andrew. "I want to hear the news." But the Oliver College station provided no more information. The downed officer was still fighting for his life, the young announcer said. His comrades in the Oliver Police Department were still baffled by the accident and by the disappearance of Sergeant Pruitt's bicycle, a blue Schwinn ten-speed. Joan wondered whether Pruitt was part of Oliver's bicycle patrol. Would they use a sergeant for that?

"Did you know him?" Andrew asked.

"Not really. I met him a couple of times. Oh, Andrew, I feel so sorry for his parents! I know how I'd feel if it happened to you." She felt her eyes begin to fill up.

Andrew reached across Grandma Zimmerman's old oak kitchen table and patted her hand.

"Mom, it's okay. I'm right here, honest."

Blinking back tears, she said, "I know. It just got to me all of a sudden."

"Guess you won't be seeing much of Fred for a while," he said matter-of-factly, and buttered his toast.

"Guess not." This is the part I've already lived through, except that Ken would have been comforting the family instead of going after some drunk. "Unless they catch the driver right away."

"Fat chance," Andrew said. He poured her a second cup of coffee. "Did you read the story?"

"Most of it. Why?"

"They don't have any witnesses at all. Even the kids who called 911 disappeared. You think they stole Pruitt's bike?"

"Maybe," she said thoughtfully. "But it doesn't fit with calling 911. Maybe the driver stopped long enough to remove the only thing he could have left any evidence on."

"And left a cop dying in the gutter?"

"They don't say he was in uniform, Andrew. He was out riding his bike. Some people have it in for bikers. And I'll bet he looked dead. The driver thought he was dead, and then he thought, why stop? Why ruin my life? What difference can it make?" She was warming to it. "But if I'm the driver, and I stop to pick up the bike, I must have something to put it in. So I'm driving something big—a station wagon, or a van, or a pickup."

79

"Yeah, or a Winnebago."

"Or a moving van. Or a car pulling a trailer."

Andrew's eyes lit up. "Or a Honda with a bike rack."

"I suppose. And you may be right about the kids, too. Or somebody else could have ridden off on it while they were calling 911."

"I'll bet Fred's really looking for those kids," he said. "So, Mom, tell me about Bruce. You haven't said anything about yesterday."

That's right, Joan thought. And there was nothing in the news about Camila, either. Are they keeping that quiet for a reason? Or did she show up, after all? Or did the news about Pruitt bump what was already of scant interest to Oliver?

"I think he's all right, but things keep happening up there. Last night they couldn't find Camila. The police came over to the Osbornes, and I didn't get home until late."

"So, is she back?" Andrew didn't volunteer where he'd been that late, and Joan didn't ask. The only reason she had any idea of his schedule was that they were saving the cost of a dorm room by having him live at home. He was a good kid. She didn't want to cramp his style just because her budget was tight.

"I don't know. Kyle Pruitt's bigger news in Oliver. But they'll tell me at the Senior Citizens' Center if it made the news up there." Most of the old folks, Joan knew, watched the TV news out of Indianapolis as faithfully as they checked the obituaries in the local paper. Quickly, she scanned page two, glad to see that none of her old regulars had died over the weekend. She stashed her lunch in her shoulder bag and set off on foot for work.

As usual, she cut through the park that separated her street from Oliver's tiny downtown, but nothing about the park was usual anymore. Few trees remained standing since the tornado that had torn through the park last summer. Instead, huge piles of firewood the town had cut from the stricken trees would fuel the handsome limestone fireplace in the new picnic shelter for many years to come, and excess wood had been offered to townspeople with fireplaces and woodstoves, as well. Memorial donations were being sought for new trees. Joan had given money for a sycamore in memory of her parents, and she was touched when Andrew and Rebecca together donated a maple in memory of their dad. It would be a good twenty years before these saplings provided much shade, though. She'd be almost old enough then to attend the Senior Citizens' Center for her own sake. Meanwhile, the sun beat down on her when she walked to and from work. July and August had been scorchers, but she rejoiced in September's relative cool; today she was hardly perspiring when she arrived at the center.

"Welcome back, Joanie," old Annie Jordan greeted her. Annie was already ensconced in her usual seat by the window, with her knitting needles flying. Four needles today, and a tube of bright red worsted yarn hanging below them, one of many new mittens Annie supplied her grandchildren every year. When Annie pulled out one needle and turned the mitten to start knitting on the next, Joan saw a cable already twisting its way up the back of the mitten.

"You weren't sick, I hope," said Margaret Duffy, the old teacher who had helped her get the job as director of the center. "We worried about you."

"Thank you, Margaret, but I was fine. Had a little family business to attend to."

Margaret nodded, folding her hands in her ample lap. It was hard to imagine Margaret really worried. She was one of the calmest people Joan knew. Always had been, even when dealing with thirty sixth-graders.

"You take off to see Rebecca's fiddler?" Annie asked. Rebecca had made a big hit with the women of the center when she'd come to Oliver for the quilt show and had helped them finish the quilt the orchestra raffled off.

"Yes, as a matter of fact, I did."

"You think he's good enough for our girl? We don't want her mixed up with anyone who won't treat her right."

"He seems like a fine young man." She wasn't about to

tell them the police had practically accused Bruce of doing away with the competition.

"Well, then, I hope he beats the pants off all the rest of 'em." Pulling a cable needle out of her topknot, Annie turned another twist in the red cable.

"Me, too." Joan smiled at Annie and sat down at her desk to work through the mail. As others began arriving for the day's programs, it became clear that the unscheduled topic of the day would be Kyle Pruitt and his parents, whom these folks clearly knew well.

"Sam and Barbara are dear people," one woman said. "I hate to see them have to go through something like this."

"Salt of the earth," a man answered her. "I used to work for old George Pruitt, before he gave up the family farm. He expected to hand it down to Sam, but Sam never took to the farm. Had his heart set on being a mechanic. And he's a good'un."

"I wouldn't trust my Buick to anyone else," another man said.

"Barbara's such a homebody," the first woman said. "All she ever wanted was a house full of children, but she never had but Kyle, and him late in life."

"That's mighty risky," Annie Jordan put in. "Could have been a Down's baby, you know."

"That's what the doctor told her, but she was bound and determined to have him, and then that was the end of their family."

"Probably decided they'd better stop while they were ahead," Annie said.

"All I know is she's been scared something would happen to him ever since he joined the police force. It'll half kill her if he doesn't make it."

Poor woman, Joan thought. A new worry crept into her mind. I'm getting awfully old to have a baby. Do I have the right to risk another one at my age? Still, if Fred wants children of his own . . . they'd do amniocentesis, of course. But could I bring myself to act on it, if we got bad news? Is there nothing simple about this whole business?

"You're a million miles away," Annie said, and Joan jerked herself back.

"I'm sorry, Annie."

"You thinking about all the fuss and feathers up there in Indianapolis?" Margaret asked.

Relieved to change the subject, Joan asked, "What did you hear?"

"You know, about that missing violin. Why, is there more?"

She never missed anything in school, either, Joan thought. "Well, I don't know, exactly," she said. "Last night they couldn't find the violinist who owned it. I listened to the local news this morning, but it was all about Sergeant Pruitt." So maybe Camila did show up, after all.

"Brazilian, isn't she?" asked Alvin Hannauer, the retired professor of anthropology who had known Joan's father when he was visiting faculty at Oliver College all those years ago. Like Margaret, Alvin was a member of the center's board of directors.

"Yes," Joan said. "Camila's from Rio de Janeiro." She pronounced the Rs as she always had, not with the Portuguese H sound that had entranced Andrew—though, of course, it was really Camila who had entranced Andrew.

"Those Brazilians are an impulsive lot," said a trim retired army officer who played at bridge and worked at charming the ladies several days a week. "Like as not, she threw up her hands and took the first plane home."

As she had at the Osbornes' house, Joan felt oddly obliged to stand up for Camila. "I can't believe that. Bruce—that's my daughter's fiancé—said she was all broken up when she discovered the violin was missing, but she came out on the stage and played on a borrowed instrument so beautifully that if the audience had been voting, the whole competition would have been over right then and there. I can't believe she'd throw all that away."

"I heard she was a millionaire banker's daughter," the retired officer said. "Why would a girl like that care about winning a rinky-dink Hoosier fiddling contest? Let her daddy snap his fingers, and she'd hop on a plane just like that."

Joan had a hard time picturing Camila hopping when anyone snapped his fingers. "Maybe," she said. "But she seemed to take her career pretty seriously. It's no rinky-dink contest, either. The first prize is something like thirty thousand dollars. And in addition to the money, the winner gets concert bookings and the kind of prestige that can jump-start a solo career. It means far more than the prizes. Besides, I can't believe even a wealthy Brazilian would leave a Stradivarius behind."

"If she left it behind at all," the army man said. "If you want my opinion, it flew south ahead of her."

"You think it's a scam, then," Alvin Hannauer said.

"Hell, yes. Pardon my French, ladies, but I wouldn't trust a Brazilian as far as I could throw him. If this one's disappeared, that's all the more reason to think there's something phony about her missing violin. And I'll tell you one thing for damn sure. If I handled their insurance, it would be a cold day in hell before I'd pay out on *that* claim."

It wasn't anything Joan hadn't heard before, but it left a bad taste in her mouth. She wished now the subject had never come up.

"Look who's here, Joanie," Annie said from her seat near the window.

Joan looked out to see Fred coming down the sidewalk. She headed him off at the door. "Do you want to come in? Or talk outside? They'll be all over you this morning."

"Part of the job." He followed her into the center, and the questions rained on him as if he were a politician arriving at a press conference.

"Lieutenant, any word from the hospital?"

"How is he?"

"Is he still alive?"

Fred waited until they stopped. "He's alive," he said quietly. "That's all I know." He rubbed the back of his neck and closed his eyes for a moment.

He's been up all night, Joan thought. Leave him alone. Can't you see how he feels?

She needn't have worried. These folks didn't follow up with a dozen useless questions. They nodded and murmured to one another as if the center had turned into a hospital, or a funeral parlor. The bridge players sat down at their tables, and Annie carried her knitting to a good kibitzing spot behind them.

"Come on in, Fred," Joan said, and held the door to her tiny cubicle. He dropped onto the sturdy chair she kept for him. "Want me to find you a cup of coffee?"

"I'm floating in coffee."

"You up all night?"

"No, but I didn't sleep much. We canvassed the neighborhood for witnesses, but we didn't find anyone who saw or heard a thing. It's hard to believe nobody was on the street at that hour, but it happened down at the end, toward the arboretum. The few folks who live down there were watching the news or eating supper, if they were home. I doubt that it made the kind of noise a two-car collision would. No skid marks."

She got it. "No screeching brakes."

"Exactly. And one side of the street is classroom buildings. Not much open at that hour except the library, farther away."

"No students walking around?"

"If they were, they're not coming forward. The dorms are on the other side of campus. So's the pizza place."

"You think the driver stole the bike? Or the kids?"

"Or a third party, who may even have seen the accident." Again, he rubbed the back of his neck. This time he yawned.

"Can you get some sleep?"

He shook his head and looked into her eyes. "So, tell me about yesterday. Bruce okay?"

"I guess. But we had some more excitement up there last night. Camila—"

Fred's pocket beeped. She passed her phone to him across the mail cluttering her desk. He hit the numbers, said his name, and listened.

"I'm on my way." Without another word, he kissed her once, hard, and left.

Her lips still tingling, Joan watched him stride past the bridge tables and out the door.

I'll have to get used to it, she thought.

12

he phone was ringing when Joan walked into the house
with a handful of junk mail. She recognized Bruce's
voice even before he identified himself.

"Bruce, are you all right? Has anything happened?" What
a dumb question, she thought. But he answered as if it made
sense.

"I'm fine. I'm calling to tell you that I made it into the
finals."

"That's wonderful!" Dropping the mail on the table by
the door, she tossed her shoulder bag into the corner, kicked
off her shoes, and tucked her feet underneath her on the sofa.
"Tell me all about it."

"There isn't much to tell. We'll start the last part of the
competition tonight. The good news is that all the finalists
win substantial prizes."

"Who are the others?"

"You know Nate."

"Oh, good. I thought he deserved to make it."

"I agree. I don't think you heard Vivienne Rambeau or
Hannah Weiss. Vivenne's from Montreal—you met her at the
picnic—and Hannah's from Tel Aviv. Oh, and Katsuo Tanaka, from Kobe."

"No, I didn't hear any of them. Isn't there one more finalist?"

"Camila, of course, if she shows up in time to play. The police still haven't found any sign of her. Everybody is so concerned about her that the judges have promised to let her play both her concertos last, out of order, if it turns out that she's been absent for some reason she couldn't control."

"And if she doesn't show up in time?"

"Then she loses out, except for the stipend she'll get as a finalist."

"Would someone else take her place?"

"No, they're just rearranging the schedule. Vivienne plays Mozart tonight, and she was scheduled to play the Tchaikovsky on Friday. But if Camila doesn't surface by tomorrow, Vivienne will have to play her big concerto tomorrow night, after Nate and I play Mozart, and I'll play the Brahms on Friday night instead of Saturday. They're bending over backward for Camila. It won't make much difference for me, but it's going to be hard on Vivienne."

"Hardly a picnic for Camila, either."

"Of course. That's why we all understand."

"One of my old ladies at the center said this morning she hoped you'd beat their pants off."

Bruce laughed. "I'll try. Can you come to hear me? I can get you tickets."

"Any night but tomorrow. Orchestra night."

"That's when I'll play the Mozart, but the Brahms will be Friday or Saturday, depending on Camila."

"I'll be there for that, at least. I don't know what to tell you about Fred and Andrew, though. I never know about Andrew, and Fred's working on a hit-and-run—someone hit one of his sergeants when he was out riding a bicycle."

"Did the sergeant see the car?"

"I don't think he can talk. He may not make it."

Bruce was silent. Then he said, "Tell Fred I'm sorry. And let me know if you want more tickets."

Joan promised, and they hung up. What a week this was

turning into. Uwe would indeed arrive Wednesday afternoon—
that was only tomorrow. His Indianapolis driver would bring
him down, and Joan would escort him around Oliver, feed
him supper, and take him back after the orchestra rehearsal.

"I would very much like to see an American orchestra at
work," Uwe had told her.

"This is just a little community group, Uwe," she'd said.
"Not a professional orchestra like the Indianapolis Symphony."

"I used to play in a little one like that in Germany. They
have a charm of their own."

Alex, charming? Uwe would find out soon enough. And
now she realized that she'd better plan what to feed him. Not
that she could live up to the level of food he'd probably been
getting at his host family's. She'd have to put something in
the slow cooker. Maybe her never-fail pork roast, with onions
and dry mustard. Or beef. She'd check what was on sale. Too
bad she couldn't ask Fred to bake some of his sourdough
oatmeal bread. Unless, just maybe, he'd already baked on
Sunday, before Sergeant Pruitt was hit, and had frozen a loaf
or two. A German would appreciate that dense, flavorful
bread. She'd ask.

Her eyes traveled to the things she had tossed on the table
and floor, and the mess she hadn't picked up when she'd hurried off to work in the morning. And to the viola she hadn't
touched all week. At least he won't hear me alone tomorrow
night. The viola jokes aren't all wrong: How do you get a
violist to play a passage pianissimo tremolando? Mark it
"solo."

There were leftovers for tonight, at least. She could take
the next hour to practice, not for Uwe, but for her own sake.
No, she'd better go pick up the meat for tomorrow first—it
would have to cook all night, so that she could let it cool
tomorrow and skim off the fat. And she needed some milk.

Joan slid back into her shoes, picked up her bag, and with
an apologetic glance at her instrument, took off again. In the
grocery store, she was surprised to find the mood low. Even

the usually cheerful checkout clerk was somber.

"Did you hear about Kyle Pruitt?" she said as she slid Joan's roast past the scanner and typed in the code for onions.

"Hear what?"

"He died this afternoon. It just came over the radio. It's a darned shame, that's what it is. I don't know why those fraternity boys can't wait till after dark to start partying. And after twenty-one. All that underage drinking—dumb kids don't know what they're doing, and don't care." She slammed the plastic gallon of milk onto the end of the counter.

"Is that who hit him?"

"You watch, it will be."

So they still didn't know, she thought.

13

The plastic loops dug into the fingers of Joan's left hand while the fingers of her right grew cold from the handle of the milk. She hadn't been able to stop at three pounds of onions when the price on five was so much better, and the pork roast had looked so good that she'd bought a large one. By the time she reached her little house, she almost wished she'd driven to the store.

Andrew greeted her at the door. "Mom, Sergeant Pruitt died. It was on the radio."

"I know. The checkout clerk told me."

"You think Fred'll be here tonight?"

"I doubt it. We'll hang loose." I'm not about to call him now, she thought.

"What did you bring? I'm starved." He relieved her of her load and peered into the plastic bag.

"That's for tomorrow, except the milk."

"Tomorrow?" He put the milk in the refrigerator.

"Uwe Frech is coming to supper before orchestra. So we're eating early."

"What's Uwe doing in Oliver?"

She explained about the school and the senior center while she started the roast in the slow cooker and warmed up the leftover stew. Andrew set the kitchen table for two without further comment, and they ate quickly, getting it out of the way rather than savoring the food.

"You need me for anything, Mom?" he asked, carrying his dishes to the sink.

"Thanks, Andrew, I'm fine."

"I'm off, then." And he was, lifting his bike from the back porch to the driveway and pedaling off. By the time he came home, it would be dark. Good thing he had a bike light.

"Be careful!" she called, but then hoped he hadn't heard her. Turning her back on the door, she stashed the remains of the supper in the refrigerator and plunged her hands into hot sudsy water. She wasn't about to turn into a hover mother just because she sort of knew the victim of one freak accident.

Or was it an accident? Bad enough that it was a hit-and-run. What if someone took advantage of the fact that Pruitt was vulnerable on his bicycle to kill a cop? Had he been investigating someone who didn't want to be found out? Or had he made enemies in the past? Or did someone just hate cops? Maybe the checkout clerk wasn't wrong. Maybe it was fraternity boys, out on a bender. Or maybe they'd had problems with Pruitt before. Surely no one would go out after men on bicycles in general.

Joan realized suddenly that she'd been washing the same plate over and over. She rinsed it, stood it in the drainer, and reached for the next.

Stop thinking, she told herself. He'll be fine.

But she scrubbed the pot in which she'd warmed up the leftovers with more vigor than it needed, and left the stove the cleanest it had been in a week.

She was rosining her viola bow to practice when the phone rescued her from her own good intentions.

"Fred! Are you all right? Have you eaten?"

"Not yet. We've been kind of busy. You still want to feed me?"

"Sure, come on over."

Retrieving the last of the stew from the refrigerator, she

cut a couple of potatoes and an onion into it and sliced a
plate of pears and one huge King Luscious apple from the
local orchard while Fred's supper cooked and the coffee
brewed. Not fancy, but he wouldn't starve.

He didn't seem to notice what he was eating, and said
little until he had finished. Finally, though, he leaned back in
her old kitchen chair and looked at her with tired eyes.

"What a day. You heard about Pruitt?"

"Yes. Was that the call you got this morning?" No, she
remembered, that couldn't be right. They'd said the sergeant
died this afternoon.

"No. This morning the officer who was watching him
thought he was about to tell us something." He shook his
head.

"But he didn't?"

"I don't think he ever regained consciousness. Not really.
Officer Root was in love with him, and she heard her name
in the first sounds he made."

"Poor girl." Joan remembered Jill Root. "It must be
dreadful for her."

"I feel worse for his parents. They won't find another son
to take his place."

She winced, thinking of Andrew.

"He died at half past four. So now we've got a homicide.
That's bad enough, but he's one of our own, and we don't
have the first scrap of evidence. Not so much as a broken
headlight. Nothing from the vehicle on his clothing, either. I
don't think it even touched him. I'm convinced his injuries
came from the momentum of his fall. He left blood on the
curb, and there was gravel and dirt in all his wounds, but
that's all. If there's any other physical evidence, it's on that
damn bicycle."

"Which you don't have."

"Which disappeared into thin air, along with the witnesses, if there even were any. Today we reinterviewed all the
residents in that area and buttonholed every passerby from
noon to seven, and got zip. Tomorrow we're going back into

the school with the college student who saw those kids. We've got to find them."

"Nobody's answered your appeals?" Dumb question, she thought.

He shook his head. "It's human nature to be scared of getting involved. But this isn't New York or Chicago. I thought when I came to Oliver things would be different. I was wrong." He stared morosely into his empty coffee cup. She held out the pot, but he waved it away. "Gotta go back. There's not a damn thing I can do, but I can't just sit around."

"Oh, Fred."

"Cut it out!" He stood up abruptly. Halfway to the front door, he turned back. "Sorry."

"It's okay."

The door closed on her words. She cleared the table automatically and washed up for the second time, while her thoughts churned.

I know he's upset. But he didn't have to take it out on me.

Grow up, Joan! He's feeling terrible. He even apologized. Just don't push him. Be there for him when he feels like this, that's all. Give him some space.

Sure. And who's going to be there for me? I don't want to feel more alone married than single.

When her alter ego didn't come up with any good retort for that one, she didn't feel that she'd won an argument, but that she'd lost . . . what? Fred? Or only a fairy-tale image of him?

Not wanting to brood in silence, she flipped on the college radio station and recognized the last measures of the slow second movement of Mozart's *Sinfonia Concertante* for Violin and Viola, which she had occasionally attempted at home with a violin-playing friend. For a few moments more, the music matched her low mood exactly, and then the third movement's Rondo danced it out of her. She turned the radio off again and opened her viola case to practice, beginning not with the viola parts in her orchestra folder, but with the music she had just heard.

An hour later, she came up for air. Her arm and back ached, but her spirits had lifted considerably. She wiped the rosin off the viola and the strings, loosened the bow, and packed them both back in the case, covering the viola gently with the viola-shaped blue silk top Rebecca had quilted and sent her for Christmas.

As awful as it would be if someone took my instrument, she thought, I could find another one this good. But how desperate would I feel if I lost one as good as Camila's? What would I be willing to do to get it back?

14

On Wednesday, Uwe wowed them at the Senior Citizens' Center with his European charm and a tape of himself playing the Paganini caprice Bruce had performed in the classroom. Joan found unexpected tears in her eyes and turned away, hoping no one would notice.

But after accepting thanks from a number of the old people, Uwe asked her, "Are you all right?"

"I was just sad for you. This was the first time I heard you play. I didn't have any idea how good you were. Now it seems that much worse that you were kept from competing."

"Thank you," he said quietly. "And now, do we go to the children?"

"Oh, Uwe, I hope that goes as well here as it did up in Indianapolis. They may be a little distracted. In fact, they may already have had a visit from the police."

On the way to the school, she told him about Kyle Pruitt's death, and the disappearance of the boys who had called 911.

"You think those boys will come to hear me?"

"It's possible. There's only one school in the county now. I don't know what grades will be in your audience today, though."

"Maybe I can help. The kids in Indianapolis are all watching for Camila's violin."

"And for Camila?"

"I haven't visited any schools since she disappeared. But I think the ones Bruce and I talked to must be looking for her, too."

Joan could believe it, having watched the dollar signs light up in their eyes. Pulling into the familiar parking lot, she felt she should be lugging her viola and the box of orchestra folders. "This is where we'll come tonight for the rehearsal."

"The school sponsors the orchestra?" Uwe looked at the sprawling concrete Alcorn County Consolidated School building.

"No, we pay to use the auditorium and the timpani. The rest of us bring our own instruments."

In the principal's office, Cathy, a pretty girl who looked about fourteen, was assigned to escort them to the band room. When Uwe shook hands with her, she dimpled up at him and burst into chatter.

"I've been so excited ever since I heard you were coming. I even made Marybeth trade jobs with me in the office. Marybeth didn't care—she thinks the Beatles are classical music." She trotted beside him, taking three steps for each of his long ones.

Joan lagged behind. No question about where she belonged.

"So, Cathy, do you play the violin?" Uwe asked, smiling down at her.

"No, but I just love it! And I can't wait to hear you play for us!"

Was it possible that she didn't even noticed his hand?

Uwe didn't laugh. "Maybe you'll help me demonstrate my instrument to the other students, then?"

"Really? You mean it? Marybeth will just die when she hears."

This time Uwe's laugh burst out in the long, empty hall.

"I hope not." He looked at her seriously. "I heard someone young already died here this week."

"You mean Sergeant Pruitt? But he wasn't *young*. He must've been almost forty—my dad was on the football team with him ages ago. Isn't it awful? Someone ran over him and just left him there in the street to die. When I get my license, I won't even do that to—to a rabbit."

"I hope you never hit anything," Uwe said, and had to stop suddenly to keep from running over her when she turned in front of him without warning.

Don't count on it, Joan thought.

"Here's the band room. Better get in quick."

Joan made it into the room just in time to escape the mob of teenagers whose bulging backpacks nearly doubled the floor space they required.

The orchestra director, a woman about Joan's age, welcomed them warmly and invited them to follow her to the podium. Although more inclined to hide out at the back of the room, Joan tagged after Uwe and Cathy down the carpeted steps into the well of the funnel-shaped room, reminiscent of European university classrooms and an ideal setup for a band or orchestra, in which it was important for every member to see the conductor. Pictures of the high school band over the years covered the walls, and a shelf of large trophies attested to its success. She watched students handing chairs in from some other room, bucket-brigade style, and others passing music stands back out, presumably to make space for Uwe's audience. Many of the younger students were already sitting on the floor in front of the chairs, their backpacks on their laps. Maybe it wouldn't be a total loss to sit down front with Uwe. She'd be facing the audience and could keep her eyes open for a couple of towheads and watch their expressions when he made his speech about helping the cops.

"It's going to be pretty crowded in here," the director said. "I hope you don't mind. We're squeezing all our instrumental students in today—winds and strings, starting with the middle schoolers and going on up. They don't get a chance to meet a professional performer very often. The strings just about never do."

"I'm happy to be here," Uwe said.

Scanning the faces of the kids who continued to crowd into the room while the noise level increased, Joan shook her head. She'd already spotted a dozen or so boys who met the description Fred's witness had given of the two boys he had seen. Any attempt to watch them all at once was doomed before it started.

I suppose I could ask the teacher to put all the towheaded boys in one corner. She swallowed a giggle before it got away from her. And what did Fred's witness mean by "towheaded," anyway? The white-blond her mother had saved that word for? Or just any boy with light hair? That would include lots of these kids, not to mention the ones who weren't in band or orchestra. They could hardly take dozens of boys out of school for a lineup.

"Mrs. Spencer?"

She jerked her attention back to see Cathy holding what was surely the only empty chair in the room for her. "Thank you," she told Cathy, who promptly claimed a spot on the floor next to Uwe and flashed a "look at me now" smile at her schoolmates.

The bell shrilled again. The orchestra director tapped her baton on a stand for quiet, and got it. She did a good job of introducing Uwe and the violin competition, emphasizing that he had to be one of the best young violinists in the world even to have been allowed to enter it.

Uwe stood to wild applause. They're showing off, Joan thought. But he soon had their attention, with an older version of his talk to the little kids.

"If Cathy, my lovely assistant, will help me here"—blushes from Cathy, whistles from the boys—"I'd like to show you an instrument with hundreds of parts to it. It's not hard to understand why only a few people can make violins that sound as wonderful as the Stradivarius that was stolen from one of our top competitors last week. Or why they are so valuable, even to people who don't love music, as I hope all of you do."

This time he explained a little about violin making, woods, and varnishes, and discussed theories about how aging and playing could improve instruments, or wear them out. "We don't know exactly what will happen to any violin in the future, but we do know some simple things we can do to preserve them. Who can tell me why you don't leave your violin near a hot stove?"

A boy in the back row waved his hand. "To keep the wood from drying out."

"Right. And why you don't want it to get damp?"

"That'll wreck it, too," said a girl. "I got mildew on my bass once."

The give-and-take continued. When it came time to demonstrate the sound of the instrument, Uwe turned to Cathy. "You play the violin, Cathy?"

"Oh no, not me." She put her hands behind her.

"Then we will start with you." And with some quick tips on how to hold the instrument and the bow, he overcame her embarrassment and had her making acceptable sounds in only a few attempts.

If his hand doesn't heal right, Joan thought, he's a born teacher.

"Let's give her some applause for an excellent first lesson," Uwe prompted, taking the violin back, and they did. He consulted briefly with the orchestra director and turned back to the students. "Is Stan Cracraft here?"

"Yo!"

"Come down here, Stan, and show them how Cathy can sound if she studies hard for five or ten years."

A slender boy of sixteen or seventeen, Stan trotted down the steps. From the red mark below his left jaw, Joan guessed that he was the star of the high school orchestra. He accepted the violin and bow without hesitation, checked the tuning, and began playing what had to be Bach. Nothing dramatic, but every note clean and in tune. This time Uwe didn't have to ask for applause.

"What a great violin!" Stan said when he handed it back to Uwe. "I wish I had one that good."

"I'm lucky to have it, but it's nothing compared to the Strad Camila Pereira lost."

"What happened to it? And her? Where did she go?"

Right on cue.

"Nobody knows," Uwe told the room. "All the kids in Indianapolis are keeping their eyes open for her, and her violin. You should, too, if you go up to the city—there's a big reward." He described Camila to them. "You know, kids see a lot of things other people miss. Some kids your age were real heroes right here in Oliver. They called the paramedics when they saw that policeman in the street. Then they disappeared, just like Camila. Maybe they're afraid. But no one thinks they did it. The police hope they saw something that could help. Tell them that, if you know who they are. And tell your parents or teachers or the police if *you* see or hear something strange. That's how they find lost people. And lost violins."

Joan saw lots of big eyes, and some kids with eyes half-closed, whatever that meant. Maybe they were sleepy at the end of the school day. Or maybe they were trying to act cool.

"Okay," Uwe said. "You see I can't play for you, and I'm grateful to Cathy and Stan for demonstrating my instrument. But I also brought a tape. So I want to end with some violin music I played before I was so stupid to break my hand playing Frisbee. This is a caprice written by that great violinist, Niccolò Paganini." He pressed the button, and the music poured forth.

Again, the students were generous with their applause. The orchestra director thanked them for coming, and then the bell rang. The herd charged for the door, except for a few who hung around asking for autographs.

Cathy was one of those. "You were so great!" she told

Uwe while he signed the notebook paper she'd borrowed from a friend. "Wait'll I tell Marybeth what she missed!" And Uwe signed another, for the absent Marybeth.

"That went well, don't you think?" Joan asked him on the way home.

"I think young Stan could have a future."

"I'll see what we can do about recruiting him into the symphony."

While Joan finished fixing supper, Uwe set out on foot to see the sights of Oliver.

"Uwe," she called after him, and was glad to see him stop and turn around. "We have to eat by six or I'll be late."

When he waved his cast at her, she relaxed and checked the inevitable Wednesday messages waiting. Only one cellist had begged off, and her croak sounded like genuine illness.

Then she heard Fred's voice, sounding tired. "Joan, I'm staying away tonight. I'd be lousy company again, and I couldn't make it in time anyway. Maybe we can connect after you take Uwe home. Say hi to him for me." Nothing personal, but then, Fred didn't get personal when he didn't know who might hear him.

She was sorry not to have some time with him, but relieved not to have to wonder how he'd act tonight. With a light heart, she boiled some new potatoes, skimmed the fat off the meat and reheated it, and sliced cucumbers and tomatoes into a tossed salad.

Uwe arrived on time, and Andrew moseyed in.

"How's the hand?" he asked at supper.

"It doesn't hurt," Uwe said. "That's all I know until the cast comes off."

"I never should have thrown that Frisbee at you." Andrew's eyebrows scrunched together in the guilty look Joan remembered so well from his childhood escapades.

Right, she thought. Not to mention at the windows.

"No problem." Then Uwe looked at his hand and laughed. "I don't mean that, do I?"

"Thanks. I'm really sorry, man."

"I know. But the doctor thinks I will play again."

"That's good." Andrew's brows relaxed. Was it possible she hadn't told him Uwe's good news before now?

Guilt was still doing good work, though; Andrew volunteered to clean up. With no compunctions about accepting his offer, Joan took off immediately after supper, comfortably on time for a change. At least Uwe wouldn't hear Alex explode on that score.

15

Actually, Alex was more than cordial in her welcome, and Joan didn't worry about Uwe while she sorted out people's problems. The missing trombone folder turned up in the midst of the string box. Why did so many people leave the music? Not surprisingly after Alex's outburst the previous week, the cellos had taken theirs home.

This time Alex praised their good work.

"I knew you could do it! Why don't you practice like that all the time!"

She gives with one hand and takes away with the other, Joan thought. But it's better than last week, and the cellos are smiling.

The rest of the rehearsal went better than usual, and Alex didn't blow up even once. At a particularly beautiful place in the Unfinished, when the whole orchestra seemed to be responding more to the music than to its technical challenges, Joan felt herself transported, and forgot the observer for whom their efforts had to have fallen far short of perfection. When he crossed her mind again, she relaxed. We are who we are, she thought, and we're not pretending to be any better.

Afterward, Uwe waited by the outside door with the boxes of folders while Joan brought the car around.

"I wish I could help you carry them," he said, but it was clearly impossible, one-handed as he was.

She waved his concern aside. "I'm used to it. Besides, they aren't that heavy, now that more people are finally taking their folders home to practice. I just hope enough of them do before the next concert."

"You sounded better than I expected," he said while she opened the car doors.

"Really?" Rats, she thought. I wasn't going to ask for his opinion.

"Yes. I told you I played in such an orchestra. But yours is better."

In spite of herself, she enjoyed hearing it, but she was determined not to fish for more praise. All in all, the drive to Indianapolis passed pleasantly. They agreed that she would drop him at the Osbornes' house, where she could ask how Bruce's performance of the Mozart concerto had gone.

The Osbornes were turning into their driveway when they arrived. At the curb, the blue sedan in Joan's headlights disgorged Cindy Lloyd and Nate, in a tux and carrying his violin.

That's right, she thought, all the finalists played Mozart tonight.

"Hey, man," Uwe said. "How'd it go?"

"He was superb!" Cindy answered for him.

Even in the dark, Joan was sure Nate was rolling his eyes. He jerked his head toward the house, and Uwe followed him.

"Joan! I thought you weren't coming." Bruce loped toward her, also in formal concert dress, with his violin case on his back, hanging from a shoulder strap. He hugged her. "Didn't you have a rehearsal?"

"That's right. But I brought Uwe back, and I couldn't resist finding out how your concert went. If the Osbornes are having a party, I won't stay."

"No party. Polly invited Nate and his mom over for a cup of coffee. Come on in. You know she'll be glad to have you."

"How was the Mozart?" They started up the front steps in Cindy's wake.

"Okay."

"And Camila—any news?"

"Yes, but not about her."

But the news had to wait while Polly welcomed Joan with her usual enthusiasm and seated her on the sofa next to Cindy Lloyd, with a cup of that elegant coffee. Over by the kitchen door, Bruce was chatting amiably with Uwe and Nate. Even from that distance, Joan could see dark circles under Bruce's eyes, and a drawn look to his whole face. Was he losing sleep? Or was it just his preperformance jitters again? Maybe he hadn't kept his supper down. Would that affect his eyes?

"Here you go, boys." Emerging from the kitchen again, Polly handed Bruce a tray of sandwiches and cookies. "Help yourselves and pass 'em around."

"You pass." Bruce picked up a substantial beef sandwich before handing Uwe the tray. "I'm too hungry to be nice."

Like a waiter, Uwe hoisted the tray over his shoulder on the palm of his good hand and began passing it with considerable flair, offering it to each person with a deft spin of his fingers.

Bruce took his sandwich over to the ottoman and sat at Joan's feet. "Polly knows I'm always starving after a concert."

"Bob told me why. Is it that bad every time?"

"Just about. And with the pressure in this competition, I don't even try to eat ahead of time."

"I always make Nathan eat before his performances," Cindy said, beaming in his direction. "He needs his strength, just like an athlete."

"I don't seem to have any choice about waiting," Bruce said cheerfully between bites. "My mom gave up on me years ago when she saw what happened to her good food before a recital."

"Maybe I should try that," Nate said. Cindy's mouth pursed.

Joan changed the subject quickly. "So, Bruce, what's the news you were going to tell me?"

"Oh, you haven't heard our bombshell?" Polly said. "Tell her, Bruce."

He snagged a handful of cookies from the plate on Uwe's tray. "Camila's family is arriving from Brazil tomorrow. With her boyfriend, no less." Biting into a cookie, he shook his head. "It was bad enough being interrogated by the police. I can just imagine what it's going to be like when her folks hear I'm a prime suspect."

"You don't need that now," Uwe said. "You play Saturday?"

"No, Friday. But how can I work between now and then? It's going to be a madhouse around here. Sorry, Polly."

"I know exactly what you mean," she said. "We'll do our best to protect you, but you're probably right."

Feeling suddenly shy, Joan hesitated to make the obvious suggestion. But why not? All he had to do was say no. "Would you like to come home with me tonight? Nobody will be home to bother you during the day, and we'll bring you back tomorrow night if you like, or, if you'd rather, when we come up on Friday. We're not going to miss that concert!"

"Good idea," Uwe seconded. "It's a quiet little town, Bruce. Nothing to disturb you."

"Don't I owe it to the Pereiras to stay?" Bruce asked, but his eyes begged someone to contradict him.

Nate obliged. "No! You know you didn't do anything wrong. You owe it to yourself to give the best performance you can."

His mouth curved up in the faintest of smiles. "Then, after I beat you, there will be plenty of time to let them ask you questions."

"The Schmalzes have been going a little crazy today," Polly said. "Violet still doesn't know whether they expect to stay at her house, and Harry's sure they're going to blame him for not protecting Camila. I imagine they'll stay in a hotel, but of course they'll want to see where Camila was and where all her things still are."

"Except the violin," Bruce said, staring into space.

"Well, yes, except that. And I'm sure they'll want to see for themselves how close together our houses are."

"No wonder they suspect me." He stood up and brushed the crumbs off his black trousers. "Joan, if you really mean it, I think I'd better go with you. I'll need to pack a few things."

"Sure. If you forget anything, you can probably borrow it from Andrew."

"Except a violin," Uwe said, and grinned.

"I've never held so tight to my violin in my life," Bruce said. "Until we know who took the Strad, I'm not letting go." Tucking the case under his arm, he left the room.

"I have to take off now, too," Cindy said. "I've got a client in Louisville on the brink of making an offer on a house I've been trying to unload for months. But I'll come back up for as many of the final concerts as I can. Give your mother a hug, son."

When Nate unfolded himself from a chair clear across the room from her and obliged, Joan thought his embrace showed real affection.

"Have a safe trip." Polly ushered Cindy out the door.

Relaxing visibly, Nate helped himself to seconds—or was it thirds?—from the tray Uwe had set down on the coffee table. How could he put away so much and still look like Paganini? Maybe he'd only faked eating before his concert.

"So, Nate, how did Vivienne do tonight?" Uwe asked.

"Okay, I guess. I was too wrapped up in my own playing to be any judge. You were supposed to be my spy, remember? But you sold out."

"I need the money."

"Me, too, believe me."

"You've already won some, as a finalist." Uwe tapped Nate's shoulder with his good hand. "Congratulations."

"Thanks, but I have a long way to go. I played okay tonight. What do you think of Hannah Weiss?"

"Very precise. Safe for the judges."

"You don't sound very enthusiastic."

"I'd rather hear someone take chances, the way the three of you do—you and Bruce and Camila."

"But who knows what she'll pull off in her concerto?" Nate tossed his head.

"Who you talking about?" Bruce had changed to blue jeans when he came back carrying an overnight bag, his violin over his back and his tux on a hanger.

"Hannah Weiss."

"Relax, Nate, you can play rings around her." Bruce grinned. "It's me you have to watch out for, and I'm taking my technique into seclusion. I'm gonna come up with a whole new approach to defeat you." He turned to Polly. "Thanks for understanding."

"We're pulling for you, Bruce." She hugged him and Joan at the door.

Joan opened the wayback of the old Honda wagon for Bruce to stow his violin and bag. Quite a comedown from the Osbornes' Volvo, not to mention their house. And his own family probably lived as comfortably as the Osbornes.

I will not apologize for not having as much money as a doctor.

"Joan, this is really nice of you," he said when they were finally rolling along the highway between fields of dry cornstalks. The cool September evening breezed through the car's open windows and ruffled their hair.

"It's the least I can do, and it's going to be fun to have you there. Of course, Rebecca left home before I moved to Oliver. It's never been home to her."

"Will I see Andrew and Fred?"

"Andrew, anyway." At least they wouldn't have to share a bedroom. Not for the first time, she was grateful that her little house could sleep three adults in separate rooms. "Fred's harder to predict. That sergeant who was hit on Monday died yesterday."

"Did they catch the driver?"

"Not unless it was tonight. Fred's taking it pretty hard,

and all the police are working overtime. I don't know whether you'll see him at all."

"It's okay. I'm getting away from people, remember?"

"If he does come over, he may be kind of cranky." She felt disloyal for even mentioning it. But it wouldn't be fair to Bruce to take him from one stressful situation into another, especially if he might blame his presence for causing Fred's mood. And would it even be fair to Fred?

"I can imagine," Bruce said.

Was she going to go through life with Fred apologizing for him? Had she felt like this when Ken was upset? Why couldn't she remember?

"Bob Osborne lost a patient last week. He came home pretty upset. My dad's like that, too. I learned a long time ago how to roll with it."

Then she did remember how it had been, sitting up with Ken into the early morning hours after he'd buried a good friend, or sometimes after he'd heard something that he couldn't tell her about without breaking confidence. She, too, had learned to roll with it.

I can again, she thought. I just don't have to like it.

16

About all a stranger could see of Oliver by the time they arrived that night was that it was small. To Joan, though, the path of the past summer's tornado was visible even at night, when streetlights no longer hidden by shade trees could be seen from one end of her block to the other. Half a block away, she was glad to see that Andrew had turned the porch light on for her.

Or was Fred there, late as it was? What mood would he be in tonight? When Andrew opened the door to them, her disappointment battled her relief.

"I was starting to get worried about you, Mom. Well, hi, Bruce. Come on in." He stood back and closed the door behind them.

"I made her late," Bruce said. "I'm hiding out here for a while."

Andrew's eyebrows rose.

"Bruce will tell you all about it," Joan said. "I'm going up to check the spare bedroom." That was putting it mildly. The small spare room had hardly been touched since Rebecca's visit.

To her relief, it wasn't bad. She wiped off the thin layer of dust, made the bed with Grandma Zimmerman's blue and white sawtooth quilt, and set clean towels on her own old maple dresser.

When she went back downstairs, Andrew was making noise in the kitchen and Bruce was browsing in her sheet music.

"You play the *Sinfonia Concertante*? We should try it together while I'm here. Or these Mozart violin-viola duos—I've always loved them."

"I love them, too. That's why I'm not going to let you hear me murder them."

"Uwe said you guys were pretty good."

"He was being generous. Anyhow, he didn't hear me by myself."

"You mean when we're in the same family, we'll never play together?" His eyes, as blue as Fred's, were teasing her now.

"I don't know about never. But I'd have to know you a whole lot better."

"I'll get my mom to work on you. We've played violin together for years."

"That's different. She heard you make your first squawks."

He laughed. "She sure did! I don't know how any parent lives through that stage, especially on a quarter-size violin."

Joan tried to stifle a yawn, but it got away from her. "I'm too tired even to think about it."

Bruce nodded. "I'm still too wound up to sleep. Would it bother you if I played down here for a while? I'd use my heavy practice mute."

"Make yourself at home, Bruce, but leave the mute off. I often fall asleep to music on the radio or a CD."

She was almost beyond hearing the cadenza that floated up the stairwell when she remembered that she hadn't checked the answering machine for a message from Fred.

In the morning, Andrew fixed pancakes for breakfast, as if it were Sunday. By the time Joan came downstairs from her shower, he and Bruce had the meal on the table and were talking as if they'd known each other for years. And there was no light blinking on the machine.

She sat down and helped herself. "Andrew, did Fred call last night?"

"Oh, yeah. He said he'd see you sometime today. I told him you were taking Uwe back. I didn't know about Bruce."

"Thanks. I'll give him a call." From work—there wasn't time to talk now. She poured local maple syrup on her short stack. "You're on your own today, Bruce."

"That's the idea." He looked very much at home, in gray sweats and running shoes. "Andrew showed me where you keep things."

"Good."

"But I was wondering if you'd like company on the way to work. I like to run in the morning, and I could see Oliver."

Andrew choked on his orange juice. "Run? Mom?"

She glared at him. "I'd love the company, Bruce, but I don't run unless I have to. Walking's my speed."

"Sure. I'll run back."

And then some, she was sure. No wonder he was such a string bean.

They left Andrew with the dishes and set off on her usual path through the neighborhood and the park. Another beautiful blue September morning. A few of the trees that had survived the tornado were showing hints of the colors to come in October, and a new sycamore was already dropping leaves that looked too big to have fallen from such a little tree. At this hour she seldom saw anyone in the park but occasional runners and dog walkers out for exercise. This morning, though, a woman coming toward them from the downtown side of the park was wandering on and off the path. Was she drunk?

"It's a little early in the day," Joan said aloud, but Bruce broke into a run.

"It's Camila!" he yelled back to her.

Who? she thought for a split second, and then she, too, saw, and ran after him.

When she reached them, Bruce was already holding Camila's hands. This was not the beautifully groomed, alert young violinist they knew, but a vacant-looking woman with matted hair and rumpled clothing. Her face was clean, but bare of makeup.

"Camila, are you all right?" Bruce asked urgently.

She stared up at him as if trying to focus her eyes. "Bruce?"

"Where have you been? How did you get here? We've been so worried about you!"

Big tears rolled down her cheeks. "I—I don't know." Then she reached up and clung to him. "I'm lost!"

"It's all right, Camila. You're not lost anymore." He held her and shook his head over her shoulder at Joan, but there was a big smile on his face.

"You're safe," Joan said quietly. "We'll help you."

Camila looked at her blankly and said something that sounded like Portuguese.

"Your mother and father are on their way," Bruce answered, as if he'd understood her.

"My violin!" Camila cried. She pulled away from Bruce. Her eyes, no longer vacant, were suddenly wide and wild. "Where is my violin?"

If Joan hadn't been sure before, she was now—Camila had nothing to do with the disappearance of her violin. So where was it? What had happened to her? Where had she been since Monday? And how had she turned up in Oliver's park, of all places?

"We'll find it," Bruce soothed her, putting an arm around her waist. "Everything's going to be all right now. Don't you worry about a thing. We're so glad you're safe."

She cuddled up to him like a child seeking comfort, and peered at Joan. "Who is she?" Even her voice sounded like a little girl's.

"Why, that's our friend Joan." Bruce spoke to the small

child he was sheltering. "You met her at the picnic. Remember the picnic?"

"Oh. Yes. Hello, Joan."

"Hello, Camila. We're awfully glad to see you."

"Where are we?" Less panicky now, she was looking around.

"This is a park near my house. Would you like to see my house?" Taking her to the police station in this state might shock her.

"I have to find my violin. I need to practice for the competition."

"I'll lend you mine," Bruce said. "It's at Joan's house. You can practice there. Come on, I'll show you." Letting go of her, he held out his hand.

She took it, still childlike. "Thank you."

"I'll be there in a few minutes," Joan said. "I want to tell Fred where we're going."

"Good idea." Holding Camila's hand, Bruce set off slowly across the park. Joan watched them for a moment and then headed straight for the police station.

"Mrs. Spencer is here," the desk clerk phoned upstairs. "She says it's urgent."

"I'll be right down." Fred pulled on his jacket. Was she upset at him? Couldn't she cut him a little slack right now? Or was it really urgent? God, he thought, don't let anything happen to Joan. She's the one bright spot in my life. But she must be all right if she's here in person.

Praying it was true, he hurried down the steps to the first floor to find her waiting on the old wooden bench by the desk. She was dressed for work, so maybe it was routine, after all. He couldn't tell from the brightness of her eyes whether she was upset or happy to see him. Part of him wanted to kiss her, and part of him wanted to shake her for scaring him like that. In front of the desk clerk, he settled for taking her hand.

"Joan, are you all right?"

Her mouth curved up, and her eyes smiled with it. "Oh,

Fred, I'm fine. I didn't mean to worry you. But you're never going to believe what just happened in the park." She paused, as if not sure where to begin. "Bruce is here for a day or two, and he was walking me to work."

"He's hurt?"

"No. We found Camila!"

"The violinist? The missing Brazilian? Here?" It made no sense at all.

"Yes, can you believe it? She was just wandering around in the park, kind of lost. She doesn't seem to know where she's been or where she is now. All she can talk about is her violin. I left Bruce walking her back to my house. I was afraid it would freak her out to bring her here."

Probably. "Did she have the violin?"

"No, she asked us where it was, because she said she had to practice for the competition. Bruce told her he'd lend her his, and that he'd take her to it. She went with him willingly enough. She called him by name, but she didn't recognize me until Bruce told her who I was. Maybe not even then."

"How did she get there?"

"She has no idea. At least, she didn't when we found her. She seemed kind of dazed at first, but I think she was coming out of it a little by the time I left."

"And where did she say she'd been?"

"She didn't. I'm sure she doesn't know. Something's happened to her, Fred. She's not the person you met at that picnic. I can't imagine how she could play the way she is now. But oh, Fred, this will take a lot of the pressure off Bruce. The Indianapolis cops have all but accused him of kidnapping her." Her relief was obvious. "And her parents are arriving today."

"From Brazil."

"Yes, with her boyfriend."

"Stay here—I'll be right back. Or do you have to be at work?"

"I can call and explain."

He nodded and spoke to the desk clerk. "Get Mrs. Spencer an outside line, please. And, Joan, don't tell them what's up yet. Can you do that?"

"Sure. They'll probably think it's personal. I suppose in a way it is."

"Good." Leaving her to it, he went back upstairs to clear this business with Captain Altschuler before he got in too deep.

The chief of detectives, like so many of his colleagues this week, looked gloomy when Fred knocked on his open door and went in.

"Any news?"

"Not about Pruitt. But we have another situation." He filled him in quickly. "I met the girl a little over a week ago, when we went up to a picnic at the host family next door to hers."

"So you already know the players."

"So to speak." Fred grinned. "Not that the other violinists necessarily had anything to do with her disappearance, or why she's here."

"You might as well follow it up from our end. Cooperate with the IPD and whoever else they've called in. The FBI involved?"

"Not as far as I know. I haven't heard anything about a ransom demand. Not that they'd publicize it."

"Right. Keep me posted." Warren Altschuler's homely brow furrowed even deeper. "And don't let it interfere with your investigation of Pruitt's death."

"No, sir." Fat chance of that. They'd been over the same ground so often by now that it was trampled, but no new leads had developed. He thought personally that nothing short of a miracle would make much difference in that investigation. Bad enough that Pruitt was young, and one of their own. But how could he tell Kyle's parents the police were helpless to find the driver who hit their only son? And how would the rest of Oliver react to having a high-profile case seem to push

Pruitt's death onto a back burner? The media circus would do exactly that, no matter how much effort continued in the police department, unless he had some kind of breakthrough soon.

Back at his own desk, he picked up the phone.

17

With that miserable bench hitting her in all the wrong spots, Joan was relieved to see Fred come back down the steps toward her.

"All set," he told her, and led the way out to his own car, not one of the police units. "I've been talking to Indianapolis."

"What did they say?"

"We agreed that we should have her checked out at the Oliver hospital. They'll bring her family down here to ID her." They descended the worn limestone steps outside the police station.

Joan stopped dead. "We know who she is!"

"Of course, but it's not a bad idea to have her folks with her when she goes back up there. If she's ready to go back, that is."

"I think she'll want to go. She's already worried about practicing for the competition." She followed him around the corner.

"And if I'm ready to release her." He held the passenger door until she reached for her seat belt, then closed it for her and got in behind the wheel. "I want to pick her brains some first."

"I don't know, Fred. She doesn't seem to have any to pick right now."

"I'm a patient man. Look how long I've been waiting for you." He smiled and stroked her cheek.

She leaned over for a quick kiss while he started the motor. "You're a prince, Fred Lundquist, and I'm lucky to have you."

"Even the way I've been acting?"

"That's not you. That's—I don't know what that is."

"A temporary aberration, I hope. This business with Pruitt is driving us all a little nuts."

"And now we're dumping Camila on you."

"Yeah. But finding her alive sure as hell beats finding Pruitt dying."

When they pulled up in front of the house, the Mozart pouring through the open window promised a lot of brain to pick.

"Listen to her!" Joan said. Whatever had happened to Camila obviously hadn't harmed her playing. But when they went in, it was Bruce who met them with violin and bow in hand and Camila who was sitting empty-handed on the sofa. She still looked almost as blank as she had in the park.

Bruce introduced them to her as if they'd never met.

Taking her cue from him, Joan said, "Fred is a policeman, Camila, and our good friend." She sat down beside her. "He's here to help you."

Fred showed her his badge. "Do you feel up to answering a few questions?" he asked gently.

Her eyes turned to Bruce.

"It's all right, Camila," Bruce said. "I'm right here." He laid the violin and bow in their case and sat down on her other side, taking her hand. She nodded hesitantly.

Joan was glad to see Fred take the chair across from Camila. No need to loom over her, as scared as she looked.

"Tell me your name, please," he said.

"Camila Pereira," she said softly, and looked relieved, as if she'd passed a test.

"And where do you come from?"

The wide smile broke forth. Wherever she'd been since Monday, she'd had a toothbrush. She didn't stink, and her face was clean, but her clothing smelled stale, as if she hadn't changed it. She seemed not to notice. "From Rio de Janeiro, in Brazil. It is a beautiful city."

"I believe you," Fred said. "Do you have a family?"

"Oh yes. I live with my mother and father." With each response, she seemed more confident and natural.

"What do you do in Brazil?"

"I am a violinist." No hesitation there. She tossed her head, but the hair that had rippled merely flopped.

"That's wonderful. And what brings you here?" She looked blank again. "To America," he added quickly.

"I came to play in the violin competition. With Bruce"— she looked up at him—"and the others." Her eyebrows puckered. "But I don't know where I am. I need to go back. I need to play my next concert." Her agitation increased. "My violin! My violin is missing! I must find it!"

"When is your next concert?" Fred asked.

She relaxed. "Not until Wednesday night. Isn't that right, Bruce? If I make the finals, I play the Mozart on Wednesday. Then the Sibelius on Saturday."

Bruce nodded. "That's the schedule. And, Camila, you did make the finals."

She showed no surprise. What day did she think it was? Would she panic if they told her she'd already missed Wednesday? Careful, Fred, Joan thought.

"Do you know how you got here?" he asked instead. "Who brought you here?"

"I came here with Bruce," she said. "From the park."

"Uh-huh. And how did you get to the park?"

Her eyes clouded over, and she shook her head.

"What's the last thing you remember before the park?"

"A car. I was looking for my violin. But I don't know where I was. Why can't I remember where I was?" Her voice rose, and her eyes begged them.

Fred leaned forward. "Camila," he said carefully, "I'd like for a doctor to check you. I think something has happened to you. I think that's why you can't remember."

"I know you," she said suddenly, and smiled at him. "You were at the picnic."

"That's right." He returned her smile. "Joan brought me."

"Yes," she said, and turned to Joan. "And your son was there, too. Andrew. A cute guy."

On cue, the front door flew open and Andrew burst into the room, his hair wild. Breathing hard and perspiring, he might have been running. He stopped short and gaped at them. "Camila! What—what are you doing here?"

"Hello, Andrew," she said, with some of her old manner back. "We were just talking about you."

"You—you were?" he croaked, his voice not quite breaking. His eyes focused on Camila. "How did you get here?"

"I walked here from the park, with Bruce. But what are *you* doing here? Come, sit here and tell me." She patted the sofa next to her, not noticing, or maybe not caring, that Joan was already occupying that space. Whatever was wrong with Camila, her personality seemed intact.

"No, I can't. I—I just came back for my lab notes. I'm late for class." They watched him race up the stairs. He reappeared almost immediately with a backpack over his shoulder. In those few moments, he had mopped his face and generally pulled himself together.

"Is she okay?" he murmured to Joan.

"Looks like it."

"That's great! Look, I'm sorry, but I can't miss this lab. Tell me all about it tonight, okay?"

"Sure," she said, and followed him to the door. He flung himself onto his bike and pedaled off furiously.

Fred raised an eyebrow. Joan shrugged.

"Such a big hurry," Camila said, and laughed. "In Brazil, my boyfriend would not leave without a kiss. But Andrew is a little shy. He's very young, no?"

"Some days he seems about ten," Joan said.

"Oh no," Camila said seriously. "He is much older than ten." Intact in some ways, but damaged in others, Joan thought. She wouldn't have missed that little joke before.

Bruce laughed. "You're right," he said. "Andrew is almost twenty."

"I knew it!"

Fred leaned forward again. "Camila, would you like to see your family?"

"They're in Brazil. They had to miss this competition."

"I have good news for you."

"Good news?" Her eyes weren't quite focusing.

"Yes. They're coming here to see you."

"Here?" She looked around the room, frowning as if trying to recognize it.

"Very near here. Will you come with me? I'll take you to them."

"I don't understand. My father had important business. He couldn't leave Brazil."

"You're more important to your father than his business. Camila, listen to me. We want you to see a doctor. I will take you to the hospital. Your family will meet you there, at the hospital. They want to be sure you're all right."

She turned to Bruce, still frowning. "Can I trust him? Is he telling the truth?"

"Yes."

"Will you come, too?"

"If you want me to."

"Then I will come." She stood up, and swayed slightly. The two men stood quickly and reached out to her. She took Bruce's arm. "I feel a little dizzy. I think it is good if I see a doctor." Then her smile lit her face. "And I will love to see my family!"

Fred sent her to the car with Bruce and hung back for a moment with Joan. "Can we drop you at work?"

"Please, and I hope you'll rescue Bruce. He came here to get away, not to play nursemaid."

"Her folks will be here before long."

"But, Fred, don't you see? That's exactly the stressful situation he was trying to avoid until after tomorrow night, especially if the Indianapolis police already have filled their minds with Bruce as the bad guy."

"He's a grown man, Joan." He brushed a wisp of hair back from her forehead.

"I know." She shook her head. "It's just so unfair! Bad enough that Camila loses out, but why should Bruce have to?"

"Crime is like that. I'll do what I can."

She hugged him. "I knew you would."

Bruce and Camila were already sitting together in the back. Fred tucked Joan into the front and drove off. She didn't say much in the car, but waved to them when they dropped her off at the center. Wouldn't her old ladies have a field day if they knew what was going on?

18

*A*nnie Jordan was waiting for her, looking mock fierce. "When they said you'd be in late, some of us worried about you. I told 'em you were probably just out gallivanting with your man." She followed Joan into her small office.

"I'll never put anything past you, will I, Annie?"

"So who was the redhead in the back with the girl?"

Couldn't be any harm in telling her that much. "That's Rebecca's Bruce. He's spending a day or two at my house before his final concert—just getting away from it all."

"With another girl?" Count on Annie not to miss much, but she obviously hadn't recognized Camila, even though her picture had been in the papers and on the TV news. Not that the girl in the car much resembled that picture.

"Fred was giving her a ride." Keep it casual, she told herself, and stood flipping through the mail on her desk.

"So why was Rebecca's young man with her?" Annie wasn't giving up.

"Bruce runs in the morning before he practices. Fred will drop him off somewhere, and he'll run home. Honestly, Annie, if he were messing around with another woman, you can't believe he'd be doing it in Fred's car!"

"Not that she was much to look at. Couldn't hold a candle to Rebecca."

You should see her when she's herself, Joan thought, remembering her own first reaction to Camila. "There you go. And Bruce isn't looking at anyone else."

"Uh-huh. All men look."

"He's going to meet women all his life, you know. What kind of marriage would it be if she couldn't trust him?"

"Like most of 'em, I expect. You gonna bring him around to see us?"

"Maybe next time. It's up to him."

"I want you to introduce me."

"I will," Joan promised, and settled down to work.

At noon, she took her tuna salad sandwich and joined the people eating the government-sponsored nutritious food served at the center—what Annie called "eats for old folks." Today's heavenly smelling chicken pot pie was more than Joan needed before a full supper, but she accepted a cup of coffee.

"Now they're blaming the fraternities again," a man was grumbling when she sat down. "Seems to me, whenever folks don't know who did something, they lay it on the Greeks."

"Most times, they're right," another man said. "Those kids have too much time and too much money for their own good."

"And some of 'em don't have the sense God gave a goose," a woman said. "My grandson's fraternity got him so drunk it most killed him."

"I'll grant you it was probably a drunk," the first man said. "But there's no more reason to think a fraternity kid hit Kyle than someone who stopped off after work for happy hour."

Ah, so Kyle Pruitt was the topic. Somehow, Camila's sudden appearance had wiped him from Joan's memory. Since finding her in the park, she'd been trying to imagine how Camila had turned up in Oliver, of all places. She was such a flirt—was it possible that Oliver College students had lured her away, and then somehow kept her here in their fraternity house since Monday?

Could it have been a prank, or even an initiation stunt? She was a pretty girl, and she'd had enough publicity. Every once in a while some stunt that got out of hand made the news and a local chapter would be disciplined, but this was serious business. Not that Joan knew much about such things from her own college days; there had been no fraternities or sororities at Oberlin.

For sex? Some of those stories concerned parties and date rapes, in which the victims knew their assailants at least casually, and the men claimed that the women sent ambiguous signals, meaning yes when they said no, and that they'd been justified in acting on what they were sure the women meant. That might fit with Camila's personality, except that she was so intent on the competition. It was hard to imagine her leaving Indianapolis for a flirtation, much less voluntarily staying in Oliver that long.

"What does your friend on the police force say?" the first man asked. "They find those kids yet?"

"Not that I've heard," Joan said. "But I don't think they know for sure that the kids saw anything that would help. Only that they spotted Sergeant Pruitt in the street and called 911."

"I'd like to shake some sense into their heads," said the woman whose grandson had almost died.

"Wouldn't help," Annie said. "They're probably scared to death as it is."

Probably, Joan thought, and wondered whether Uwe's encouragement would reach them. Even if they hadn't been at his talk, the word might get around the school.

"Why do people act that way?" the woman said, as if she hadn't heard Annie. "Even kids."

Right. Why would Camila leave with someone? She didn't seem to remember a gun, or any other kind of force.

Joan thought back to the last time she herself had made such a mistake. She'd thought Andrew was in danger and hadn't hesitated. What if Camila had thought she was being taken to rescue her missing violin? Wouldn't she have gone anywhere for that? Or what if she'd heard something that made her think she could find it on her own? She hadn't mentioned another person, though, only a car. Could she have heard something that made her think the violin was in Oliver, and rented a car to drive there herself? What if someone had sent *her* a ransom note, for the violin, and said she had to drive somewhere alone to deliver the money? Maybe she hadn't been headed for Oliver at all, but somewhere else, and had had an accident on the way and hit her head? She'd been lying by the side of the road, like Kyle Pruitt, only nobody had seen her, and she'd finally come to by herself and wandered into town. That would explain her confusion, and why she'd been gone so long.

Well, yes, Joan thought, but she's too clean, and she doesn't act hungry. Maybe Bruce fed her and found her a toothbrush while I went after Fred, but how did she wash her face before we saw her in the park?

So what did happen to leave her so blank? And where has she been since Monday? Her family must be wild—I know I would be. What will they say when they find her in this shape?

"Is anybody going to the calling hours this afternoon?" Annie Jordan asked.

Joan hadn't even scanned the paper. "When is the funeral?"

"Tomorrow at ten. You might as well go. Nobody will be here tomorrow morning."

Joan looked around the table. Heads were nodding. "Then I should see whether anyone from adult day care wants to attend it. *Their* staff can't just take off." She crumpled her sandwich bag and flipped it neatly into the wastebasket. "I'd better go tell them I'll sub."

"She's quite a girl," she heard Annie announce to the others as she left.

The entrance to the adult day care was around the corner. Except when the staff was locking or unlocking the building, the connecting door to the senior center was used only in emergency situations, so as not to add to the confusion of the already confused day-care clients, who were not free to come and go without staff supervision. But the same fragrance of chicken pot pie teased her nostrils when she walked in.

As always, the folks seated at the homey-looking dining room table needed varying degrees of help. Some had finished alone, some were being coaxed to eat a few last bites, and one man was being spoon-fed by a thirty-something woman who glanced at her watch while she held another spoonful of pot pie at the ready.

"Come on, Charlie," she said in a kindly enough voice. "Have another bite. It's awfully good today." She checked her watch again, as if it could have changed in those few moments.

Uh-huh, Joan thought. "You need to be somewhere? I could do that for you."

"Oh, would you mind? I really wanted to go to the calling hours at Snarr's this afternoon. The Pruitts live down the block from the house I grew up in. Kyle used to walk me home from school. I can't believe he's gone."

"I thought the service was at First Methodist."

"It is, but the visitation is at Snarr's. I can't go to the service, because I have to work, but I thought I'd have time to speak to his folks once I was done with lunch today." She slipped the spoon out of Charlie's mouth and laid it on his plate.

"Sure, go ahead." Sitting down opposite Charlie, a tall, rawboned man with gray hair fringing his mostly bald head, Joan looked into his cloudy blue eyes. He was staring off into space and chewing intermittently.

Blanker than Camila, she thought, and reloaded the spoon. At least Camila seemed to be coming out of whatever had messed her up. Charlie, she knew, would never come out of it. He still had occasional windows of lucidity, but he'd gone downhill considerably since she first visited the day care. Back then, he could be helped to carry on a conversation, and enjoyed his food.

"Good, huh, Charlie?" she tried, but he seemed to have

dozed off. She nudged him gently. No response.

"Anybody ever sing to you, Charlie?"

He opened his eyes.

"Take a bite, and I'll sing to you."

He opened his mouth, and she spooned in more pot pie.

"Charlie, my boy, oh, Charlie, my boy," she sang to the old tune, and he chewed the chicken. Aha. "This chicken's delicious," she improvised, spooning in more. "It fills you with joy." He smiled with his mouth still full, and dozed off again.

"Charlie, wake up, oh, Charlie, wake up," she sang, and nudged him again. But after he chewed that bite, his head immediately dropped, and he snored gently. She was afraid to persuade him to take more for fear he'd end up choking on it. Gently, she wiped his mouth and untied his bib. Chin on his chest, he slept on.

Almost as if he were drugged, Joan thought later, as she left the day care. Drugged. She felt silly not to have thought of it sooner.

Of course, Camila had been drugged, and now she was coming out of it. What was the name of that drug she'd read about? The one they called the date-rape drug. The one that left young women wondering why they found themselves in the wrong place, missing time, sometimes naked, and often frightened, but too embarrassed to complain, because they thought they must have drunk too much and felt at least partly to blame for whatever had happened to them. Fred would know, she was sure.

19

Fred knew plenty of names for the drug he wanted Camila tested for: roofies, roach, rib, the forget pill, the date-rape drug, the love drug, Rohypnol. Easily bought in Mexico, among other countries, the powerful sedative could be dropped into a drink of almost anything, unbeknownst to the victim. The ultimate Mickey Finn, it didn't so much knock the victim out as make her unable to resist or remember anything that was done to her. And it was cheap, which made it a favorite of penny-pinching students looking for a cheap drunk, or a more aggressive sort of good time.

He sighed, and turned toward the hospital. He supposed it was bound to happen. Up to now, they'd had no problem with roofies in Oliver. But if the drug had made its way to this small college town, they could expect the rate of acquaintance rape to increase dramatically. Detection was a nightmare because of the amnesia the drug induced in the victims. Prevention lay in educating people, especially women, not to accept mixed drinks from anyone they didn't trust completely, and not to leave a drink where anyone could drop something into it. But he didn't expect college students to listen to him. The women would have to educate each other to be less trusting, and they'd probably start doing it only after enough of them had been victimized.

Behind him, Bruce was chatting with Camila, who sounded closer to normal all the time. Whatever she'd been given didn't seem to have done any major damage. She was lucky. If, as he suspected, she'd been kept drugged for days, and if someone had guessed wrong about the dose, she could have been in convulsions by now, or dead.

Or maybe someone *had* guessed wrong. Maybe she'd been left for dead, but her system had fought the stuff off, and she'd come to and managed to escape.

"Where are we going?" Camila asked loudly.

Fred's eyes met Bruce's in the rearview mirror. "To the hospital," he said, in as calm a voice as he could pull out of his own worries.

"I'm not sick! I need to go home! I need to practice!"

"That's right," Bruce said. "But something is wrong. You need to see a doctor first."

"Can he help me play the violin?"

"Maybe," Fred said. "It depends on what's wrong."

"But this isn't the way to the hospital. I visited Uwe in the hospital. It didn't look anything like this." Her little girl voice was back, and in the mirror her eyes were wild. "Where are you taking me?"

Fred pulled over and turned off the motor. He turned around to face her. "Camila, what town do you think this is?"

"What town?" She looked puzzled.

"Do you see the tall buildings of downtown Indianapolis?"

She looked around at the quiet residential street, with grassy front yards and modest houses. "No." She grabbed Bruce's hand.

"Camila, this is Oliver, Indiana. It's a little town south of Indianapolis. This is where Joan lives. I live here, too. I'm a detective in the police department, and I'm going to help find out what has happened to you. Somehow, you came from Indianapolis to Oliver. Do you remember how you came here?"

"No." Barely audible.

"You told us you remembered a car."

She hesitated. "Yes."

"What do you remember about the car?"

"It was fast. I like to drive fast, but not that fast."

"Why did you drive so fast, then?" Keep it gentle.

"I didn't."

"Who drove the car?"

But again, she shook her head.

"Was it late at night? Was it dark outside?"

"No."

"Were you afraid?"

"A little. It was too fast."

"Were you hungry?"

"I don't think so. I don't remember."

"Are you hungry now?"

"A little."

"But I'm not driving too fast?" He smiled at her.

She laughed. "You're not driving at all!"

"You're right. I'm going to drive you to the hospital now. But it won't be the big one in Indianapolis. It's just a little hospital in this little town. And your parents will come here, too, to this little hospital. They were so worried about you."

Fred could see the wheels turning.

"It takes a long time to fly here from Brazil," she said. "How long do I have to wait for them?" Time to tell her.

"Not long, Camila. You've been missing for several days."

Her eyes filled with tears. One spilled down her right cheek, and Bruce wiped it with his finger.

"What day is today?"

"This is Thursday," Bruce said.

"But I was supposed to play on Wednesday! I missed my concert!"

"It's all right. They understand. They will let you play last. They said so."

Tears spilled from both eyes, and she shook her head.

"No, they will never believe me. I have lost the competition."
Shoulders slumped, she wept without sound.

"They'll believe *me*!" Fred said, and started the motor.

At the hospital, she hung back, unwilling to get out of the
car. "I'm not sick. Take me home. I need to practice."

Fred and Bruce exchanged glances. Would they have to
keep going through it over and over?

"I wonder whether your family is here yet," Bruce said.

"They're really coming?" She looked back and forth to
them.

"They're really coming," Fred said. "You two stay here,
while I ask whether they've arrived." And warn the hospital
what's going on.

Halfway to the entrance, he heard a scream behind him.
He spun around and saw his rear passenger door fly open.

Camila stumbled out of the car and launched herself at a
tall, dark, well-muscled young man running toward her from
a Lincoln that had pulled up behind Fred's Chevy. Her
brother? No, the boyfriend. Fred had forgotten he would be
there, too. Bruce followed Camila out of the car, but the dark
young man reached her first.

"Camila!" Catching her before she could fall, the young
man picked her up and swung her around in a bear hug and
planted a most unbrotherly kiss on her mouth. Rapid Portuguese poured from him. Camila's words came more slowly,
but her smiles and tears flowed freely.

A uniformed driver held the door while a well-tailored,
silver-haired man who had to be Camila's father helped her
youthful mother, dressed in an immaculate linen suit and
carrying a neat flight bag, from the car. Tipping his cap, the
driver closed the door and returned to his seat. These people
didn't look as if they could possibly have been sitting on a
plane all the way from Rio de Janeiro, even in the relative
comfort of first class. Fred felt rumpled.

He gave them a few moments together, and then went
forward, holding out his badge rather than his hand, and hoping their English was better than his Portuguese.

"Mr. and Mrs. Pereira? I am Detective Lieutenant Lundquist, of the Oliver Police Department. We found your daughter here in Oliver."

They nodded, and both began talking.

Fred held up his hands. "I'm sorry. I don't speak Portuguese."

Camila translated. "My mother says thank you. My father asks what have you done to catch these bad men?"

From the intensity with which he'd spat the words out, Fred would have given odds that he hadn't put it that way.

"The Indianapolis police have been handling the case. My first step is to get medical attention for your daughter."

"Yes, she must see a doctor," said the boyfriend. "She is—not right."

Camila took his hand and smiled up at him. "This is my boyfriend, Hodrigo Machado—no, you say Rodrigo. And this is Bruce Graham, a violinist in the competition."

No one bothered to translate, but her father bristled and her mother looked worried.

"Why is he here?" Rodrigo asked angrily. "The Indianapolis police told us about this man. They think he took your violin."

"Oh no!" Camila said. "Bruce is my friend. He would never do such a thing."

This time Rodrigo translated.

"I think I'd better leave," Bruce said. He bowed slightly to the parents. "Good-bye, Camila. I'll be at Joan's house later today, if you need me for anything." And he ran off toward the park.

Camila's father erupted.

"He says, why do you let him go?" Rodrigo asked Fred. "He will complain to his good friend, the Brazilian ambassador, if the police do not soon punish the man who did this to his daughter." Clearly, he had said much more.

"I know this young man, and I have no reason to suspect him," Fred said carefully. "He's not going anywhere. Right now, the most important thing is for Camila to be seen by a doctor. Please come with me." He waited for the translation, and then turned his back and led the way up the steps.

They followed. He hadn't been sure they would. For the moment, at least, concern for their daughter was winning over the desire for vengeance. He hoped it would last, especially when the doctor brought out the rape kit. Time to involve a woman officer.

Jill Root came willingly.

"If you need me," she said when he called her from the car, but when she arrived a few minutes later, she thanked him. "I know I asked to work on Kyle's case, but we keep running into brick walls. I need to *do* something." Her eyes glistened.

"I wasn't sure you'd be on duty this afternoon."

"I'll go over to Snarr's tonight, Lieutenant. It's not as if I were his wife. We hadn't even announced our engagement. I'm all torn up, but I don't have any official right to stand at his parents' side. I need to work."

When he introduced her, relief was visible on the face of Camila's mother. Had she worried that he would watch the exam? Or did she not trust the young male doctor? Whatever her concern, Root's presence seemed to ease her tension. She stroked the shoulder of Camila's hospital gown as if to reassure herself that her daughter was alive and safe, and spoke quietly to her.

Fred had already told the resident what he suspected, and why.

The young doctor had nodded. "It's possible. That drug is a benzodiazepine, and her behavior and responses are consistent with benzodiazepines. We've had a fair amount of experience with other benzos, usually with people who get addicted to them. We'll test for them here right away, to be sure we shouldn't be looking for something else, but we'll have to send up to the IU Med Center to narrow it down to a specific drug. They take their sweet time when it's not an emergency."

Fred's jaw clenched. "Possible rape isn't an emergency?"

"Not a medical emergency. She's in no danger at the moment, and whatever she was given seems to be wearing off."

Fred knew it was true. "If we're right, can you give me any idea when she received the drug?"

"Not really. I've heard of it, but I've never seen a case of it before. We can ask the Med Center about that, too, but it depends on whether she had one dose or several—you say she's been missing for several days. If the first dose hadn't worn off by the time she got a second dose, that would make a difference in her response to the second, and so on. If there were more, it might take longer for her to get back to normal. I don't know the half-life of Rohypnol, if that's what it turns out to be, and I can't check it in the PDR because it's not legal here."

"The longer it takes, the less likely we are to pick up on whatever trail there is. Her dad's threatening us with the Brazilian ambassador."

"I'll do what I can, Lieutenant, but considering her improvement, you'll have more luck with the Med Center than I will, even if I find physical indications of rape."

"We'll want the clothing she was wearing. We asked them to send clean clothes down with her mother."

"The nurse put it in a paper sack. She'll give it to you."

In the waiting room, Camila's father was pacing and talking nonstop to her boyfriend, who seemed to be trying to calm him. They broke off when Fred entered the room.

"I've spoken with the doctor, Mr. Pereira. He thinks your daughter was drugged. He will test her blood here, and I will have a police officer carry a sample of her blood to a laboratory in Indianapolis that can test it in more detail." Fred waited for the translation. "Now I need your help."

Both men stared. Apparently the father understood a little English, after all.

"Will you please come with me to the police station? I need information from you for our official investigation." He hoped his formality would have the right ring for a Brazilian banker. Apparently it did, and they were soon following him in their chauffeured car. Most of the information he expected them to provide was already on his desk, courtesy of the Indianapolis police, but he wanted to defuse this angry father by demonstrating conscientious attention to the daughter's case.

For the moment, he left Mr. Pereira and Rodrigo with sober Detective Terry, who methodically spelled Moacir, Isadora, and Camila Pereira aloud as he entered their names and addresses—local and home—into the computer.

Fred took Sergeant Ketcham to one side and handed him the IPD faxes from his desk. "I want all the details on the missing violin. It's a Stradivarius, worth who knows how much. Camila couldn't tell the IPD much about the insurance when it disappeared, either because she was too stressed out or because she didn't know. Let's hope her father has that information. And we need to pump them both about anything she told them before she disappeared—any leads to finding the violin, any men she was interested in and might have left with. I'd like to separate the father from the boyfriend for that, but the boyfriend's acting as interpreter."

"My Spanish might be close enough to his Portuguese. For that matter, I'd expect a Brazilian banker to speak Spanish."

"I didn't know you could." More of Johnny Ketcham's hidden talents.

Ketcham's eyes smiled behind his wire rims. "It doesn't come up much. I take it you think the girl's on the up and up?"

"I do now. Somebody doped her and confined her, at the very least. I'll get a picture of her as she looks now. I want that circulated in town along with the publicity shot that's closer to how she looked when she disappeared. She's been unaccounted for since the daylight hours on Monday, and she herself has some vague memories of riding in a car. Someone may remember seeing her. Hit the campus first."

"You're thinking students?"

"Maybe."

Or maybe someone who already knew more about her

than what was on the news when her violin was stolen. Somebody with a connection to Oliver. He didn't much want to think about the young men with Oliver connections who knew her.

How coincidental was it that squeaky clean Bruce Graham, the IPD's prime suspect because he'd hung around Camila and had been on the scene when the violin disappeared, just happened to be in the park when Camila appeared? Joan and Rebecca would hate it if it turned out to be Bruce, but if Bruce had drugged and hidden Camila to increase his own chances of winning the competition, say, or abducted her because he had the hots for her, Rebecca would be better off without him. It had probably been easy for Bruce to persuade Joan to bring him down last night, and wouldn't have been hard for him to rent a car before that, except for working it into his schedule. Maybe if his schedule hadn't been so tight, Camila would still have been doped up. But he and Joan had been together all last night.

Uwe Frech no longer had a performance schedule, and he'd been in Oliver on Wednesday. Even with his bum hand, Uwe probably could have driven her down. And he'd been hurting for money and disappointed at losing his chance at the competition. Had he taken it out on Camila?

And then there was Andrew, obviously taken by Camila the day he met her. Andrew, who was dumbfounded to see her in his mother's house, and who sped off on his bike after stammering only a few words to her. Andrew, who could have borrowed his mother's car without her knowledge while she was at work. Andrew, an Oliver College student who worked in a biology lab.

Andrew, the thoroughly decent kid whose mother Fred was going to marry. He knew he ought to let Warren Altschuler know the rest of it. Let the IPD handle this case and clear Andrew, whose innocence he didn't doubt for a minute. But he knew he wouldn't. The least he could do for Joan was investigate it himself, and risk being called down later for not declaring his conflict of interest.

20

L eaving Camila's men in the capable hands of Ketcham and Terry, Fred took his camera back to the hospital. The odors that met his nose when he opened the emergency room door evoked Kyle Pruitt's death watch.

What kind of clod am I? I shouldn't have left Root here again.

But she was coming toward him with a smile on her face. "Good news, Lieutenant. The doctor says there's no sign of rape. They're giving her some meds anyway, just in case, but they don't think it happened. She wasn't tied up—no marks. But you're right that she was drugged with some kind of benzodiazepine. Could be roofies."

"How's she doing?"

"Better, I think. She didn't fall apart during the exam, and she sounds more adult all the time, if that makes sense. The only thing that sounds like a rape victim is that she's getting intense about feeling filthy. She wants to shower and shampoo her hair before anybody else sees her, especially the people up in Indy. But the ER's not set up for that, and they don't want to admit her just to take a shower."

"I'll see what I can work out. I don't want to let her leave Oliver yet if I can help it. I'd like to pass her through town and see if she can remember anything before she turned up in the park this morning.

"Like recognize where she was held?"

"Exactly. I'm going to take a few shots of her as she is now. Then I want you to take the camera to Sergeant Ketcham and tell him what's in it."

"Yes, sir."

"Then run a blood sample up to the IU Med Center. The doctor will tell you where." If they drag their heels up there, I'll get Camila's father to sic the Brazilian ambassador on them.

She nodded, and headed for the door.

Dressed in clean clothes, but with her hair still oily and matted, Camila put up only a little fuss about being photographed as she was.

Root jollied her along. "This is one time you don't need to smile, because if anyone saw you during the past day or two, you wouldn't have been smiling." That evoked a smile, but then Camila looked worried, and Fred clicked rapidly.

"What time is it?" Camila asked.

Fred checked his watch. "Almost noon." His stomach growled. He wondered when Camila had eaten last. She had said she was a little hungry. Could it be that whoever had been holding her had missed feeding her breakfast, and that's why she had been drug-free enough to escape?

"How far are we from Indianapolis? Maybe I could play for the judges this afternoon." Her earlier agitation had faded.

"It's not far, but are you in any condition to play? The doctor says you were drugged, and some of the drug may still be in your body. Everybody will understand if you can't play yet, but if you play badly, won't that eliminate you from the competition?"

Camila quickly translated for her mother, who was tugging at her sleeve. Then she said, "Can you take me back to Joan's house? Bruce will let me try his violin."

"Good idea. And I don't think Joan would mind if you used her bathroom to clean up."

Her face lit up. "Oh yes! I'm so dirty. I smell bad even to myself." Another improvement. Earlier, she hadn't seemed to notice.

"I'll call and ask her, but I'm sure she'll be glad to let you bathe there." And I'll be glad for you to recover that much more while you're still in Oliver, Fred thought.

He debated briefly whether to leave her at Joan's before picking up her father. With her mother as chaperone, could even that angry father object to her spending time in the same house as Bruce? Yes, he could. Better take the women by the station to pick up the men. And give Bruce a few more minutes of practice time. Bad enough that they'd all land on him at all. He called Joan from the hospital.

"Sure," she said. "Give her the blue towels in the linen closet. The shampoo's on the shelf inside the shower curtain. There's a clean hairbrush on my dresser, too, if her mother didn't bring one."

"We'll manage. And thanks."

The Lincoln followed him to Joan's little house. At the sound of Bruce's violin through the open windows, Camila's father stopped dead on the sidewalk. Fred didn't need a translation of his angry words.

"You tell Mr. Pereira that this is an opportunity for Camila to test her ability to play the violin," he said to Rodrigo. "I personally guarantee her safety."

His back stiff and his jaw tight, Mr. Pereira subsided.

With violin and bow hanging from one hand, Bruce opened the door to them and stood back to let them file into Joan's modest living room. Trying to look at what would soon be his home through their eyes, Fred thought they must think they were slumming. At least it was clean; had Joan charged through the house in preparation for Bruce's visit? Or Uwe's, more likely.

"How do you feel?" Bruce asked Camila.

"Much better, thank you." She smiled. "But dirty. I'm

going to take a shower, and then I'd like to borrow your violin. Maybe I still can compete this afternoon if I have one good practice first. I've played that Mozart concerto for years."

"Sure. You know you're welcome."

Camila's father's eyes were boring holes into Bruce, but he held his tongue.

"Camila? Mrs. Pereira?" Fred led the way up to Joan's bathroom. Obediently, he sorted out the relatively new blue towels from the other, more worn colors in the linen closet and pointed out the shampoo. Then he left them to it.

Downstairs, Bruce had laid the violin in its open case and was standing beside it, near the front door. The two Brazilians, Moacir Pereira on the sofa and Rodrigo Machado on the big upholstered chair that was Fred's favorite, were speaking Portuguese.

Ketcham had reported that they'd said separately they had no idea who might have abducted Camila. She'd been all but engaged to Rodrigo for a couple of years. Both her father and Rodrigo claimed that the relationship was happy. Remembering Camila's rush to Rodrigo's arms, Fred was inclined to believe it. As for the violin, Ketcham said it had been insured for approximately half a million dollars. According to her father, it was underinsured and they'd been planning to have it reappraised. In an insurance fraud scam, they would just have taken out another million on it.

The violin was the IPD's worry. For all Fred knew, it had no connection to Camila's disappearance except to shout to the world that she was the daughter of a wealthy family.

"Did Camila tell you what the doctor found?" he asked her father and Rodrigo now.

"No. What?" Rodrigo didn't bother to translate.

"She was not physically injured. And there were no indications of rape."

When Rodrigo translated, Mr. Pereira's face crumpled, and he buried it in his hands.

"Thank God," Bruce said quietly.

Pereira's head jerked up. He said something soft to Bruce.

"He asks if you were worried, too," Rodrigo said. His tone sharpened. "You care for Camila?"

Bruce's face flamed. For a little too long, he was silent. Then he said, "Only as a friend. She didn't deserve all this."

Camila's father, looking suddenly old, held out his hand to Bruce and said something.

"He believes you." But from the stiffness in his voice and face, Rodrigo did not. "He wants to apologize for thinking that you would hurt his daughter."

Bruce took the hand and held it. The young man and the older man stared into each other's eyes for a long moment. Then both nodded and smiled.

By the time Camila and her mother came downstairs, peace reigned. Bruce had been persuaded to play and had chosen a sweet, haunting tune Fred didn't know. Eyes closed, Mr. Pereira was leaning back against Joan's sofa, beating time with his right index finger. When the women entered the room, Bruce lowered his violin, and Mr. Pereira opened his eyes and beamed.

Camila, dressed in yet another fresh outfit, ran to her father and embraced him. Still visibly damp, her hair already waved down her back, with a few dry tendrils curling around her face.

"I feel so much better now that I'm clean! But I'm starving." She translated for her parents.

Her mother shook a finger and scolded her. Fred didn't need a translation. She sat down next to her husband, crossed her ankles, and folded her hands in her elegant lap.

"My mother says first I must practice. I sometimes think the violin competition is even more important to her than to me." Camila smiled and held out her hands for the violin.

Bruce took it carefully from its case, quickly checked the tuning with his thumb, adjusted the shoulder rest, and tightened and rosined the bow for her. "Here you go."

She tucked the violin under her jaw competently enough,

but when she aimed the bow at the strings, its tip caught on the edge of the bridge. Extricating it awkwardly, she lifted the bow onto the G string and played a simple G-major scale. Fred winced. Camila's own dismay showed on her face. It wasn't that the notes were wrong, exactly. But she wasn't pulling any tone out of the violin. She sounded like a beginner playing a school rental instrument, not a budding virtuoso on the fine violin they'd heard through the window. Her mother made soothing sounds.

Camila tried again, this time a bit of Mozart Fred recognized, though he couldn't name it, but with equally discouraging results. Her puny tone wobbled as the bow skittered along the strings, and many of the notes were sharp, as if she couldn't control the fingers of her left hand. She probably can't, Fred thought, much less her bow arm.

A big tear ran down her left cheek into her mouth. "This sounds terrible!" Lifting her head, she held the violin out to Bruce, who took it from her. "What's wrong with it?"

"It's not the violin," Fred said gently. "It's the drug, the one that made you forget. We talked about it, remember?"

"I didn't forget the music!"

"No. But the drug has affected your coordination."

"I will never play again?" She was horror-struck.

"I'm sure you will. But you'll have problems until the rest of the drug leaves your body."

"When?"

"In a day or two, maybe. We don't know how much you took."

"I didn't take any drugs!"

"I should have said we don't know how much someone gave you. Or how many times you were drugged since you disappeared."

She wiped her cheek and dabbed at her eyes. For the first time, Fred noticed that she had taken the trouble to make up her face. On the sofa, Mrs. Pereira broke down in sobs. Bruce, ever resourceful, handed her a clean cloth handkerchief from the pocket of his sweats. She sat up, blew her nose loudly, and began laying down the law, her eyes flashing. But she was no longer scolding her daughter.

Rodrigo had been translating for the Pereiras. Now he turned to Fred.

"She says we must telephone to tell the judges that they must let her play both the Mozart and her big concerto on Saturday night."

Bruce tried to speak, but Rodrigo waved him to be silent. "You will tell them why they must allow it, she says. Camila is a wonderful violinist. This American crime must not be allowed to take the prize away from her. If necessary, we will call the Brazilian ambassador."

A tigress defending her cub. Maybe all mothers were stage mothers at heart.

Camila's father drew a neat leather case from his inside jacket pocket and took out a card. He spoke quietly to Rodrigo.

"He will pay for the telephone. He has the number for the competition, but he asks you to place the call and speak to them."

Nodding, Fred accepted the telephone calling card from Pereira's manicured fingers. They were going to have to hear it from the official source. When he said he was with Camila Pereira and her family, he was put through to the director of the competition's sponsoring organization. By all means, the director said, they wanted to give Camila every opportunity to recover from her ordeal.

"Please convey to her and her family our deep shock at what has happened to her, and our great joy at knowing that she is safe. As soon as we knew she was missing, we met with the judges to discuss what would be fair to her. We decided to allow her to compete last, and to perform both the Mozart and her other concerto together on Saturday night, if she is able to do so at that time. If, by Saturday night, Camila is still unable to play, she will receive the award for the sixth-place finalist and any other awards she may have earned along the way."

When Fred explained and Camila translated, her mother accepted the decision as fair. One hurdle out of the way. Now he had to keep them in Oliver long enough to see what Camila could remember of her captivity—if it had even taken place in Oliver. But if not, why would she have shown up in the park this morning?

His stomach complained again, this time with more reason. It was well past noon. If he could persuade them to eat lunch in Oliver, Camila would have another hour of recovery. Would it make her more or less likely to recognize where she'd been held? He'd heard of state-dependent memory, and had even seen it work once, when he'd had to get a man drunk again to help him recall the details of a murder he'd witnessed while under the influence. Still, Camila had been almost completely blank when she'd surfaced in the park, and there was no way he was going to feed her more roofies, if that's what she'd had. His only hope was that she'd still been relatively clearheaded in the car that brought her to Oliver. If so, she might eventually remember where she'd been driven.

He explained what he wanted to do, and recommended Wilma's Cafe for lunch. "It's plain food, but it's clean, and Wilma makes a good cup of coffee." Not that he knew what kind of coffee Brazilians liked.

"No!" Rodrigo exploded. "We're getting out of this town."

And away from Bruce, Fred thought. He thinks Bruce is beating his time with her.

"But I want to eat," Camila said. "I was hungry all morning, and now my stomach hurts." She hugged her middle and translated what was going on.

They all talked at once. Camila's father overruled Rodrigo's objections. He spoke in the quiet voice of a man accustomed to being obeyed.

Camila embraced her father and smiled up at Fred. "He

says if his daughter is hungry, we will eat. And we will all cooperate fully with the police investigation. From now on, we will do what you say."

"Good. Your driver can follow my car," Fred told them. "But Camila will ride with me. If she recognizes anything on the way to the restaurant, I don't want to miss it."

No longer resisting, they loaded into the two cars. Bruce stayed behind to practice. At the last minute, Fred picked up the program booklet of the competition from the table at the end of Joan's sofa, and, feeling like a heel, lifted a recent snapshot of Andrew from the stack of family pictures that Joan kept promising to put into her album.

"Keep your eyes open," he told Camila as he turned the key in the ignition. "If you see anything that looks even a little familiar, speak up." Could she? he wondered.

They drove for a few blocks.

"This park!" she cried, pointing suddenly in front of his nose. "I remember this park."

"What do you remember?"

"I was . . . lost. And Bruce and Joan found me there."

"Good. That happened this morning. And before that?"

"I don't know."

"You're doing fine. Keep watching."

But she was silent. He left them at the restaurant to go back to the station and have copies made of the pictures. When he returned on foot, they all seemed less tense than before. Food will do that for you, Fred thought, his own stomach protesting. Again he drove, giving Camila the front window seat. This time her parents and Rodrigo crowded into the back. The driver stayed behind with the Lincoln.

"This won't take long," Fred promised. "Oliver is a small town. We'll start with the campus area."

They rode in silence past academic buildings with beds of red and gold chrysanthemums, Oliver College colors, and wound through the campus and back out onto fraternity row. Fred held his breath, but Camila said nothing, although he could see that she was paying close attention to buildings on both sides of the street. At the edge of campus, he turned toward the road that would take them back to Indianapolis and the most likely route for Camila to have traveled on her way into town.

Then he felt, rather than heard her tense beside him. He stopped. "What is it?" he asked her.

"Nothing. We were going so fast. A dog . . . I think it was a big dog."

"Here? Chasing you?" Any of these homes could have a dog, he thought. In this older residential section at the edge of the campus, no two houses looked alike. A frame two-story with peeling paint rubbed shoulders with a neat brick bungalow trimmed in limestone, and next door neat flower beds were outlined with geodes, ugly rocks that Fred had learned hid beautiful crystals inside. Near the far end of the block, window shades pulled to the sills closed the eyes of an old house with a FOR SALE sign in a scruffy yard that must have been a trial to the neighbors on both sides, whose lawns were lush and manicured. All along the block, mature maple and sweet gum trees tinged with fall color met across the shady street. The tornado hadn't touched down here.

"I don't know." But her agitation increased. She was staring at the houses, as if she could force her memory to come.

"Do you recognize a house? Were you held here? Was there a dog in the house where you were held?" He paused between questions to give her a chance to respond, but she was silent.

Finally she sighed and shook her head. "I'm sorry."

"That's all right. You just keep watching." He could hear Rodrigo translating softly behind them. He crisscrossed the neighborhood a few more times, but Camila didn't respond again. At least he knew where to begin circulating those photographs. Not because they were necessarily his most likely suspects, he thought—the money still had to be on the fraternities—but because the number was small enough to deal with, like the old joke about the drunk crawling around under the streetlight looking for the watch he lost halfway down the block, because that's where there was more light to see it by.

And if that does as much good as looking in school for the kids who saw Pruitt's killer, we'll be 0 for 2.

21

When Joan returned from the adult day care after feeding Charlie, a message to call Fred was on her desk.

"Had lunch yet?" he asked.

"Yes, why?"

"I'm about to grab a bite. I was hoping for some company."

"It's really quiet around here. I can take an hour." And I can tell you what I've figured out.

They met at Wilma's and sat in Fred's favorite booth, where he could sit with his back against the wall. Joan sipped Wilma's good coffee and watched him light into a burger and fries, loading on the mustard and spearing kosher dills between bites. She couldn't help wondering whether Charlie had ever enjoyed his food like that. Probably. The way his clothes hung on him, he hadn't always been so gaunt. She shook her head.

"What's the matter?"

"Thinking about another man." She grinned. "An old guy in the day care. And about Camila. Fred, I'll bet anything she was drugged. What do they call that date-rape drug?"

"Rohypnol, or roofies."

"That's the one. They ought to check her for it. And you ought to drive her around Oliver. See if she can recognize the place she was held, like a fraternity house, maybe."

He smiled at her. "I'm way ahead of you. You're right about the drug. She had something in that family, anyway. When we get the full report we'll know more. She still doesn't remember much. Before she and her folks went back to Indianapolis, I rode around town with her. She remembered the park, but didn't react to the campus, or the fraternities. She got kind of agitated in a residential neighborhood near campus, though. At one point she thought she remembered a dog, but she couldn't remember anything about it, or about any of the houses we could see."

"So it's a dead end."

"Not quite. We'll circulate her photograph around there and see whether the neighbors remember seeing her."

"And whoever took her there."

"Right." He wiped hamburger juice from his chin. "And we'll keep our eyes out for dogs."

"I suppose you'll show them Bruce's photo."

"I think we have to, don't you?" The crease in his forehead deepened.

Poor Fred, Joan thought. You shouldn't have to worry about my feelings while you're doing your job. "I know. And I've been thinking about Uwe, too, and Nate. They hung out with Camila almost as much as Bruce did. Bruce and Nate are still practicing, but it doesn't take much time to drive to Oliver and back."

"Is Uwe driving yet?"

"I don't know. I don't think so, but maybe he talked her into driving herself. If he'd told her he had a lead on her violin, Camila wouldn't have hesitated to drive anywhere to find it."

"And back?"

"I forgot about back. Still, I'll bet he could manage an automatic transmission one-handed."

"The cast on his arm will make him easy to remember. The Indianapolis police checked car rental agencies with photos of Camila, but not of the other violinists. They'll go back now with the whole program booklet, and focus on before she was missing—even before the violin was missing."

She didn't want it to turn out to be Uwe, who had lost everything through no fault of his own, and who had come through it with such grace. "Nate wouldn't have to rent a car. He could borrow his mom's, if she wasn't using it herself."

"You don't think she'd notice? Would you notice if Andrew borrowed your car without asking?"

"Probably not, but he wouldn't."

"How many miles would it take you to notice that it had been driven?"

"I never look at the odometer as long as the gas tank isn't low. But Cindy Lloyd might, if she logs her business trips. Nate would probably know whether he could get away with that."

Fred signaled to Wilma to refill their cups.

"I can't even imagine how she would feel if he did," Joan said. "Or if she heard he was under suspicion. You saw them together."

"Yeah."

"I'm not the hover mother she is, but I'd truly hate for Andrew to have done such a thing, even as a prank. He wouldn't—I know that. I'd probably defend him as fiercely as Cindy would defend Nate. The cops had better stand back if they accuse Nate. And maybe even if they accuse Bruce." She looked him in the eye. "I know you have to do what you have to do, but I'm becoming very fond of Bruce. Still, I don't feel as absolutely sure about him as I do of my own son."

"Why would Nate bring Camila here?"

Wilma came over and poured, but didn't break into their conversation with dessert specials. It was one of the reasons they kept going back—not that they had a lot of choices in Oliver.

"I don't know. Maybe he knows students at the college. Or maybe he didn't bring her here until this morning, before we found her in the park. Either Nate or Uwe could have brought her here to throw suspicion away from himself and

153

onto Bruce. They both knew Bruce was coming here with me."

Fred raised his eyebrows.

"I suppose that's pretty far-fetched," she said. "It was probably fraternity kids, no matter what Camila doesn't remember. That's what my old folks are saying about Kyle Pruitt. Except the ones who say fraternities are an easy scapegoat. They do have a point."

"We're not jumping to any conclusions about that." Fred shook his head. "This is turning out to be some week. Good thing we didn't get married when we talked about. Some honeymoon this would have been."

She reached for his hand across the table. "I don't care. I'd rather be with you during this mess than without you."

His eyes crinkled. "You mean that?"

"Yeah."

"Even the way I've been acting?"

"Yeah." She smiled, and found that it was true.

"Let's go pick up a license."

"And get married? Just like that?"

"We can wait. But if the mood strikes us, we won't have to."

They strolled over to the courthouse hand in hand. Sudden shyness overwhelmed Joan, but the young, gum-chewing clerk was matter-of-fact.

"Your date of birth?" she asked Joan. Not Fred.

"Why?" You can't think I'm underage.

"Are you under fifty?"

"I'm forty-three."

"Did you bring your rubella form?"

"My what?"

"Women under fifty need a rubella form signed and dated by the doctor. You have to pick the form up at the hospital lab. Bring it back with an ID with your date of birth and eighteen dollars in cash."

"No blood test?"

"No. Just the form."

Rubella. They don't want me to catch it while I'm pregnant. Why else would the state care? And we still haven't talked about that.

Fred hugged her. "I didn't know about that. I never got married in Indiana before."

"Just as well we didn't wait till the last minute. You'd think they could keep the forms in the clerk's office."

"Come on, we might as well pick it up." They walked to his car, and he drove to the hospital, leaving her in a NO PARKING zone with the motor running while he ran in. At least she didn't have to worry about getting a ticket.

When he came back, she told him, "Fred, I just thought. Rebecca will need one, too, if she decides to be married here."

Solemnly, he handed her two slips of blue paper. "I think of everything."

"You do, don't you? Have you already lined up the preacher?"

"That's your department. You're the one who wants the traditional fuss."

"All right. But right now, I couldn't care less about tradition."

"That's my girl."

It was high time to get back to work. Late in the afternoon, though, she did manage a couple of brief phone calls.

Dr. Cutts's nurse, Liz MacDonald, said she could come in first thing Friday afternoon. "Or right before lunch."

"No, I'm subbing for some folks who will be going to the Pruitt funeral, and I don't know when they'll get back."

"Oh, I know. Isn't that a shame? My younger sister had a big crush on Kyle when they were in high school. But he never married."

"You make him sound old. He wasn't even forty."

"Well, I am, and some days I feel like ninety."

Joan laughed. "I'll see you tomorrow, if you're still alive by then."

The call to the church she had attended a few times was even briefer, since she wasn't on chatting terms with the secretary.

The minister had time Friday afternoon, if it could wait until then. They set the time early enough to let her make it to Bruce's concert afterward. Everyone else was taking the morning off; she could take some time at the end of the day.

She decided that the gossips at the center couldn't have any idea who was on the other end of the line, much less what the calls concerned. With Liz, she had asked for enough time to fill out a form, and the rest of the conversation, like so many these days, had concerned Kyle Pruitt's death. With the church secretary, she had asked to see Mr. Young, whose name she knew from the Sunday bulletin on her occasional visits. There must be other Mr. Youngs in Oliver. Not that Annie Jordan couldn't have put two and two together. Nobody else listened as closely as Annie.

But why do I even mind if they figure it out?

The phone rang then, and Joan picked it up. The boy on the other end of the line sounded like Andrew before his voice changed. And he sounded worried.

"You the lady come to school yesterday?"

"Yes." She smiled.

"With the guy with the fiddle?"

"That's right."

"I heard what he said, and I had to call you. The orchestra teacher told me where to find you. She's okay."

"I'm glad to hear it."

"But I don't want to get nobody in trouble, you know? So I didn't want to talk to a teacher." Oh? "Then I thought of you."

"Uh-huh."

"I mean, that fiddler said to tell someone. And you've got a nice face, you know?"

"Thank you."

"I'm kinda worried about these kids."

"What kids?" she risked.

"There's two kids on my school bus. Only they quit riding the bus."

"Why did they do that?"

"I figured they were out sick, but then I saw them at school, just not on our bus. I know they didn't move, 'cause we drive past their house on the way to my house, and the same old junkers are in their yard."

"Uh-huh." Joan had seen yards like that, especially out beyond the edge of town.

"Then I saw them riding to school. And you know what they're riding?"

"What?"

"Bikes. Both of 'em. They used to have one old bike between them. Sometimes the big kid would ride his brother on the handlebars, but he was gettin' too heavy, you know? Only now the little kid's got the old bike, and the big one's got a new one. A blue ten-speed. Not real new, but they never get new stuff."

Joan held her breath. Was this what she hardly dared to hope it was?

"That wasn't so weird, but they're not putting their bikes in the bike rack like you're supposed to. This morning they hid them in some bushes. And the little kid acts scared of his big brother. He never used to. So I started wondering. They quit riding the bus on Monday, and I saw the blue bike on Tuesday. I heard about the bike the cops are looking for, you know?"

"I sure do. You did the right thing, to tell someone."

"You won't get 'em in trouble, will you? They're not bad kids."

"No, but someone needs to talk to them. Who are they, and who are you?"

"Let's leave me out of this, okay? And promise me you'll talk to them first, before you tell the cops."

"I promise." Can I keep that promise? Never mind.

"They live out on Quarry Road—you know that road?"

"Yes." I'll never forget it. "Where?"

157

"Before you get to the quarry. Maybe half a mile out of town, in a trailer on the right just after the road curves to the left. It says Johnson on the mailbox."

"And the boys' names?"

"Adam and Timmy. Timmy's the little brother."

"Were they there—?" But the dial tone interrupted her question.

Joan sat thinking of what she had promised. She'd had to say it, or this kid would have stopped right then. Look at the way he'd hung up. Was she bound by a promise made under duress? No. But would it hurt to keep it? She hadn't said she wouldn't tell the police, only that she'd talk to the boys first. Still, Fred wasn't the anonymous police.

Her fingers dialed his number automatically. "Fred Lundquist, please."

"I'm sorry, ma'am, he's not available. Would you like to speak to another detective?"

"No, I'll try him later." He must be out helping canvass the neighborhood where Camila reacted to something, she thought. This might not amount to anything, anyway. I'll just drive out there after work and check.

22

At five, she closed up the center and walked home through the park, enjoying what was left of the day. In a couple of months the sky wouldn't be so blue at five. Bruce waved to her from her new porch swing, and she suddenly remembered her other promise, to take him back to Indianapolis tonight, if he wanted to go back.

"How did it go?" Joining him on the swing, she shut her eyes and yielded to the movement. With Bruce doing all the work, it did funny things to the back of her neck.

"Not bad. Camila's dad was ready to tear me limb from limb at first, but we parted friends. She's doing better already, but she wasn't ready to perform when she left."

"What a shame. Bruce, I'm so sorry. Instead of the refuge I thought I was offering you, you ended up in the middle of it all."

"It would have been worse in Indianapolis, before they'd seen her."

"I suppose. Do you want to go back tonight?" She opened her eyes and saw that his were closed.

"No, if you don't mind, I'll stay over again. Once they all left, it really was peaceful here. I've been getting a lot of work in."

She grinned. "I can see that."

"And relaxation. Just as important."

"I'll leave you to it, then." She stood up. "I'll be back to fix supper."

She willed the old Honda to start one more time, patting it on its dashboard when it did. Last summer, when she'd been so worried about Andrew, she hadn't been able to appreciate the curving, wooded beauty of Quarry Road. Now she could enjoy glimpses of steep hills and gullies and occasional houses, big and little, tucked back in the woods away from traffic. After a sharp left she spotted a battered mailbox and deciphered *Johnson* in its flaking paint. The rusting cars in the yard were almost as good a landmark. She pulled into the rutted driveway. The old mobile home was nestled among some of the biggest sassafras trees she'd ever seen.

Should she go up to the sagging porch someone had built onto the front? Feeling eyes on her, even thought she couldn't see anyone, she stood still and soaked in the natural beauty, marred only by human habitation. Around her, the leaves were already changing color. Poverty would be easier to endure, she thought, if you could see flaming sassafras from every window.

She didn't hear the man open the door, but there he was, tall and thin, standing on the porch in clean, faded jeans and a plaid shirt. His light brown hair, clipped short over his ears, very likely had been blond when he was a boy. Fred's towheads might well be his sons.

"Mr. Johnson?" She went forward. "I hope I'm not coming at a bad time."

"Good as any," he said softly, and waited.

How could she begin? I had an anonymous phone call that suggests your boys may be tangled up with a cop killing? She wished she'd thought it out ahead of time. Somehow she'd expected to be talking to the boys, not their father.

"My name is Joan Spencer. I wonder if I could talk to your boys."

"They in some kind of trouble?" His voice didn't change, but she thought he gripped the porch support harder.

"Nothing like that. It's a long story."

"I got time." He stepped back, and gestured for her to join him on the porch, at least, but when she climbed the rickety steps, he was holding the door open.

She followed him into the house and paused while her eyes adjusted to the dimness. Like the man, the simple furniture was worn, but clean. She sat down in one of two cushioned chairs with wooden arms. Over in one corner, hard to ignore, a shotgun leaned against the wall.

"Get you a cup of coffee?"

"I wouldn't want to put you to any trouble."

"No trouble. It's on the stove."

"Yes, please." *He can't very well shoot me if I'm drinking his coffee.*

She could see him moving in the kitchen. He poured two mugs of steaming coffee from a large graniteware coffeepot like one her grandmother had owned, and handed her a mug. She sipped her coffee black, careful not to burn her tongue, and was amazed. "Mr. Johnson, this is wonderful! What's your secret?"

He melted. "No secret. Ma always fixed Swede coffee like this for church suppers. You just stir a raw egg into the grounds before you dump 'em into the boiling water."

"I'm going to try it." She didn't have to fake her appreciation. *Would Fred's mother have fixed "Swede coffee" when he was growing up?*

He watched her over the rim of his mug, and waited.

"I visited the school the other day, with a violinist from the International Violin Competition of Indianapolis. He told the students about violins and such. I don't know whether your boys heard him."

"Not that they mentioned."

"Well, the kids got to asking him about that violin that was stolen from one of the competitors—a valuable one."

"Stradivarius, wasn't it?"

That surprised her. "Yes, it was. You can understand why they were interested. So he told them what he knew about that, and about the violinist who disappeared after that. He said that the schoolchildren he'd talked to in Indianapolis were watching for any sign of her or her violin, and what a big hero anyone would be who noticed anything that might lead to finding her or her violin and told some adult about it. But he'd heard about our local mystery too, so he told them what heroes the boys would be who called 911 when Sergeant Kyle Pruitt was hit, if they ever came forward and told what they'd seen, and especially if they were able to help the police find who hit him."

"I heard about that, too." His hackles were rising. "What makes you think it's got anything to do with my boys?"

"Maybe it doesn't. But I had a phone call today from a boy. He told me about Adam and Timmy because he didn't feel comfortable talking to a teacher or the police."

"About what?" Now he was on his feet, shaking a finger down at her nose while waving his mug of hot coffee all too close. "They're good boys! They ain't done nothin' wrong!"

Joan resisted the urge to pull back into the cushion of her chair. "I believe you. The boy who called me seemed to think they might turn out to be the heroes that violinist was talking about. Is it possible? Do they ever stay in town after school?"

He sat down and parked his mug on the floor. "No, they ride the bus home."

"That's what made the boy who called me wonder. He said he usually rides the same bus, but they haven't been on it the past few days. They've been riding their bikes, instead."

"They've only got the one bike. Sometimes they ride it together, if they miss the bus to school—in an emergency, you understand. Then Adam rides it home, and Timmy comes home on the bus."

"Did they do that on Monday, do you know?"

"Could be. I leave before they do of a morning. Monday I got some overtime. They was here when I come home for supper." No sign of a mother in this household. She wasn't going to ask.

"Mr. Johnson, would you mind very much if I asked your

162

boys about this? I don't want to scare them. I'm nobody official. But if they saw something that will help the police, and if they can bring themselves to tell what they saw, they really will be heroes. I don't know whether there's a reward out, but it wouldn't surprise me a bit."

"When you put it that way . . ." He smiled for the first time, revealing teeth that needed a good dentist and probably never would have one.

Where were the boys? Joan hadn't seen any sign of them, and yet their father didn't seem at all worried.

He went to the door, stuck two fingers in his mouth, and whistled. "They'll be here." He came back in, but didn't sit down again.

Sure enough, in a few moments she heard young voices outside. Then the door opened to admit two boys with burr cuts, their short, fine hair so pale as to be almost invisible. The little one stopped short when he saw Joan, and the big one had to put on the brakes not to run over him.

"Come on in." Laying his hands on their shoulders, Mr. Johnson propelled them toward Joan's chair. "This lady wants to talk to you."

They looked scared. Were they that used to being in trouble?

"I won't bite, honest." She smiled at them. "I hear you might be heroes."

They looked at their father, doubt written all over their faces.

"You tell her what she wants to know."

"Yes, sir," said the older one. Adam, her caller had said. He might be fourteen or fifteen. His voice hadn't changed, and he was still a foot shorter than his father, but he already had the same lanky look. Timmy, though slender, was rounder than his brother. They wore jeans and plain T-shirts, a red one and a blue one, both faded. They weren't as clean as their father, but what boys are, especially a couple of hours after school?

"Last Monday a man was hit while he was out riding his bike in Oliver, near the college."

Adam stared straight ahead, but Timmy's head swiveled toward his brother.

"Some boys called 911 and gave him the only chance he had to live. Afterward, a college student saw a couple of boys who looked like you two near the accident. The police still don't know who hit the man, who was a police sergeant. They're hoping the boys could tell them what they saw." She let the words hang in the air.

"That was on the TV," Mr. Johnson said. He leaned against the door, releasing their shoulders.

"That's right. Boys, if you were the ones who saw the accident, and if you called 911, you're not in any kind of trouble. You're already the good guys. But if you tell us what you know, you can help solve a crime. Won't you do that?"

"That was no accident!" the little one burst out.

"Timmy—" His brother's hand shot toward him, but Timmy dodged it.

"I told you we oughta tell." He turned huge blue eyes on Joan. "That old car sped up to hit him. They did it on purpose!"

"They?" Joan asked.

"Somebody," Adam said. His voice was dull. "I couldn't see who was driving. We were too far down the street. I don't think they sped up, but they were going fast, and they never even slowed down."

"What did you see?"

"Just a white car, tooling away fast."

"A license plate?" Probably too much to hope for.

Adam shook his head. "Too far away."

"What kind of car?"

"Maybe a Ford."

"A station wagon," Timmy said. "And somebody wrote on it."

"Graffiti?"

"Yeah, kinda."

"So what did you do?"

"I rode over there—I rode my bike to school that day," Adam said. "The guy looked dead. So I knew we had to call 911. We rode over to the college library. They've got a pay phone in the lobby, and 911 calls are free, did you know that?"

"No, I didn't. And then you rode back to see the cops come?"

"An ambulance came," Timmy said. "I thought that was dumb. We told 911 he was dead."

"But he wasn't," Joan said. "He was still alive. You gave him the only chance he had. It's a good thing you acted as fast as you did."

"See?" Timmy said. "I told you we had to, Adam."

"Had to what?" Joan asked.

"Borrow his ten-speed."

Joan saw storm clouds gathering on their father's face. "You certainly did," she said. "That was exactly the right thing to do. Riding two of you on one bike would have been too slow. What happened to the ten-speed?"

Both boys studied their scuffed sneakers.

"Son?" Mr. Johnson growled at Adam.

"When we got back, a man was standing there." He didn't lift his eyes. "I was scared he'd say I stole it."

"And then?" Joan prompted.

"Then I heard the sirens. I didn't want to get arrested. So we took off fast."

"On the ten-speed?"

"Timmy rode ours and I rode that. I was gonna take it back later, but he was gone and I didn't know where he lived. Then I heard the police were looking for us, and I was real scared."

"Where is it now?"

"Out back, in the woods. It's okay, Dad, honest."

"The police want to see that bike," Joan said. "But I'm

sure they're not going to arrest you. They want to see whether the car that hit Sergeant Pruitt left anything on the bike that will help them find the car."

"Like what?"

"Paint, maybe. I don't suppose they'll find anything else."

"I did," Timmy said.

"Did what?" his father said.

"Find something else. I put it in my pocket, for a souvenir." He pushed his hand deep into his jeans pocket and pulled out a bit of broken plastic. Yellow plastic, curved.

"Where did you find it?" Joan asked.

"On the street, by the bicycle. I picked it up while Adam was picking up the bike."

Watching his father's face, she rushed in. "That's wonderful, Timmy. That's just the kind of thing that could crack this case wide open. And the bike, too, Adam. You boys did just right. First you got help, and then you took care of the evidence." She hoped she wasn't laying it on too thick.

"You been riding that bike?" Mr. Johnson towered over the boys.

"Some," Adam said, not meeting his eyes.

"You been riding it to school?"

"Yes, sir."

"We'll take it back in the pickup, right now."

"Yes, sir."

"Mr. Johnson," Joan said. "I think the police will want to see it before it's moved again, and certainly before any paint from the pickup can get on it. I know Lieutenant Lundquist, who's in charge of this investigation, and I'm sure he'd like to come in person to meet your boys."

"You think so?"

"I really do." And who knows, maybe Kyle Pruitt's family will let them keep the bike. "Let's give him a call."

"Uh—the phone's not working just now." Shut off? she wondered. He'd be much too proud to say so.

"I'll find him, then, and bring him right back."

23

*H*ad she made a mistake, not taking the piece of plastic with her? Leaving it with Timmy had seemed like the right thing to do at the time, but now, negotiating the curves on the way back into town, Joan wasn't sure. She tried to remember what she knew about the chain of evidence. Did it even apply to something that had already been removed from a crime scene? But she was sure she was right in persuading Mr. Johnson not to load the bicycle into his truck. She hoped it wasn't too late, and whatever traces the white car had left on the bike hadn't already been destroyed when Adam hid it in the bushes at school and the woods at home. Even so, her heart sang at the prospect of offering Fred a lead, any lead.

She pulled into the last empty visitor parking spot at the police station, passing by closer spots marked RESERVED FOR POLICE. Not that anyone would ticket her when she arrived with news like this, but habit was strong.

"No, ma'am," the civilian desk clerk said. "He's not back yet." And he's much too busy for you, the bored look on her face said plainly. "Can I take a message?"

"I've found Kyle Pruitt's bicycle," Joan said flatly.

The clerk sat at attention and punched her switchboard. "There's a woman down here asking for Lieutenant Lundquist. Says she's got Sergeant Pruitt's bike. Yes, sir. I'll tell her, sir." When she turned to Joan again, her whole demeanor had changed. "Would you take a seat, please? Captain Altschuler will be right down."

Joan sat down on the hard wooden bench and wondered whether it had been designed with malice aforethought to poke suspects in uncomfortable places. Or were suspects rushed right in, unlike innocent citizens with information for the police?

This time she didn't have to wait long. She recognized the man coming down the stairs in a dark blue suit, who looked as though he might have been a prizefighter—nose a little mashed, and off center. Fred said Warren Altschuler was tough, but fair.

Joan stood up and held out her hand. "I'm Joan Spencer, Captain."

He shook it. "Warren Altschuler," he said in a voice full of gravel. "What's this about Pruitt's bicycle? Did you bring it here?"

"No, but I can take you to it."

"Are you sure it's his?"

"Oh, I think so. The boys who called 911 have it."

"You found them, too?" When she nodded, he called to the clerk. "Alice, track down Lundquist and tell him to report back here. He deserves to be in on this."

"Yes, sir."

Altschuler's homely face creased into a smile. "Come on up and tell me all about it. Can I get you anything? Coffee?"

"No, thanks."

He led her into an office a little larger than Fred's and offered her a straight chair that was only a minor improvement on the hall bench.

"Tell me all about it."

She began at the beginning, with Uwe's visit to the school, today's phone call, and then her trip out Quarry Road. He leaned forward with his elbows on his desk.

"Did you actually see the bicycle?"

"No, but the boys described it as a ten-speed. The kid on

the phone said it was blue. What I did see was a piece of plastic one of the boys picked up off the street at the scene and has been carrying around in his pocket. It looked like part of a parking light."

"You didn't bring that with you?" A half-question.

"No, I didn't know whether I should. I'm not sure they would have trusted me with it, anyway. I told them I'd bring Fred back. And I said they'd be heroes if they preserved the evidence that cracked this case. Kind of corny, but they're just kids, and I wanted them to feel good when the police arrived. They're poor, Captain. No working phone—that's why I came back here. You think there's any chance of a reward?"

"A reward for what?" Fred walked in.

"Mrs. Spencer's found you a lead on Pruitt," Altschuler said, smiling broadly.

"And you're asking the department for money?" Fred sounded stern, but his eyes were crinkling.

"No. I asked for you."

"Fill him in on the way," Altschuler told her, and they left.

"What did you come up with?" Fred asked as they walked downstairs.

"Oh, Fred, it's the boys you've been looking for. They have the bicycle and what looks like a piece of the car!"

A few minutes later Fred was her passenger, with a police van following to bring back the bicycle. Joan gave him the long version and, when she dared to take her eyes off the curves, enjoyed the expression on his face.

She drove home alone, leaving Fred with the awestruck Johnson boys. He would come back in the van with the uniformed officer and the bike.

Bruce had switched from the Brahms to finger exercises and was flying through some that she remembered taking at a crawl, back in the days when she still practiced seriously enough to do them at all. When she opened the door, he grinned lopsidedly at her without pausing. Taking the hint, she tossed her shoulder bag on the sofa and headed for the kitchen. He went back to Brahms, and again she heard that different cadenza she'd thought she'd dreamed in the Osbornes' living room. He'd found a new one—or written one himself, the way violinists used to do, the way Brahms's friend Joachim had written the one almost everybody played. Now he was switching back and forth between the Joachim cadenza and this new one. Hadn't he decided yet which to use on Friday?

Supper was almost ready when the violin broke off.

"Don't stop on my account."

Joan hadn't heard the door, but that was Fred's voice.

"Give him a break, Fred." So, Andrew had come in with him. "If you'd been working as hard as Bruce all day, you'd be begging for an excuse to quit."

Joan smiled, listening to the two of them and Bruce. They sounded like family already. Feeling good, she tucked up her back hair, but ignored the stragglers around her warm face, in the probably vain hope that the occasional blasts of steam they'd received while she was cooking had bent them into some semblance of curls.

Fred came into the kitchen and kissed her on the back of the neck, sending little shivers down her spine.

"If I never loved you before, I do now."

"You got it?"

"We got it. There's no question about it; it's Pruitt's bike. The vehicle that hit it did leave white paint on it, so we can probably trust the rest of the boys' description. You were right about the parking light, too. The department will come through with some money for the kids, and I'm sure Pruitt's parents will want them to have the bike when we're done with it."

At the table, they shared the news, but Bruce and Andrew were more interested in Camila. It figured; she was prettier than Kyle Pruitt.

"So what happened? What was she doing here?" Andrew

asked, and they told him, with Fred filling in the bits Joan and Bruce couldn't.

"I still don't have any idea what she was doing in Oliver," Joan said. "Did you learn anything from the neighbors this afternoon, Fred?"

"No, if they even were the neighbors. Her memory was still too spotty to mean much. She may have been held somewhere else entirely."

"You think she'll eventually remember how she ended up here?" Andrew asked, helping himself to the last of the roast. Either Bruce wasn't such a bottomless pit, or he was holding back out of politeness. Or maybe Andrew just beat him to it. It would be all right. She had shamelessly spread frosting out of a can onto an Amish angel food cake she'd bought on the way home. It should be plenty big enough for all of them. The Amish made generous cakes, with a hint of almond she loved.

"Maybe," Fred said. "I don't think anyone knows for sure. All we can do is wait and keep nudging her with questions."

"You know her family will do that," Bruce said. "And Rodrigo."

"And the IPD," Fred said.

"Her mother may keep them off her back until she has her chance to play Saturday night," Bruce said. "She's not out of the competition yet."

"That's good," Andrew said.

"For her, sure. But I'd better not lose any of my edge between now and then. Camila at her best is awesome."

"She is, isn't she?" Joan said. "But so are you." Loyalty aside, she meant it.

"Thanks."

"Are you going to keep working tonight?"

"No, I'd kind of like to hang out with you guys. Get to know you all better, if you have time."

"Sure," Andrew said. "The pressure's off, now that I finished that lab."

"Not tonight," Fred said, but he was whistling when he went back to the station. Although Joan wondered what progress he could make at this hour, she was so glad to see him feeling good that she didn't ask.

On Friday morning the sun shone brightly and a brisk wind tore leaves off the trees. Joan kicked at them and sniffed autumn in the air as she walked to work. She spent a peaceful morning at the adult day care, feeling more useful than usual. Fred hadn't even suggested that she attend the funeral.

No one mentioned having seen her name in the paper, which had run a brief article about Camila's sudden appearance in the park. After feeding Charlie again, she walked over to Dr. Cutts's office.

"I had rubella as a child," she told Liz MacDonald. "So it's not a problem."

"Not good enough. We need medical records to prove it."

"They're long gone. What can I do?"

"Well, you could have the rubella titer done, but that costs fifty dollars. It'd be a lot cheaper to let us give you a rubella shot."

Ridiculous, Joan thought. But in the back of her mind, she knew that it wasn't.

"When did this happen?" Liz MacDonald prepared the injection and swabbed her arm.

Joan thought back. "I was eight years old. I remember, because half the third grade came down with it that year."

"Not the German measles, the man."

She's dying to ask who he is. "We've been seeing each other quite a while now." Ouch.

"There you go. All done."

"Thanks."

"I'll be right back."

At least Rebecca won't have to have the shot. I know we did that when she was little, and I still have her medical records. Somewhere. I'll have to find them.

When Liz returned, the blue paper bore her clear signature

and an illegible scribble that had to be Dr. Cutts's.

"I hope you'll be very happy."

"Thank you." Joan smiled and tucked the form into her bag.

The center was so subdued after the funeral that she felt conspicuous in the red shirt she had chosen for the day care. Not that Charlie had seemed to notice it—or her, for that matter. But he had eaten better than the day before.

She left work early and walked over to the church, a modest frame building with a steeple—the kind Rebecca had always drawn as a child, even when her father was pastoring a congregation that called a flat, school-like building its church home. But Joan had been glad to discover that the minister's sermons weren't as old-fashioned as the building. He wasn't Ken, but she could listen to him from time to time.

He met her in his shirtsleeves at the door to his study.

"Mrs. Spencer? I'm Eric Young. Come in, won't you?" His cheerful face glowed all the way up to his rising hairline. In good shape, he looked to be in his mid-thirties.

She followed him into a study furnished simply with a desk, a couple of armchairs upholstered in what looked like real leather, and a tall shelf of books. The chair he offered her squished comfortably when she settled into it.

He took the desk chair and leaned forward. "How can I help you?"

Poor man, you don't know whether I'm coming to ask your theological advice, or to unload the burdens of my life on you. "Marry me."

He looked startled, and she grinned.

"I'm sorry, I couldn't resist. My husband was a minister, and he used to talk about all the women he'd married."

He smiled. "You said 'was.' " His eyebrows rose.

"He died young."

"I'm sorry."

"Thank you. The first years were hard, but we're doing all right."

"You have a family?"

"A daughter and a son. Andrew is living at home while he's in college here, and Rebecca lives in New York. They've both heard you preach—Rebecca was in town for the quilt show last year. Her fiancé is a finalist in the Indianapolis violin competition this week. I think they may want to be married here, too, but I don't know when."

"Back up there a minute."

"I really did come to ask you to marry me. I'm engaged to Fred Lundquist, who's on the Oliver police force. I hoped we could be married in the church."

"Did you have a date in mind?" He reached for a date book.

"It's a little up in the air because of Rebecca, but we don't have to wait for her. Mr. Young, some days I'm afraid to wait. I'm afraid he'll be the next police officer killed."

Her eyes filled with sudden tears, and she fumbled blindly in her bag for a handkerchief. He slid a box of tissues across the desk and waited while she wiped her eyes and blew her nose.

"Where did that come from?" she said finally. "I didn't mean to cry on your shoulder. I didn't expect it to hit me that hard."

"I'll be happy to do your wedding anytime," he said. "The only wedding scheduled here in the next few weeks is tomorrow morning. So, tell me a little about the groom. How long have you known him? How did you meet?"

He was a good listener, and by the time she left his study, she was glad she hadn't told Fred she'd settle for a quick ceremony in the clerk's office. At the minister's suggestion, she went downstairs to look at the modest room the church offered for receptions. Not that she could imagine a big wingding. Tables covered with white tablecloths were already set up for Saturday's wedding, and at the far end of the room a familiar flaming head was directing a young man hanging colored streamers from the ceiling.

Joan's previous encounters with Catherine Turner, the town's only caterer, had been anything but pleasant. When she'd first met him, Fred had still been seeing Catherine, who had held it against Joan ever since for coming between them. She hoped Catherine wouldn't notice her now.

No such luck. Her hands full of rolled-up streamers and her red hair flying, Catherine came over to her. "I was just thinking about you."

"Me?" Unlikely, Joan thought. What's she up to this time?

"Mm-hmm. Ever since the police showed me your son's picture yesterday."

"They did *what*?"

"I'm surprised Fred didn't tell you." She was clearly enjoying herself.

You tell me, or I'll probably strangle you with my bare hands. Oh, why does this woman succeed in making me so angry, every time? And what on earth is she talking about?

"He had people going up and down my street yesterday, showing pictures of that violinist who disappeared, with some pictures of young men, and asking whether we had seen her with any of them. I recognized your son from that time you brought him to church. I'm so sorry he's under suspicion. I've often been glad I never had children. It's such a terrible disappointment to parents when they go wrong." She turned her back on Joan and called some direction to the fellow hanging the streamers.

Stunned, Joan stumbled up the stairs and out of the church. Eric Young had already left for the day—he probably had a rehearsal tonight for that wedding—and what could she have said to him, anyway? My fiancé suspects my son of committing a crime, and he's told his old girlfriend before telling me?

24

*J*oan's thoughts tumbled through her head as she walked home from the church. She knew that Andrew would never do such a thing. So why didn't Fred know? And why didn't he tell her he was circulating Andrew's picture with the others? How *could* he let her hear about it from Catherine?

Is that why Fred was asking what it would take to make me notice if Andrew used the car? And I said I wouldn't. Great. He couldn't have used it the day she disappeared, though. I drove it up to Indianapolis Monday morning, and stayed all day. Fred knows that.

If he remembers. That was the day Kyle Pruitt was hit. Fred didn't come over that night at all. He probably doesn't remember that I had the car. Not that Andrew couldn't have borrowed someone else's.

But he didn't. And I don't believe Bruce did it, either, or Uwe. It's easier to imagine a group of kids in a fraternity daring each other to pull a stunt like that.

Uh-huh. That's why they get blamed for everything that happens around here. You're not being fair.

Maybe not. But it wasn't Andrew!

Fred arrived shortly after she got home, but with Andrew there, she felt constrained from bringing up what was at the top of her mind. Seething, she fed them sandwiches.

When Bruce didn't even approach the table, she knew better than to push food on him, but he accepted a cup of tea in the living room. She left him hunched over it and hurried into her bedroom to change into her good shoes and do her hair for the evening. Time was getting tight. Fortunately, Bruce had thought to bring his tux along. If he'd had to go back to the Osbornes' to dress, he would have had to leave on Thursday, or she would have had to put off seeing the minister.

And I might not have seen Catherine at all, she thought. Then I wouldn't have known Fred suspected Andrew. Would that have been good or bad? I hate this whole business.

"You ready in there?" Fred called.

Think of Bruce. This is his night. And we're the only family he has here.

She took a deep breath. "Coming."

Fred drove, with Joan beside him, and Andrew, Bruce, and the violin in back. Looking pale, Bruce sat straight and still in his sweats, with his fiddle between his knees. The tux rode in a garment bag behind Fred.

Joan's fingers reached automatically for the radio knob, but she pulled them back. Music was the last distraction Bruce needed. She wished she knew him well enough to know whether talking would help or bother him. He had said he was nothing like Camila, who wanted someone with her before her performance. She decided to stay silent.

Andrew showed no such qualms. "You find that car yet?"

"Not yet," Fred said. "But we know it's a white Ford wagon, and we have a sample of the paint and a piece of its right front parking light."

"What's the next step?"

"We're checking repair shops and parts shops. No luck close to home, but we're branching out. It's just a matter of time."

"Suppose the driver doesn't notice it, or he just doesn't bother fixing it?"

"We're not the only police department watching for it. If it's driven on the public roads, someone will spot it."

A muffled sound behind her made Joan turn around. Taking one look at Bruce's too-white face, she told Fred, "Stop the car."

They were still rolling on the shoulder when Bruce flung open his door and disposed of his tea on the gravel. He wiped his mouth with a handkerchief from the pocket of his sweatpants.

"Thanks." Looking a little better, he pulled the door shut. "Afraid I cut that a little too close."

"You want to wait here a minute?" Fred said.

"No, I'll be okay now."

"You're sure?"

"I'm sure."

Fred pulled back out onto the road. The whole episode had taken only moments.

Bruce was looking more like himself by the time they dropped him at the Hilbert Circle Theatre, where he'd play with the Indianapolis Symphony.

"I hate to go off and leave him like that," Joan said as she watched the tall figure with violin and garment bag slung over his back disappear into the building. Despite all the glass on the front of the building, he was soon invisible.

"He's done it before," Fred said. "He'll be fine."

She was sure it was true. But how could he put himself through it over and over?

In the lobby, elegant chandeliers, cream-colored paint with touches of gold leaf, and a lush carpet befitted the finals. Even the audience buzzed at a higher pitch than at the semifinals. And they had dressed for the occasion. Here and there, Joan saw men in black tie and women in long dresses and sequins. She was glad she had worn her pearls, which she'd inherited from her mother. They were the only good jewelry she owned, except for the modest diamond engagement ring and gold wedding band she'd quit wearing several years after Ken's death. Her feet sank into thick carpet as she followed the usher down the aisle, and she inhaled enough perfume to choke anyone with allergies.

As Bruce's family, they had rated good tickets, smack in the middle of the tenth row. Seated between Andrew and Fred, she looked around, but she didn't recognize anyone yet. Bruce would play on the second half of the program tonight, but they had arrived early enough that only a few Indianapolis Symphony Orchestra penguins in black and white were noodling onstage. In between trumpet runs, she recognized the oboe solo from the second movement of the Brahms. Get it right, she thought. He deserves the best you can do.

A sudden worry hit her. "Bruce didn't mention running through his concerto with the orchestra."

"They did it Wednesday afternoon," Andrew told her. "He's hoping they won't rush him. He and the conductor had some different ideas about what the tempo ought to be."

"It's the conductor's job to follow the soloist."

"Sure, but if the conductor speeds up the orchestra when he's not playing, he'll sound as if he can't play that fast when he comes in the way he wants it. And the orchestra starts this concerto, not the violin."

"Where did you learn all that?"

"From Bruce. I like him, Mom. He sure beats some of the losers Rebecca dated in high school."

Joan laughed, remembering. "They weren't so bad, really, just young. I'm amazed she didn't kill you a time or two back then, you gave her so much grief."

"It paid off, didn't it? She waited for a good one."

Fred's hand squeezed hers. His eyes were laughing down at her. She smiled back, resolving to believe in him, to believe that whatever he was doing with Andrew's picture had some perfectly logical explanation.

"There you are!" Arriving at the seat just beyond Fred, Polly Osborne looked smashing in a simple black dress that could have gone anywhere, and a double strand of pearls.

Joan resisted fingering her own single strand.

Bob Osborne wore a suit that might well have come straight from work. They shook hands all around.

"How is he doing?" Polly asked.

"Seems calm enough," Fred said.

"If you don't count throwing up on the way." Andrew shook his head. "And he didn't even eat supper."

"He'll make up for it afterward. You'll come back to the house? We're hosting a little party for him."

Joan exchanged the kind of glance with Fred that made her feel married already. "Sure, we'd love to." She would wall off her anger; deal with it later.

"You'll have to tell us all about Camila," Polly said. "We were so glad when we heard she was safe. Is it true that she just walked up to you and Bruce?"

"It's true. He was walking me to work through the park, and there she was."

"And she doesn't remember a thing?" Bob asked.

"Not much," Fred said. "The doctor thought her memory might return, but he couldn't predict how long it would take. He found benzos, but we haven't heard back yet what kind from the blood we sent to the IU Med Center."

"I'll see if I can speed that up a little," Bob said. "I don't know whether I have any influence, but it can't hurt to try."

"I'm so sorry her family landed on you," Polly said to Joan.

"Not on me, on Bruce and Fred. I was at work, and missed them."

"Bruce was worried about them. Did they tear him limb from limb?"

"Close," Fred said. "But by the time they left, he had them eating out of his hand."

"I hope it doesn't affect his playing."

"I don't think it will," Joan said, and hoped it was true. "He got it over with yesterday. Until the last hour or so today, he seemed pretty calm."

A few rows ahead of them, Uwe was squeezing past the early comers. Reaching his seat, he looked back and waved his good hand at them.

"There's Uwe," Joan said. "I want to tell him that his school talk brought that phone call about the Johnson boys."

But the sound of the oboe's A told her it was too late. When the orchestra had turned by sections, the conductor came onstage with Hannah Weiss, the first finalist of the evening. Forgetting the voice that would announce it, Joan consulted the program quickly, before the lights dimmed. Hannah would play the Mendelssohn concerto, often the first big concerto any violinist played, and the first concerto Joan remembered ever having accompanied, back when she was in the high school orchestra.

Hannah, wearing red satin, tuned quickly and stood ready. The violin solo began immediately in this concerto, Joan remembered, over what her father used to call "deedle-deedles" in the strings.

At first sweetly, then vigorously, Hannah played the lyrical theme that made up most of the Allegro molto appassionato. Her intonation was precise and her arpeggios exact, but the passion was missing. This music should make you want to weep, Joan thought, remembering not that early school performance now, but the only time she'd ever heard Itzhak Perlman play, when he, too, had chosen the Mendelssohn. He gave us soul, but Hannah's only playing notes. No wonder Bruce isn't worried about her.

Hannah redeemed herself with the lively last movement, in which her clear, rapid technique stood her in good stead. But Joan, while enjoying the music, had already dismissed her as a medal contender.

The break between the first two performers was too brief for a real intermission, and the concertgoers stayed in their seats.

"Wow!" Andrew said. "Are they all that good?"

"The other finalists I've heard are even better," Joan said. "Unless Camila isn't back to herself by tomorrow."

"Bruce is that good?" He sounded awed.

"Wait'll hear you hear him when it counts. But he'll play last tonight."

Katsuo Tanaka would play the Beethoven concerto, the voice announced. He bowed to the audience and turned to the orchestra to check his tuning against the oboe. Then he stood with his head down, waiting.

The soft boom boom boom boom of the first timpani notes sent shivers through her, as they always did, and Joan found herself hoping that this young man would do Beethoven justice, even if he was competing with Bruce. When the violin made its entrance, a clear, sweet tone promised that he would. Joan played along mentally with the violas during the triplet passage she had once practiced for another orchestra and another soloist until it had flowed effortlessly from her fingers and bow, and then she relaxed into the beauty of the violin. Katsuo was playing so far beyond her abilities that all she could do was listen.

By the time he had danced through the last movement, she applauded as enthusiastically as anyone in the appreciative audience. If she hadn't had a good idea of what was yet to come, she would have thought it impossible for the judges to choose anyone but this young Japanese man as the gold medalist.

The lights came up, and Polly leaned over. "That's the best I've heard him play. I thought Bruce was definitely better on the Mozart."

"It doesn't matter what you think," Bob said. "Only the judges get to vote."

"That's why we've never hosted a finalist before. I would have chosen a couple they passed over. This is always so exciting."

Joan remembered that she wanted to find Uwe. But then she saw him making his way toward them through the crowded aisle. He slid into the row in front of them and stood facing them.

"How's the hand?" Bob asked.

"Much better." He looked down at the cast. "I have almost no pain."

"Good. Your surgeon tells me he expects you to make a full recovery."

"That's what he says. But here I am, down in the audience instead of up there."

"And you had a good chance, I know," Joan said. "Uwe used a tape of his playing when he talked in Oliver," she told the others. "It was truly excellent. But, Uwe, I wanted to tell you what happened after you were at the school." She described the phone call and her drive out Quarry Road.

"So now I have some evidence I might never have found if you hadn't come to town." Fred shook Uwe's good hand warmly.

They talked on until the lights began to blink for the end of the intermission. Joan's own stomach began to churn.

Bruce came onstage in his tux, looking serious, but no longer so pale. He smiled and bowed before making a quick check of his tuning. Then he stood with his violin under his arm while the orchestra began the long tutti introduction to the Brahms. Joan hoped they were taking his tempo. It certainly wasn't fast.

And now he was playing, and they were following him beautifully as he played arpeggios against the oboe, bassoon, and flute, and then the strings. The violin began a lyrical theme echoed in the strings, and she was lost in the interplay. Crashing chords, multiple stops, runs, trills, octaves, and a singing tone suggested nothing of the wan, sick child in the car, but a master fully in charge of his instrument.

She held her breath when the orchestra introduced the cadenza. Would he use the sure-fire Joachim, or surprise them? The first arpeggios told her that he'd chosen the new one. Like the familiar cadenza, it blended the themes of the first movement into a beautiful, musical whole while showing off Bruce's technical ability. Softer than the Joachim, she thought, although with this one in her ears the familiar one blurred in her memory. Trills she recognized brought the orchestra back, and the long first movement was over.

Bruce wiped his face with a pristine handkerchief and nodded to the conductor, and the first oboist introduced the theme to the slow movement with long lines and a clear, beautiful tone. Responding, the violin didn't play the theme, but played around it with such a sweetness that tears pricked Joan's eyes.

Dah, da da-da *dah*, the driving last movement began, and scarcely paused for breath until its electric finish. Without consciously deciding to stand, she found herself on her feet shouting "Bravo!" All around her, others in the enthusiastic audience were standing and clapping. Bruce bowed deeply and shook the hands of the conductor and concertmaster, and then the conductor waved to the first oboist to stand before he brought the entire orchestra to its feet.

"He's great!" Andrew shouted in Joan's ear through the applause.

"I wish Rebecca could have heard him," she said when it finally ended, and Bruce had left the stage. "She would have been so proud."

"The bank's not open on Sunday. Couldn't she fly out, even if she has to work Monday?"

"You're right. After tonight, I can't believe he won't be one of the medalists." She wondered how much a ticket would cost on such short notice. Fred would say it's only money, she thought. But that depends on whether you have it.

It took a while to make their way to the lobby, and considerably longer to collect Bruce, waylaid by congratulatory handshakes that it would have been a shame to interrupt. Eventually, though, he went back for the garment bag that now held his sweats, Fred brought the car around, and they piled in.

The street in front of the Osbornes' was so full that they had to park several doors down, across from the Inmans' house. In the driveway, Joan saw Gail Inman's white station wagon with the logo on the door, and suddenly realized what Timmy Johnson had meant by graffiti on the car he saw—it had to have been the logo of some business. She turned to tell Fred, but he was already halfway to the Osbornes' door, matching strides with Bruce and Andrew as if she weren't there.

But Cindy and Nate Lloyd were getting out of the blue sedan that had squeezed into the space in front of them. Joan greeted them warmly.

"Bruce was terrific!" Nate said. "Gave me something to live up to."

"He was, wasn't he?" Joan said, falling into step beside them.

"And that took guts, to play his own cadenza."

"Was it his? It was beautiful."

"Yeah. He was debating all week whether to risk it."

"So that's why I heard him practicing both of them. I wonder how late he decided which one to use."

"I didn't see Camila," Nate said. "Will she be at the Osbornes' party?"

"I don't know. Her family brought her back here yesterday, but I don't know whether she's staying at the Schmalzes' or in a hotel with her folks."

"It's too hard to practice in a hotel," he said. "She'd be better off with a host family. The Inmans have been terrific to me and Mom. Clyde Inman likes Camila a lot. Maybe she could move in with us."

"Nathan couldn't wish for a better host family," Cindy said. "They've given me a room of my own for whenever I can make it up here. These homes are so big; it wouldn't surprise me if Camila's family were staying with the Schmalzes."

Camila, at least, was staying with them, Polly Osborne told them at the door, but they'd called to say she wasn't coming. "I guess it's all she can do to try to get ready for tomorrow. She's not up to facing a crowd tonight."

Crowd was right. Even the Osbornes' huge living room had standing room only. Joan spotted Bruce and Andrew at the buffet table. Andrew had eaten plenty at supper, but poor Bruce needed it. He certainly seemed to be relaxed now, alternately eating and accepting more congratulations.

Feeling a little lonely among so many strangers, Joan found her way to Fred, who was standing with his back to a wall, always his preference in a crowd.

He smiled at her. "Had enough?"

"I have, but Andrew's still stuffing his face."

"I expect a long day tomorrow, and I'm fading fast."

"I'll get him." She made her way through the crowd and waited her turn to hug Bruce. "It was wonderful, Bruce. I hope we can make it back tomorrow. Tell Rebecca I'll give her a call late tonight."

He blushed as only a redhead could. "I already talked to her."

"Of course you did. Where's my head? I'll talk to her tomorrow. Come on, Andrew. Fred's getting antsy."

When Fred dropped them off and they went inside, her message machine was blinking. Rebecca, she thought, but the voice was younger than Rebecca's.

"Mrs. Spencer, this is Cathy. You came to our school, remember? And Uwe gave me a lesson. I saw your name in the paper this morning. I really need to talk to you. Please call me, okay?"

But it was too late at night. Cathy would have to wait.

25

*J*oan dragged herself out of bed early on Saturday to catch Rebecca before she went to work. "He was really great last night, Bec. We were all so proud of him. You should have heard Andrew go on."

"Oh, Mom, I wish I could have been there!"

"That's what I'm calling about. If you want to come to the awards ceremony on Sunday, I'd love to buy you a plane ticket."

"Mom, that's really sweet, but it's unbelievably expensive on such short notice. We talked about it, but he'll still be practicing today anyway, in case he has to perform tomorrow, and I'd have to come right back tomorrow night. I can't remember the schedule, but I'd be completely beat. Besides, what if I went and then he didn't medal? I wouldn't want to jinx him."

Joan smiled. "You don't believe that."

"Not really. But I don't want to do anything to put pressure on him, and he's made it plain that I'm not welcome, much as he loves me. Maybe because he loves me. It was true, what I told you about the bank, but that was only part of it. He wouldn't let his family go to the competition at all, you know. Absolutely put his foot down."

"I wondered. He just said they couldn't come. I didn't push him about it."

"They're busy, of course, but he really didn't want them there, or me, either. For you to drive up doesn't feel like such a big deal, and he doesn't know you so well, so he could handle that. Bruce's whole life could be touring and stuff, if he makes it as a soloist." Her voice sounded wistful. "I wish I could be more a part of it, but I'm going to have to get used to staying home a lot and hearing about it."

This was not the impulsive daughter Joan remembered. Maybe she was ready for marriage, at that. But what kind of marriage would it be, to a man so high-strung that her very presence wouldn't be welcome at his trials and triumphs?

No worse than showing Andrew's picture around like a criminal's! Couldn't Fred see how upset I was? He had to know how that made me feel.

No, he didn't, she remembered. He still doesn't know I know about it. And maybe knowing how I'd feel is why he didn't tell me in the first place.

Still . . . can't he trust me more than that? We have to talk.

She took her time over a bowl of cereal before calling Cathy, who probably slept in on Saturdays. But Cathy sounded wide awake.

"Oh, Mrs. Spencer, I'm so glad you called. I was about to try you again. I called you yesterday after school, but you weren't home, and then you didn't call back last night, and nobody else would listen to me." The words came out in a rush, with scarcely a pause for breath.

Uh-oh. Joan was glad she had carried her coffee into the living room. She tucked her feet up under her on the sofa.

"What's on your mind, Cathy?"

"It's about that old house—you know, the one on Prospect Street, near the park."

"There are a lot of old houses on Prospect, Cathy."

"This one's got a FOR SALE sign out front. But nobody's ever going to buy it, see, because everyone knows it's haunted. So when I thought I saw a ghost, there's no way I was going to tell anyone, like you know what they'd say, but I know I saw a face in an upstairs window. It was dim, like a ghost, you know? Only now I'm sure it was that girl. You know, the violinist you found in the park. They had her picture on the late news Thursday night, getting into a Lincoln with her parents and a real hunk of a guy! I knew she was the girl I saw in the window. And then when I told people that, no one would believe me. I even called the police, but the snippiest thing answered the phone. I know she thought I was making it up. But you believe me, don't you?"

The old Dayhuff house, it had to be. "I certainly do, Cathy. And I promise I'll check it out. This could be important."

With Cathy's thanks ringing in her ears, she finished her coffee, pulled on her sneakers, and set out across the park. The old Dayhuff house made complete sense; Camila had been coming from that general direction. And that would explain why no one had noticed a strange woman in a fraternity house, or how someone else could have hidden her. But it would have been risky, even in a house known to be haunted. What if some prospective buyer had wanted to tour the house while she was there?

She circled the old brick house, looking for signs of a break-in, but it seemed securely locked. The doorknobs didn't turn, and she couldn't lift the sloping cellar door. All the leaded windowpanes appeared intact, if dirty; no wonder the face Cathy saw had looked dim. She'd seen it "through a glass, darkly," in the words of St. Paul.

How to get inside? Of course.

She walked downtown to Floriana Real Estate, the company listed on the sign. A loud bell jangled when she opened the door, and a bored-looking blonde with too much mousse in her hair hung up the phone and straightened out of her slouch.

"Can I help you?" She popped her gum.

"I hope so. I'd like to look at the old Dayhuff house, on Prospect."

The receptionist gave Joan's jeans and sneakers the once-over, but apparently they passed muster, because she typed a few keys on the computer in front of her.

"I'm sorry, but we can't show that house until Monday. If you'll leave your name and phone number, I can set up an appointment for you then. It's a lovely old house, in excellent condition. You could move right in." Had she seen the state of the windows?

"I don't understand. It's been for sale for months, hasn't it?"

Twirling a strand of that hair, the blonde said, "Maybe there's a family illness." She clicked a few more keys. "No, this house is vacant, and we have a lockbox on the door, so the owners don't have to be there when we show it. People have all kinds of reasons."

"Couldn't you find out why?"

"It's probably in the computer, but I don't know how to find that out. We don't need to know why. I can set you up an appointment, as I said."

"Who put it in?" By now, Joan was leaning over her desk, straining to see her computer screen.

Sighing elaborately while she hauled a list out of a file in her bottom desk drawer, the woman popped her gum again and ran a finger down the list. "It's some Realtor in an Indianapolis branch of the firm."

"Look, I think someone may have used the house in the commission of a crime. Can you identify this person?"

"Really? Gosh, let me look it up." Suddenly interested, she typed rapidly, and then swung the screen around so that Joan could see the name.

Gail Inman, Joan read. That's odd, she thought. Gail did mention at the picnic that she had the Dayhuff listing. And she didn't like it when her husband paid too much attention to Camila. But she wouldn't abduct her!

Still, it's Gail who kept the house from being shown.

Or maybe she didn't. Nate Lloyd is staying with Gail. I was already wondering about Nate, and here's a possible link to him. It's not hard to picture Nate finding out how to get into

Gail's computer to send a message that would keep everyone out of his hair while he kept Camila in hiding all weekend. And Nate was there when Gail was talking about the house.

"Ma'am?" The blonde was looking at her funny. "Are you all right?"

"Oh—oh, sure. Thanks. Thanks for your help."

Time to tell Fred. Sure of finding him there today, she set out for the police station.

This time the clerk at the desk called for Fred almost before she asked to see him.

"He'll be right down, Mrs. Spencer. Won't you have a seat?"

Joan thanked her, but decided to stand rather than wait on that bench.

"What brought you out so early?" Fred said after he'd kissed her hello right there in front of God and everybody.

"Oh, Fred, I think I found the house."

"The . . . you mean where Camila was held? Where? How?"

"It's the old Dayhuff place, on Prospect." He looked blank. "A brick house with limestone windows, near the park. There's a FOR SALE sign out front."

"Oh, that house."

But from the expression on his face, she doubted that he had the foggiest idea which house she meant.

"Come on, show me. And tell me why you think so." He held the heavy front door for her, and automatically headed for his car.

Why not? It would save a little time. She started with Cathy's phone call. "The girl's a little flighty, Fred, but I thought she might have seen something, especially when she said she recognized Camila's face on the news."

"Mm-hmm."

"Then I checked with the real estate firm, and learned that the house couldn't be shown until next Monday."

"Really." His tone was neutral, but his pupils widened.

He turned onto Prospect.

"I got the receptionist to show me who put that into their computer, and when she called it up, the name on the screen was Gail Inman."

"Who's Gail Inman?"

"The Realtor across the street from Camila's host family. She mentioned this house at the picnic—you met her. She's a member of the same firm—I guess it's an Indianapolis company with a branch down here, although this receptionist talked as if it were the other way around. Gail's hosting Nate Lloyd."

"So maybe she was too busy to show it this week."

"Maybe, but they have a system that lets any real estate agency show it. They keep the keys to the house in a lockbox on the door. Anyone who knows the combination can open it. If someone else sells it, Gail will have to split her commission, but that hardly seems like a reason to keep it off the market, once they put the box on."

"That the one?" He pointed down the block.

"That's it. It's locked up tight."

He checked it as she had, and peered through the dirty windows. "Guess we'd better get that combination."

When he showed his badge, the receptionist didn't hesitate to write it down for him, though she carefully shaded her paper from Joan's eyes.

"Do you really think it was involved in a crime? I'll bet if someone got murdered in one of our houses, everybody'd want to see it. It would sell in no time!"

"Hate to let you down," Fred said, "but we don't expect to find a body."

At the house, he punched the numbers on the lockbox and reached for the keys. The front door opened smoothly; maybe the house was in better shape than the windows would suggest.

"Keep your hands in your pockets," Fred said.

Indoors, Joan admired the gum woodwork and the carved cherry mantelpiece. This was a lovely place, after all. Even the oak floors looked as if one good polishing would make them shine. Some of the Dayhuffs' old furniture was still there, draped with covers on which a thick layer of dust suggested that they hadn't been disturbed for months. But most of the dust on the floor had retreated into corners, away from the obvious traffic pattern. That figured; the house must have been shown often enough for prospective buyers to have done that much.

No sign of recent habitation downstairs—until they reached the kitchen, where several pans in the sink held the dried remnants of some soup or stew, with dirty spoons and bowls tucked into them. Empty soup cans in the wastebasket revealed the source. Nothing fresh, though. Had a homeless person broken in and found food? But if that's what had happened, why was the house so securely locked? Even though the door locked automatically when it was closed, there would have been broken glass or something to show how such a person got in.

"Upstairs," Fred said quietly.

She climbed the steep steps, following him so closely that she could feel his warmth. The stairs opened beside a linen cupboard set into the back wall at the end of a narrow hallway. Through the open door to the cupboard she saw sheets and towels neatly stacked inside, but the bottom shelves were almost bare. One crumpled blanket suggested what they had held.

Moving clockwise, Fred silently opened the doors to the bedrooms and the bathroom one after another, methodically checking each clothes closet as well. From her spot out in the hall, Joan could see that no one was sneaking out of another room to escape him.

Finally he opened the door to the back bedroom nearest her, on the side of the house that faced away from the park. "Bingo," he said.

Joan looked in. On the floor in the corner farthest from the windows, a tangle of blankets and sheets made a rough pallet. Nearer to the door was a collection of dirty glasses and bowls with dried leftovers that looked like the soup in the kitchen pots.

Then she saw it. In the opposite corner, almost hidden in the shadows, a rectangular violin case in a crisp brown zippered cover lay flat on the floor.

"Oh, Fred!" She ran over and knelt beside it.

"Don't touch it."

"But it looks like Camila's case. It might be her violin!"

"Uh-huh."

"Oh. Of course." Where was her head? Not that they could get much off a violin case—or could they? The handle was a smooth surface. "You expect to find fingerprints on it?"

"Maybe, but they'll probably turn out to be Camila's. I want photos of this room exactly as we found it, and I want our techs to check everything, not just the case, before it's disturbed. But first we need a search warrant, especially for this room and the kitchen. Until we get it, we just have to sit tight."

"How long will that take?"

"Maybe an hour. Maybe more. I'll call the prosecutor." He pulled a cellular phone from his pocket, punched the numbers, and spoke into it.

Without trying to listen, she heard him say "violin case" and then "food." Of course, he'd want to test the remains of whatever Camila had been given to eat and drink. His second call was to Captain Altschuler, and the jubilation in his voice was a joy to hear.

Joan resigned herself to waiting for the warrant and the police to arrive. For lack of a more comfortable spot, she sat down at the top of the stairs. His calls completed, Fred joined her and took her hand in his big paw.

"Looks as if the kid who phoned you had it right."

"Uh-huh. Even if there's no violin in the case. Someone lured her here by promising to take her to her violin. So she brought her case along to take it back."

"Funny no one mentioned that her case was missing."

"Not really," she said. "The case wasn't stolen in the first place; that's why she didn't miss the violin until she arrived at the Indiana Repertory Theatre with her case to play in the semifinals. I saw her carrying it home that night. But later one of the judges lent her a violin to practice on. She must have left that one at the Schmalzes' in its own case when she disappeared. With another fiddle case in the room, maybe no one noticed for a while that hers was missing, but I'll bet her family knows the difference. And I'm sure the judge who lent her a violin has taken it back by now."

"If you're right, this case is probably empty." He looked at his watch.

"I know. Especially if it was fraternity guys from down here who kept her here. How could they get to her violin?"

"How could they get into this house?"

"All they'd need was the combination. Any cute guy could distract that blonde in the office long enough for one of his pals to sneak a peek at the combination."

"She wrote it from memory."

"Easier yet. He tells her he's studying real estate law and—oh, I don't know what line he'd use. But the man who tricked Camila into coming here would have thought of something."

26

*E*ventually the warrant arrived, and with it a small army. Some of them began their search down in the kitchen, where Joan could hear pots banging, and the rest started working in the room where the violin case still lay unopened on the floor. She had lived through some of this routine before, although not without a body in the next room. What a difference it made to know that Camila was safe in the bosom of her family, instead.

She moved out of the way, but once they were all in the bedroom, she sat back down at the top of the stairs. There was probably no point in waiting, really. Fred knew everything she did. But he had asked her to stay, and until he asked her to leave, she intended to wait for the great opening of the violin case.

Wouldn't it be something if the Stradivarius were in it? she thought. Dream on.

She was leaning against the banister when he called her. "Joan, come on in and see this."

"Okay." A little stiff, she got to her feet and went into the room.

"I told them they had to wait for you." The blue eyes crinkled into a smile. "If that kid hadn't trusted you, who knows how long it would have taken us to find this?" Still wearing thin plastic gloves, he unzipped the cover, opened the latches on the case inside, and lifted the lid. The others crowded around and stared.

Joan gasped. Cushioned on crushed velvet, a violin that exactly fit the case lay inside a silk bag with a drawstring at the scroll end. Again, the cameras clicked. Fred picked up the violin, loosened the drawstring, and slid the silk off.

"Is it hers?" he asked her.

"I think so. I never saw it this close before, but it looks right." It looked more than right; it was a thing of quiet beauty. Whether or not there was musical magic in Stradivari's varnish, as some said, its translucent quality gave a warm reddish glow to the instrument. She felt she could look deep into the wood of the spruce top and curly maple sides. "Let me see the back, Fred."

He turned the violin over. The back, also curly maple, glowed even more warmly than the top. Didn't they say there was a flame to it? Joan could see why. And without knowing much about it, she could appreciate the workmanship. Even she could see that the two-piece back was split exactly down the middle. And the purfling that ornamented the edges was elegantly beveled and precisely aligned at the points.

Fred peered through one of the f-holes. "I don't see a label."

"You can't always see them. Besides, labels don't mean much. They copy his labels in all the imitations. Fred, we have to take it to Camila. She'll know instantly if it's hers."

"I can't imagine dusting it for prints; besides, the handle of the case was wiped clean, and the violin has probably been in the bag the whole time. The police report said the bag was missing with it. Do you want to hold it?"

"Could I?" What a thrill, if it truly was the Strad. She took it from him with more care than she ever gave her poor viola and was surprised by how light it was, even compared to most violins. Rubbing her hand gently over the smooth back, she felt the wood trying to vibrate. When she tapped it, it seemed to want to sing. "It's so alive."

"The bows are in the case, too."

"No, I couldn't." She handed the violin back to him, and relaxed. "If this isn't Camila's Strad, it's somebody's beautiful instrument. How many of those would you expect to find in this house?"

"Strad?" said one of the officers. "You think this is the missing Stradivarius?"

"Sure looks like it," Fred said. He was grinning openly now. "We'll notify the IPD and see how they want us to proceed from here."

"Fred, what if they want to hang onto it, as evidence? Camila's supposed to perform tonight, if she's up to it. She ought to have her own violin as soon as possible."

"You're right. I'll tell the IPD we're taking it up, and they can be there when she identifies it. If it's hers, there's no way her mother will let them take it from her. That woman's a tiger."

"I'd love to see that."

"Let's go, then." He slid the violin back into its silk bag and tucked it into the case. Then he turned the crime scene over to the others, and they left, with Fred carrying the violin under his arm.

They stopped by the station long enough for Fred to check in again with Warren Altschuler and place a couple of calls to Indianapolis. Sitting across his desk from him, Joan could hear Camila's shriek when he told her he thought they had found her violin.

"Yes, I'm leaving now to bring it to you. Yes, I know how to find the house."

In the car, he said, "She sounded much closer to normal than when they left on Thursday."

"That makes sense. Did you ever hear what the drug was?"

"Roofies, as we thought, and now we can test what's left of the soup in the house for them. They ought to be wearing off by now."

"Sure, but enough to play the violin at that level?"

"I don't know."

"Even if they're completely gone, she's missed almost a whole week of practice."

"No one is making light of what happened to her. But taking her the violin is about all we can do for her."

"I know. Even catching whoever did it isn't going to help her."

"Not this week. But it may give her some comfort in the long run. I'm glad to have another chance to question her."

"Fred, you wouldn't! Not today, of all days."

"I'm not going to push. But if she remembers more and feels like talking about it, you can bet I'm going to listen."

Would you listen to me? she thought. But she couldn't bring herself to say what was bothering her.

Fewer cars lined the quiet residential street than on the night before, but a marked police car was parked in the Schmalzes' driveway. At least they've turned their flashers off, Joan thought as she followed Fred up to the curved stone porch.

The door flew open before they could ring the bell. The vibrant young woman in the doorway bore little resemblance to the vacant, matted creature Joan and Bruce had found in the park.

"My violin!" Camila cried, and would have grabbed it if Fred had let her.

"Let's do this indoors."

"Of course, come in." She held the door wide for them.

A small crowd was gathered in the Schmalzes' living room. Camila quickly introduced the others. Joan recognized Harry and Violet Schmalz, who looked considerably less distraught than when she had met them at the Osbornes' the night Camila disappeared. Was that only Monday? she thought. Hard to believe.

"My mother and father, Isadora and Moacir Pereira." Camila indicated the handsome, well-dressed couple and, in rapid Portuguese, introduced Joan Spencer, evidently explaining about having used her house, because their expressions instantly turned to smiles and they came forward to shake her hand.

Fred greeted them without needing to be introduced.

"And my boyfriend, Rodrigo Machado. Rodrigo, this is Joan Spencer."

"I am happy to meet you," the good-looking young man said, and they shook hands. "Camila's parents and I appreciate your kindness in her time of trouble."

Two men in suits who had been standing to one side came forward now, and Joan recognized them as the two IPD detectives who had questioned her about Bruce.

"Detective Richardson," the quiet one introduced himself to Fred. "And my partner, Detective Richards." More handshakes.

"Fred Lundquist. Doesn't that cause confusion, the two of you together?"

"It was worse when we were assigned to other partners," said Richards, the older, louder one. "Now we don't care if they mix us up. We're on the same case, see, so it doesn't matter."

Camila's eyes had hardly left the violin case.

"Here you go," Fred said, and handed it to her. "Is this your case?"

"Yes. There is a little spot on one corner—see?" When she unzipped it, Joan doubted that the tremble in her hands had anything to do with roofies. Laying the case on a table, Camila slid the violin out of the silk bag and checked it all over. Tears ran down her face, and she said, "Yes, this is my violin. How can I thank you enough?"

"Make beautiful music on it," Fred said. "But you should know that it was Joan who found it."

"And Uwe Frech," Joan said quickly. Maybe, with all their money, the Pereiras could do something for Uwe.

"Uwe? But he's here."

"He told schoolchildren here and in Oliver how they could help search for you and the violin. One girl who heard him thought she had seen your face in the window of an old house in Oliver. She told me, and that's where we found your violin."

"After the competition, it would help us if you would come back to Oliver and look at that house," Fred said.

Still clasping the violin, Camila looked dreamy. "A window, yes. I remember staring out a window. Upstairs. Was I upstairs?"

He nodded. "We think so."

"I could see the children walking to school, or maybe home after school. But I couldn't go to them."

"You were drugged, dear," Joan said.

"And I remember riding in the car, too fast. Did we hit a dog? I think we hit a big dog." The horror of it crossed her face.

"I still haven't heard about a missing dog, but I'll find out," Fred promised.

Camila's mother spoke to her, and Camila answered in Portuguese.

"She says Camila must stop talking now," Rodrigo said. "She plays tonight."

"But tonight I play my own violin!" Camila said, joyous again. "Thank you for finding it and bringing it to me." Handing the precious instrument to her mother, she threw her arms around Joan and then Fred, kissing them both.

Rodrigo began herding them to the door.

"If she remembers more, be sure to call us," Richardson said.

"Yes, of course," Rodrigo said.

And they left.

"What do you think?" Fred asked Joan as they walked back to the car. "Can she play tonight?"

"Maybe. But I don't see how she can win."

27

O n the drive back to Oliver, something nagged at Joan, but at first she couldn't make it come to the surface. This must be how Camila felt, trying to dredge up deeply buried memories. Or were hers completely erased by the drug? Would they ever return?

"Didn't she mention a dog before?" she asked Fred.

"Yes, when we were driving her around Oliver. But this is the first time she said anything about hitting it."

"What if it wasn't a dog they hit? Oh, Fred, maybe they hit Kyle Pruitt! Wasn't that the same day she disappeared?"

He nodded slowly. "And not that far from the Dayhuff house. In the right direction, too. They could have met him on the way down. That would explain why they didn't stop, if the driver was in the process of committing a felony. That's not accidental death."

"There's something I know that just won't come, and I'm almost sure it has to do with all this." She stared out the window at houses and parked cars as they came into Oliver. Suddenly a mental image of Gail's car parked in her Indianapolis driveway wiped out the ones her eyes were seeing.

Gail Inman's white station wagon, with the firm's logo on the front door. Was it possible? Had Gail been the fast driver who scared Camila? Was it her white Ford Timmy remembered? Was Gail the person who killed Kyle Pruitt? Had her car been in her driveway again today? She couldn't remember.

Fred pulled up to the station and heard her out, but he shook his head at her last question. "I wouldn't have missed a white Ford wagon with damage to the right front parking light."

"Maybe it was already fixed."

"If it was, we'll find out."

"We could ask the neighbors. The Schmalzes were so upset about Camila."

"They were probably too upset to be paying much attention to Gail's parking lights."

"How about Polly Osborne? She's another house farther down the street, but she might have noticed."

"We could start there. You have her number?"

Joan fumbled in her shoulder bag. "Somewhere in here." She dug out the slip of paper on which she'd written Bruce's name and the Osbornes' phone number and handed it to him.

"Come on in." They went up to his office together, and she parked on his straight chair while he phoned Polly. He reached her on the first try.

"Polly, this is Fred Lundquist, down in Oliver. No, she's fine. But I wonder if you could help our memories. Did we remember right that Gail Inman drives a green Cadillac? Oh, I see. Any chance you'd know whether it's been in the shop recently? Something about a fender bender?" He waited, and then nodded. "I see. Thanks, Polly. I sure had that all wrong."

"Well?"

"It's a white Ford station wagon with the company logo, all right. But she's been driving it all week, and there's not so much as a scratch on it."

"She could be wrong about that. How long would it take to get a light repaired in Indianapolis, anyway?"

"I'll talk to Richardson and Richards. Call their attention to the APB we already have out on the car. They owe us. And if you're right, the IPD will need to be in on it anyway."

"Fred, can you really see Gail Inman kidnapping Camila?"

"Who knows? We can dig into motive after we're sure about the rest of it. Maybe she thought the girl was making a play for her husband."

"She did, you know." And she told him what she'd seen at the picnic. "But . . ."

"But you don't think that's enough?"

Joan thought of Catherine Turner's fury at her. Would a person as angry as Catherine resort to something that terrible? Was Gail that angry? Was she herself?

I've wasted a perfectly good trip when I could have talked that out with Fred. But now there's no time. "I'd better go home," she said, and got to her feet. "We missed lunch, but we can have an early supper. Bruce got us a couple of tickets to the last concert. Will you come?"

"Not tonight. I'll grab a burger. I want to follow this up."

"Okay to talk to Andrew?" She said it without thinking.

"Sure. But keep it in the family for now."

"Really? You don't suspect Andrew anymore?"

"Who told you that?" He glowered up at her.

"Catherine. Somebody showed her his photograph." She tried to fight it, but she heard the bitterness seep into her voice.

"Damn! I never meant for you to know about that, least of all from her. Andrew's a good kid. I was sure he was innocent, but I wouldn't have been doing my job if I hadn't given people a chance to ID him. They didn't, of course, any more than they ID'd Bruce. I knew Catherine lived in that neighborhood. I should have told you, but it never occurred to me she'd know he was your son."

"She met him in church once."

"I would never have put you through this if I'd realized that."

"Come on, Fred. There must be other people in that neighborhood who would recognize Andrew." Her voice rose. "In a town this size, everyone knows everyone. And how could you not trust me enough to tell me? That's what really hurts."

His face was stricken, but he let her pour it out before answering. "I'm sorry. I had no idea you were feeling this bad. I was trying to protect you, but it backfired." He got up from behind his desk, took her hands, and looked into her eyes. "Can you forgive me?"

"What about the next time? Will you trust me next time?"

"I trust you with my life. And there won't be a next time. I promise never to put you in that position again."

She stretched up to kiss him. "Good. I'll hold you to that."

"You forgive me?"

"Yes." And she did. Just hearing him say the words made a huge difference to her. Not that he would never make her mad again, but that he cared about how she felt.

"And you'll still marry me?"

"I wouldn't miss it. I've got the rubella certificate, and the minister says he doesn't need much notice. Today was the only day he had a conflict. He'd like to talk with us ahead of time, though."

"What about?"

"He seems to think we're past Sex 101, but he's got a little book about how to fight fair."

"Good idea. If we'd had one of those, I might still be married to old what's-her-name."

She grinned. "You can talk about Linda all you like and I won't care."

"A secure woman. I like that." His eyes crinkled, and he kissed her again. "Come on, I'll walk you downstairs."

Walking home, she admired the crisp blue sky, crunched leaves underfoot, and sniffed the wonderful autumn smell, but she knew she would have felt just as good if it had been pouring.

Andrew met her at the red front door that still startled her, much as she liked it. "You look happy."

"I am happy. Let's go get a pizza, and then I'll take you to a concert."

He didn't need a second invitation. Shutting the door behind him, he came down the steps, and they set off on foot for the pizza place. "More violins?"

"The last three play tonight. No, just two, because they moved Bruce to last night. Nate and Camila will play tonight. She's supposed to do both her concertos."

"Can she?"

"We'll find out. Bruce got us a couple of tickets, but Fred's not going."

"Sure, I'll go. I felt sorry for her on Thursday."

"She seems a lot better today."

"You saw her?"

"That's right, you don't know. Andrew, we found her violin!"

"That's great! Where?"

"In an old house that's for sale here in Oliver. Not far from where we found her on Thursday. We took it up to her."

"So you think that's where she was all that time?"

"Looks like it. There were blankets on the floor, and someone had fed her soup. Probably roofies in it—that's the drug she was given, Fred says."

"I guess they're easy to come by. How did they lock her in?"

"No need. She was too dopey to go anywhere. When the stuff finally wore off enough, she just walked out the door."

"So who did it?"

"That's the question. Do you remember meeting Gail Inman at the picnic?"

"Not really." He grinned. "I was kind of noticing Camila, if you want to know."

"It didn't escape me entirely. Gail's a little older than I am. Nate Lloyd's staying with her, so you'll probably see her tonight, but you mustn't mention this to anyone. We don't know that she did it. We do know she's a Realtor, and she fixed it so no one would go into this house while Camila was there."

"Why?"

"Good question."

"And you think she'll be there tonight?"

"I'm sure she will. Her violinist is playing. The host families always go when their violinists play."

"You don't think . . ."

"What?"

"That she'd go off the deep end about having a violinist in the house?"

"Oh, come on."

"Stranger things have happened."

"I suppose, but I imagine it will come down to something much more straightforward. Camila made a play for Gail's husband."

"She's a flirt, that's the truth. But why would she mess around with a middle-aged man?"

She raised her eyebrows at him. "Watch your mouth, kid. I'm partial to a middle-aged man, myself."

Andrew helped her make short work of a large pepperoni-mushroom pizza and a salad; the pizza place had the crispest salads in Oliver. Comfortably filled, they walked back home for the car. Neighbors sitting out on their front porches waved, and ordinarily she would have stopped here and there to chat, but tonight there wasn't time. Quickly, she changed clothes and grabbed her pearls, and they were off.

Their seats were in the same row as on the night before, but when they hurried down the aisle behind the usher, she was delighted to see Bruce's red head sticking up above Polly's blond one.

"Want to sit by Bruce?" she asked Andrew.

"Sure."

They'd scarcely exchanged greetings when the lights dimmed. The orchestra was already silent, and the concertmaster had taken his seat after tuning.

"That was a little too close," she murmured to Andrew.

"Don't sweat it, Mom. We made it."

The applause rolled up now for the conductor and, right behind him, Nate Lloyd. He checked his strings against the oboe and stood waiting. Joan thought of his mother, who must be in the audience somewhere. Nail-biting time.

The voice announced that Mr. Lloyd would play Lalo's *Symphonie Espagnole*, but Joan couldn't have mistaken the orchestra's opening notes: Bum-bum-*bah*, bum-bum-bum-*bah*. In her head, she sang along with the violas. When had she last played this piece? Much too long ago to remember the soloist.

Nate leaned into the driving rhythm, taking the fast runs as if they were nothing. No question about his keeping up with the orchestra at any speed. More likely, they had to work to keep up with him. In the second movement, the triplet runs were, if anything, even faster. The orchestra's chords and piz-zicatti kept beating time while Nate's violin sang and danced over them. Then the low Gypsy melody in the Intermezzo, and the violin's new tune that flicked up to high notes that had to be harmonics. Nate was playing with a little smile on his face. More runs and flips and trills, and still another melody. Amazing, how many melodies Lalo had lavished on this concerto.

At last, the Andante movement, and a chance to draw breath while Nate played a melody of great sweetness, with an even more Gypsy-sounding beat. Then the Rondo's triplets swelled and waned in the orchestra before the violin began dancing over them. Joan remembered playing those driving triplets, on and on and on. It was certainly more fun to sit back and listen to Nate fly all over the instrument. He ended in a flourish of runs, spiccato, trills, finger pizzes, and one great chord that cried out, "Clap for me!"

Not that they needed to be told. Most of the audience was standing. Does that make any difference to the judges? Probably not. Has to make his mother feel good, though. Not that she'd need any help, after that performance.

The lights came up for intermission.

"See you later," Bruce said. "I'm going to catch Nate if I can." He edged past Andrew and Joan to the already-clogged aisle.

"I don't know, Mom," Andrew said. "He's awfully good."

"He is, isn't he?" Polly said, moving over to the seat Bruce had left and turning sideways to talk to both of them. "And you know, all these violinists are used to being the very best wherever they come from."

"How is Bruce holding up?" Joan asked.

"Oh, now that his competition is over, he seems amazingly cheerful about whatever the judges decide. But I don't expect him to come in fifth this time, as he did in Moscow."

"Not for lack of competition."

"No, all these top players are superb. For her sake, I hope Camila is up to them now." Polly shook her head.

"Have you seen her?"

"Not yet."

"She was better today," Joan said. "I don't think you could tell that anything had happened to her, but of course, that's a long way from playing at this level. Oh, you don't know the good news. Her violin turned up in Oliver this morning. Fred and I brought it up to her."

"That's wonderful! Not harmed?"

"No, in its own case, apparently untouched."

"I'm so happy for her," Polly said. "And ashamed of suspecting that she'd fake a theft. Where did they find it?"

Time to be a little evasive. "I don't think they're talking about that yet."

Polly didn't push, and Joan leaned back and rested her eyes for a few seconds. Then someone was tapping her shoulder.

"Mom, wake up!" Andrew said. "Bruce can't get past you."

"I'm not asleep," she protested and straightened up quickly to let Bruce slide by. "It's been a long day."

"I hated to disturb you, but they're about to start." Looking as embarrassed as she felt, he squeezed past her.

The orchestra was tuning again. The lights dimmed, and the conductor came onstage with Camila, who looked almost like her radiant self in a flowing white gown bare on top except for shoulder straps that looked strong enough to let her relax about her dress while playing. She flashed a smile and bowed beautifully to the applause.

The voice announced that Camila Pereira would play the Sibelius concerto. Amazing, Joan thought, how many great composers wrote only one violin concerto.

Camila's first melodic passage sounded appropriately intense for Sibelius, but the arpeggios that followed it were a little unsure, and her spiccato bowing not as sharp as it had been a week earlier. She had a little respite, then, while the orchestra took over. Then octave double stops before and over the low viola solo that Joan herself had once played in an orchestra so viola-poor that she had sat in the first chair.

As the first movement progressed, Camila's octaves, trills, and runs just didn't live up to her true ability. Her performance would certainly have been passable in ordinary company, but Joan ached for her.

The conductor was watching her grimly. They probably hadn't rehearsed until sometime today, to give her the best chance of being ready. What a challenge for all of them, and what a shame.

The second movement went much better, with the lush legato theme played over horns and cello pizzicatti. Camila had her tone back and was certainly musical. Only the coordination and dexterity that had let her race through the technically hard spots seemed to be affected. But in a competition in which a hairsbreadth separated the winners from the losers, that was like Bob Osborne's telling Uwe Frech that only his hand was injured.

In the last movement, she lagged behind the tempo by just that hairsbreadth, seeming to lack enough control over the bow to drive the rhythmic dance forward as it needed to move. By the time she had to play the melody in harmonics, she was far enough off pitch to be embarrassing, and her spiccato double stops were a lost cause. Gamely, she struggled on to the end, but her fatigue was obvious.

At last, with tears streaming down her face, she took only one quick bow and hurried off, to sympathetic applause. Her parents must be in the audience, Joan thought. They know how she played before. How can they stand it?

"Poor thing," Polly said. "And now she's coming back to play Mozart?"

"Looks like it," Bruce said. "They left the order up to her." Members of the orchestra had already departed from the stage, leaving a much smaller Mozart orchestra. But although the lights stayed down, neither the conductor nor Camila returned. The audience was beginning to murmur.

At last the announcer's voice spoke. "Ladies and gentlemen, I regret to inform you that Miss Pereira has been taken ill and will be unable to continue."

A collective "Ohhh" rose from the audience. The orchestra left the stage considerably faster than the audience could file out of the theater.

"What a shame," Joan said.

"She probably would have won the gold," Bruce said. "But we'll never know."

"You wouldn't turn it down, would you?" Andrew said.

"No, but it's tarnished now, no matter who wins."

28

$\mathcal{I}$n the lobby, Polly invited them back to her house again.
"Thanks," Joan said. "But I think I'd better go home
and sleep." It had been quite a day, and all the walking was
beginning to catch up with her. No, it had already caught up
with her.

Polly didn't pressure her. "Tomorrow, then, after the
awards."

She hadn't intended to wait in line to congratulate Nate,
but it was a chance to chat with Bruce while avoiding the
extra drive to Polly's. It was fun to listen to Andrew and Bruce
together.

Nate accepted the praise being showered on him gracefully
enough. He looked relaxed, as well he might.

"Do you know where Camila is?" Andrew asked, when
it was his turn.

Nate shrugged. "Sorry. I think she left."

In the parking garage elevator, Andrew offered to drive,
and Joan was grateful. She'd had to do everything herself for
so long that she sometimes forgot to let go. Soon she'd be able
to count on Fred, too, except, of course, when he'd have to
put her second to the job. Just as well she knew how to fend
for herself. No cop could have much of a marriage to a cling-
ing vine.

When Andrew backed out of the parking space Joan saw Gail Inman's white Ford with the Floriana logo taking the first slow right turn down the ramp in front of them. She turned her head, not really wanting to wave at Gail tonight, but Andrew was already waving. Before she could stop him, he rolled down his window, and called out, "Hey, Nate! Nice job tonight! Congratulations!"

"Thanks!" The car oozed around the next turn and was gone from sight. Andrew had stalled the stick-shift Honda and had to restart it.

"Nate was driving? That was Gail's car." Had Nate borrowed the car, too, not just the computer? No, he was probably just riding with his hostess.

"Nate was in the passenger seat. But it looked like his mom driving."

"His mom drives a blue sedan, not a white wagon. We parked behind her last night, don't you remember?"

"Not tonight, she doesn't. Maybe she borrowed Gail's."

"Maybe." But a long-buried image was pushing its way up through the layers of her consciousness. Cindy Lloyd, offering to drive Uwe to the doctor after he broke his hand, pointing to her car. And that car was a white wagon with a company logo on it. What company? The image wasn't that clear, but she, too, was a Realtor.

Suddenly it all fit.

"Andrew, catch up to them when they pay to get out of here. And hurry!"

"What for?"

"I want to see the license plate."

"You're weird, Mom." But he sped up briefly to almost fifteen miles an hour, a breakneck descent in the confines and tight turns of the parking garage. Joan dug in her bag for a pen and something to write on.

"There they are. Slow down, so they won't know we're chasing them."

"You're the boss." He slowed on the last stretch and pulled up decorously behind the white wagon.

Joan scribbled the numbers of the Kentucky plate on the back of a blank deposit slip. As far as she could tell, neither Cindy Lloyd nor her son was paying any attention to them.

"Let's get out of here. I've got to take this to Fred."

"Does that mean I can speed and he'll fix it?"

"Not on your life. There's no hurry now."

"We'll never find the repair shop today," Fred said when she called him Sunday morning.

"Maybe not, but Realtors have to keep office hours on Sunday afternoon; that's when they hold their open houses."

"How'd you like to go house hunting in Louisville?"

"I'd love it. Until you sweet-talk the gorgeous secretary. Then I'll throw a hissy fit and get us out of there."

Maybe they'd make it back in time for the medals ceremony at five, but she couldn't count on it. Feeling the unusually cool breeze coming in her bedroom window, she put on a wool suit, just in case, with her pearls showing inside the jacket. For that matter, it wouldn't pay to look down at the heel in a real estate office. The appearance of a certain prosperity would get them much better service. Not to mention having a man along. But with her suit, she wore oxfords. A person shopping for a house should seem prepared to do some walking.

Hoping Rebecca would understand if she didn't make the ceremony, she gave the car keys to Andrew. "If I'm not back when it's time to leave, you represent the family. Fred will get me there eventually."

"This all has to do with Camila?"

"Yes." No sense in piling the rest on him, not until she was sure.

He turned away, not asking anything else.

Fred picked her up just before eleven. Church bells were ringing all over Oliver. The town, while it had only one movie theater, offered an abundance of churches, including some denominations she'd never heard of before coming to southern Indiana. Jews, on the other hand, had to go all the way to

Bloomington for services, as did the few Muslims in town, most of whom were connected to the college. Joan exchanged waves with Margaret Duffy, her old teacher, when they passed her on the sidewalk in front of Eric Young's church.

Quickly, they were out in the country, where the green wooded hillsides were dotted with red and gold. Fred drove south to Bloomington and east on 46, which wound through the hills and past Brown County State Park to Nashville, and then it was a straight shot past Gnaw Bone to just before Columbus, where he turned south on I-65. They enjoyed each other's company without needing to say much.

Near noon, Joan pulled out some fruit and cheese for lunch. They would have gone well with some of Fred's sourdough bread, but it was a long time since he'd had a day free to bake. He held out his hand for her to drop in slices of apple and little bunches of grapes.

"Pretty good service. If you don't want to 'obey,' I'll settle for 'feed.' "

"It's a deal."

When they crossed the bridge into Louisville, she was glad he was driving. Making all the quick choices without hesitation, he found his way into the city, stopped briefly to consult a city map, and didn't pause again until they pulled up in front of Floriana Real Estate.

"Very impressive."

"I memorized it ahead of time. Can't have my best girl see me get lost."

"We could have asked someone."

"Men don't ask."

She laughed. "I thought only women knew that."

"In a pinch, I might have paid a visit to the Louisville PD. A fraternal visit, you understand, nothing official. We may not have to involve them at all. Odds are good the car will be up in Indianapolis tonight, where Richards and Richardson are already primed. That would beat having to extradite a suspect across the state line."

He helped her out of the car and smoothed his jacket. She straightened his tie.

"All right?" he said.

"You look very nice." She stroked his lapels, just in case anyone was watching. Not that I have to fake it, she thought.

Inside the little frame house, the decor screamed country cute. Everything that didn't have ruffles stood or sat on curly wooden shelves nailed to the wall. A goose dressed in sunbonnet and ruffled apron stopped the open door. With tobacco-stained fingers and half a dozen earrings, the receptionist seemed like an intruder, and her computer an anachronism.

She uncrossed her long legs and stubbed her cigarette in an overflowing ashtray. "May I help you?"

Joan batted her eyes at Fred, clung to his arm, and waited.

"We'd like to see Mrs. Lloyd," he said, sounding a little stuffy and looking more than a little embarrassed.

"She's not here just now, sir. I'd be happy to ask one of our other Realtors to help you."

"Oh, Fred," Joan wailed. "I don't want to start all over again with someone else. Cindy knows exactly what we want in a house, and she's found the perfect one for us in Oliver."

"Anything you say, dear." He smiled down at the receptionist and spread his palms helplessly. "How long would we have to wait for her?"

"Won't you have a seat while I check? I don't know if she's left us her schedule." They took the chintz-covered chairs she offered while she flipped through a book and then turned on the computer at her desk. "I'm sorry, but I don't expect her in today at all. I can't even reach her unless there's an emergency."

"This is certainly an emergency." Joan wondered whether she was laying it on too thick. "We're being married in a couple of weeks. My fiancé drove all the way down from Oliver, Indiana, and now you tell me he's made that trip for nothing? We've been more than patient. Last week she told us she was having car trouble."

"That's true. She had a run of terrible luck. On Monday someone backed into her car. She drove it home, but I had to find her a loaner while she was getting it repaired. Then the loaner developed engine problems. She had to have it towed in Indianapolis Wednesday night and missed the appointment she had down here the next morning. Those folks were so upset I don't think they're going to buy the house, after all." She hit some keys and read from the computer screen. "According to my records, she turned the loaner back in yesterday, so her car must be fixed. I don't know why she's not working today."

"They took their own sweet time about it." Joan was enjoying the role of shrew. "What repair shop was that? I want to be sure to stay away from it."

"I don't know, ma'am. All our Realtors drive their own personal cars."

"Even though they say Floriana Real Estate on the side?"

"That's right."

"Joan, dear, this isn't getting us anywhere," Fred said, the model of patience. "Let's let this lovely young lady find us someone else."

"Only if she can find us someone who can show us Cindy's house."

"What house is that, ma'am?" By now, the receptionist and Fred were beginning to slide each other sympathetic glances.

"The old Dayhuff house, she called it, up in Oliver. On Prospect Street. My fiancé drove by it, but he couldn't go in."

"The Oliver office said they couldn't let me in," Fred said. "So I came back here to pick up my intended, and to ask Cindy to show it to us."

More typing. "Cindy wouldn't be able to show it to you today, either. Someone up in Indianapolis put a stop on it all this week, from last Monday morning to tomorrow afternoon."

"Indianapolis? But the house is in Oliver."

More typing. "It says here the owners live up there.

Maybe the family wanted time to remove things from the house."

"That makes sense, dear," Fred said. "I peered through those beautiful leaded windows and saw quite a bit of furniture under dustcovers. I had hoped some good antiques would be for sale with the house. But we shouldn't bother Miss . . ." He paused and raised his eyebrows.

"Twyla Owens." She handed him her card.

"Thank you, Miss Owens. You've been most helpful." He smiled down at her.

By rights, she should have melted at his feet.

"We shouldn't bother Miss Owens any further. If you like, dear, I'll take you up to look at it from the outside."

"We'll discuss it in the car," Joan said in as frosty a tone as she could muster, and she let him steer her out by holding her elbow, a singularly unsupportive courtesy. As himself, Fred might have offered her his arm.

They kept up the act until they pulled away, and then she burst out laughing. "You were good! Do you do that kind of thing often?"

"No, mostly I flash my badge and beat 'em on the head with my nightstick."

"Seriously."

"Sometimes. Though we could have found out what we needed to know with half the trouble."

"I was having fun."

"I gathered that." He smiled at her. "You're a real ham, you know it?"

"So, do you have enough?"

"We know it's her car, and that she reported damage to it on Monday. The license plate you got will confirm her ownership."

"Yes, and did you catch the part about the loaner's having trouble on Wednesday? That would explain why Camila wasn't doped up again Wednesday night." She warmed to it. "There were no marks on her, and you and I didn't find any kind of physical restraints in the house. She must have come to enough to walk out on Thursday morning."

"So we know it was Nate or his mother."

"Oh, it wasn't Nate," Joan said, glad to be sure of what she'd only suspected the night before. She'd always felt sorry for Nate, in spite of his talent. "He was still at the Osbornes' relaxing with Bruce Wednesday night when Cindy started off for Louisville before her loaner broke down. I saw her leave."

29

$\mathcal{I}$n the end, they missed the awards ceremony and performances by the medalists. By the time Fred had verified with Richards and Richardson and the Louisville PD that Cynthia Lloyd had filed no police report either in Indianapolis or Louisville about having been backed into on Monday, they just made it before the people began leaving.

Backed up by half a dozen units from the IPD, they quickly located Cindy Lloyd's wagon parked on North Meridian across from the magnificent Scottish Rite Cathedral. Fred and Richardson agreed that all marked cars should back off to where they wouldn't alarm her, but that Fred and Joan should approach as soon as they saw her and stick to her until she reached the car, where the two IPD detectives would wait to make the arrest.

"What if Bruce and Andrew come out first?" Joan asked. "Won't that seem strange, if I ignore them?"

"You'll think of something," Fred said. "After watching your performance this afternoon, I'm not worried."

"I don't know, Fred. I don't feel so good about this." Her insides were churning, not in fear, but in sympathy for the woman whose life they were about to destroy.

"Neither did Kyle Pruitt's mother."

"That's a low blow. You fight dirty."

He looked into her eyes for a moment. "This is dirty business. But I don't want to pressure you. We can do it without you."

"All right, I'll do it."

The mechanics of it turned out to be surprisingly easy. Bruce and Andrew did emerge together, and trotted down to meet them at the curb.

"Mom, you missed it. He won the silver medal! And the award for the best performance of the—what was it, Bruce?"

"The Quigley." Carrying his violin case, Bruce was wearing the silver medal around his neck.

Joan hugged him. "Congratulations, son! That's wonderful news."

"Nate won the gold," he said. "He really deserved it, especially with that last performance. I think he might have won even if Camila had been herself yesterday. They did give her the award for the best Bach performance in Phase I of the competition. You should have heard the crowd when she went up to accept it."

"Oh, that's good. I'm happy for Nate, too. Is he still in there?"

"Oh, sure. He won't be out for a while yet. There's a swarm around him. Photographers and all that. All the attention's on him now, so we got away fast."

"Do you mind?"

"Not winning first? No. This is better than I dared hope for. Andrew's driving me back to the Osbornes' to call Rebecca, and my folks, of course. And Polly's planned a shindig in my honor before I fly home tonight—you know Polly."

"We'll come by. Anyhow, I will. Fred may have to drop me off."

"Congratulations, Bruce." Fred shook his hand warmly. "I only wish I could have heard more of it."

"Thanks." Bruce seemed hardly to notice that Fred's eyes had already returned to scanning the crowd. "See you later."

Joan watched them down the sidewalk, the tall redhead who could hardly wait to call her daughter, and the familiar head of dark curls beside him. That's almost exactly how Bruce would look with Rebecca, except that he'd tower over her.

"I do like that young man," she said. "And the next time I see him, I can tell him he no longer has to worry about being anybody's suspect. I can tell him that, can't I?"

Without turning his attention away from the crowd, Fred said, "Absolutely, as soon as she's under arrest."

Joan fell silent then, and her happiness faded. For all that she'd been so eager to help Fred deal with the hit-and-run, and to remove the suspicion from Bruce, not to mention Andrew, what was about to happen hurt even to think about. And yet she couldn't fool herself into thinking that what had already happened had been totally accidental. The message in the Floriana computer proved that Cindy had planned at least part of it ahead of time. Obviously she, not Gail, had used Gail's computer to leave that message, and according to the Floriana receptionist in Louisville, she'd blocked the house from being shown ever since Monday morning.

Camila hadn't disappeared until Monday afternoon, but the violin had been missing since Sunday. Staying with the Inmans, Cindy'd had access to the Schmalzes' house keys, and that speech she'd made on Sunday about racing back from Louisville to Nate's semifinal concert had been nothing but a ruse to establish her alibi for stealing the violin. Maybe she'd thought taking the violin would guarantee her son's victory, but when Camila triumphed on a borrowed fiddle, she'd taken more drastic measures.

Kyle Pruitt had probably just come riding along at exactly the wrong time. Unless, of course, he'd noticed anything suspicious about the young woman in Cindy's car—or tried to pull it over for speeding. Had she mowed him down intentionally? And even if she hadn't, wasn't it murder if she'd killed him even by accident while committing another crime?

"There they are." Fred's voice was soft in her ear. "Let's go." He took her hand, and she started forward with him, waving to Cindy and Nate as she went. They met halfway to the door. Like Bruce, Nate wore his violin case slung over his shoulder and his medal around his neck.

"Congratulations!" Joan said with sincere warmth. "Bruce and Andrew just left. They had to tell us you won; we missed the whole thing."

"So you know he got the silver, and the Quigley prize." Nate, looking more relaxed and happy than she'd ever seen him, was gracious in victory. He would be the real casualty today, she realized suddenly, and wished she could spare him.

"Yes, and he's delighted. He agrees that you deserved the gold. Your concerto last night blew us all away."

"Thank you."

He has a lovely, sweet smile. No wonder his mother loves him.

His mother bustled up to them. "I told you Nathan was the best."

Oh, Cindy, Joan thought, how could you gloat now, of all times? And to me, of all people? I do believe it wouldn't matter to you if I were Bruce's own mother.

They crossed the street together, with Cindy needing no prompting as she chattered on. Joan tried to make her mind fly off somewhere far removed from the white Ford station wagon with Kentucky plates and the Floriana logo on the door. At least the crowd had dissipated; there would be many fewer witnesses than there would have been even a few minutes earlier.

Cindy was taking her keys out of her handbag when Richards and Richardson came from around the car in opposite directions to stand to her left and right. Fred, with Joan, was standing behind her. They had her boxed in.

"Cynthia Lloyd?" Richardson said in his quiet voice.

"Yes?" She looked up, still beaming.

"You're under arrest, ma'am." He plucked the keys from her fingers while Richards cuffed her hands in front of her. "You have the right to remain silent . . ." He droned on through the Miranda warning.

Her face, animated only a moment earlier, froze. Her mouth moved, but no sound came out.

Nate exploded. "You've got to be out of your minds! My mother hasn't done anything wrong. She doesn't even get parking tickets. This has to be a mistake. Why are you arresting her? What are you charging her with?"

"The confinement of Camila Pereira, for one, and the murder of Kyle Pruitt, a sergeant in the Oliver Police Department."

Now Nate fumed at Fred. "You had something to do with this! My mother's never even been in Oliver. She couldn't kill anyone! And she would never harm a violinist. You know how devoted she is to helping me with my career."

"Too devoted," Fred said. "We can prove that she had access to the house where Camila was held and the violin was found, and that she tried and almost succeeded in keeping everyone else out of that house all this week. And we have a witness who saw her car flee the scene after she hit Sergeant Pruitt while she was driving Camila to the house. We even have hard physical evidence that links her car to that accident. No one backed into your mom's car this week, son. She hit a cop with it, one of my cops, and he didn't make it. Even Camila remembers that she was driving too fast and hit something, and we have a piece of your mom's car that was left on the street and paint from the car on the bicycle Sergeant Pruitt was riding. We'll have to impound the car as evidence, but trust me, there's no mistake."

While Fred spoke, Nate's eyes widened in horror, and then he shut them tightly. "Mom?" he said, his whole body tensed as if against a blow. All the color had drained out of his face, except for two bright splotches on his cheeks.

Tears rolled down Cindy's thin face, but she didn't attempt to brush them away. "I did it for you, Nathan! I couldn't let her take the medal away from you. You're a wonderful violinist, and this is the last year you'd be eligible for it. I did it for you! I had to! Don't you see?" She held her cuffed hands out to him.

"I see." He looked at her now, but his voice sounded dead. "I see that you didn't trust me to win on my own. I see that you didn't really believe in me at all. I see that you've made a mockery out of this medal." His face contorted, he pulled it off and threw it on the street. Joan snatched it up just before his foot would have ground it into the pavement.

"You're going to need a lawyer," Fred said. "And if you can't afford one—"

"Oh, we can probably afford a lawyer now." Bitter tears shone in Nate's eyes. "All that prize money might as well go for lawyers, if they even let me keep it. I'm not going to touch it for myself, and I'm never going to speak to her again." He turned his back on his mother. "Could someone take me back to the Inmans'?"

Richardson jerked his head, and a IPD uniform came forward.

"Come with me, sir," the officer said to Nate.

"I'll drop you off at Polly's," Fred told Joan. "I don't know how long this will take."

"It doesn't matter. I'll ride home with Andrew."

"You okay?"

"Yes. But I don't know how you do this over and over."

He shook his head slowly. "This is worse than most."

She climbed into Fred's Chevy. The last thing she heard before he closed the door was Cindy's long wail, "Naaa-thaaan!"

30

They didn't wait for Rebecca, after all. At noon on Monday Joan and Fred walked over to the courthouse with her rubella form and his eighteen dollars. Then they spent the rest of the hour with the minister. After they discussed the wedding ceremony, Eric Young talked with them about good communication and how to fight fair in a marriage.

Joan found the idea reassuring. I tortured myself by trying not to fight this week, she thought, and by expecting Fred to know how I felt when I wasn't telling him. It was better when we got it out in the open.

"You don't have to try to settle all your issues before you're married," the minister said. "No one can. A good many of them won't even have come up yet. But you need to know how to deal with them when they do. And you need to trust each other enough not to avoid them when the time comes."

I was angry because he didn't trust me, Joan thought, but I didn't trust him with my feelings.

"Trust like that doesn't happen overnight," the minister said. "Achieving it is a lifelong process. I think you're more ready than most. I'll see you in the church tonight."

Fred walked her back to work and stopped at the door, as he so often did.

"We need witnesses," Joan said. "I'll have Andrew, of course. He's old enough to sign."

"Maybe Captain Altschuler will stand up with me."

"I never thought of that. I could ask Margaret Duffy, and just let Andrew give me away."

"And walk you down the aisle. I want to see you walk down the aisle to me."

"Oh, Fred, not with nobody in the pews." She'd come to terms with the idea of a tiny wedding. His preference, she knew. After all, she'd had the big folderol with Ken. This second time around, it would be all right to keep it intimate. Maybe even better. But to march down the aisle of an empty church? "It would feel silly."

"Not to me, it wouldn't. Go ahead, ask Margaret. And the sooner, the better. I need to get you both flowers."

Margaret agreed readily and took off to find "something right for a wedding."

"Whatever you wear on Sunday mornings will be just fine," Joan said. "This is going to be very small and informal."

"Don't you worry, I won't wear anything inappropriate. But I don't want to arrive with spots on my front, either."

When they arrived at the church a few minutes before seven, though, Joan was startled to see that the pews were not empty. Standing back in the narthex wearing her pearls and the soft blue dress that was Fred's favorite, she counted the backs of a couple of dozen heads and wanted to run the other way. Where had all these people come from? Who had invited them?

Margaret came in, wearing a simple beige suit that made her look like the mother of the bride, and carrying a white box.

"Margaret, I can't go through with this!"

"Yes, you can, dear. Here are the flowers Lieutenant Lundquist gave me for you." She opened the box and held out a plain bouquet of white spider mums.

Joan swallowed hard and took the flowers.

And so, promptly at seven, Andrew escorted his mother down the aisle to Jeremiah Clarke's familiar *Trumpet Voluntary*, competently played by the church organist. Joan carried the white bouquet, and Margaret, ahead of her, held a smaller one of rust and gold mums.

Looking a little numb, Fred waited by the chancel steps with the minister and Warren Altschuler. Both Warren and Fred wore plain gray suits with miniature mums in the buttonholes, and even Warren's homely face looked dignified. Coming closer, Joan could see Fred's blue eyes shining.

When Eric Young asked, "Who gives this woman to be married to this man?" Andrew cleared his throat behind her.

"Rebecca and I welcome Fred into our family, but our mother is not ours to give. She must give herself freely."

Joan turned in amazement, but he was already stepping back into the first pew next to Annie Jordan, who reached out and patted him on the shoulder.

From then on, there were no surprises. They'd resisted the temptation to use a sexy passage from the Song of Solomon, but Eric Young read I Corinthians 13. The vows were the familiar ones, without "obey." Fred had long ago measured her finger for a gold band, but they'd never talked about whether he would wear one, and she was pleased when Margaret produced his ring from her bouquet.

Then the minister pronounced them husband and wife, Fred planted a brief, but solid kiss on her lips, and the organist broke into the Mendelssohn. Sailing back on Fred's arm into the small sea of smiling faces, Joan felt her own face stretch into a wide smile. Most of the old regulars from the Senior Citizens' Center had come, and there were Alex Campbell, Nancy Van Allen, and John Hocking, too, from the orchestra. Who had invited them all? On the groom's side of the church she recognized Sergeant Johnny Ketcham, Detective Chuck Terry, and Officer Jill Root, who had been in love with Sergeant Pruitt. How could she bear to attend a wedding so soon?

Out in the narthex, Warren claimed his privilege and kissed the bride, while Fred hugged Margaret.

"Since we're not having a reception, maybe we ought to shake hands out here with all those people," Joan said.

"Who says there's no reception?" Margaret said. "Didn't you notice how few people were at the center this afternoon?"

"What do you mean?"

"We've been busy. Come see." She led them downstairs to the room where Catherine had confronted Joan on Saturday. Joan dragged her feet, not wanting to sully their day by thinking of Catherine. But then she rounded the bottom of the steps.

"Ohhh! It's beautiful!" The utilitarian room was filled with white and gold balloons, some tied to folding chairs, but most floating along the ceiling, dangling curly white ribbons. The tables were covered with white paper, and on one stood an honest-to-goodness three-tier wedding cake, only a little crooked. "Margaret, you did all this?"

"Goodness, no. It's from all of us together. You didn't give us any warning, so this is our wedding gift to you. Ruby baked the cake right after you told me, Lula decorated it as soon as it cooled, and we all did the rest. You should have seen Annie and Alvin blowing up balloons. They popped a fair number before they got the hang of that machine."

Fred was beaming down at her, not seeming to mind all the fuss.

"Fred! You were in on it, and you didn't say a word."

"Not me. I never would have agreed to it." But his eyes twinkled, and she didn't believe him.

"You old softy."

He took her hand in his. "You were the one who wanted to know you were married."

"Anything else I ought to know about?"

"I hope not. It was all I could do to talk the cops out of a twenty-one gun salute." He kissed her palm. "I told them we'd make our own fireworks."